GERMS OF WAR

KETAN DESAI

Indies United Publishing House, LLC

ISBN: 978-1-64456-064-8

Library of Congress Control Number: 2019950458

Indies United Publishing House, LLC
PO Box 3071
Quincy, Illinois 62305-3071
www.indiesunited.net

Germs

of

War

Prologue

Tracy stared at the biological weapon for a long time. The vial looked so innocuous, sitting quietly in the ventilated hood. Few would have suspected the pretty pink tube contained a biological weapon. Fewer still would have suspected it had enough power to destroy a large portion of humanity.

"Why is destruction so much easier than creation?" she mused softly.

Tracy had re-created this monster so she could create an antidote to it. And this was just the beginning, the first biological weapon she had created out of the hundreds of possibilities. There were many more weapons to make, many more antidotes to create.

"Time to take a break," she murmured to no one in particular.

As she stood up, she reflected on the events that led to her to work on biological weapons and she reflected on Afghanistan.

Like the vial in front of her, Afghanistan personified some of the most villainous violence as its citizens and myriad invaders were locked in perpetual warfare spanning centuries. And the violence seemed to have escalated in the past half-century. In fact, the word "savagery" would best describe human behavior over the past twenty-five years.

Lost in thought, she remembered the conversation with her mentors, "In late 1979, the Soviet Politburo, desperately trying to support a puppet communist government, ordered the invasion of Afghanistan. Leonid Brezhnev, the Soviet President, expected the Red Army to cruise easily through the Hindu-Kush Mountains.

"The Afghans did not roll over for the Red Army, and their fiercely independent spirit soon became evident. Various resistance groups, collectively called Mujahideen, sprang up. They went after the Red Army like piranhas attacking a big water buffalo helplessly thrashing about in the water. The Mujahids had powerful friends in America, Pakistan, and Iran and Islamic mercenaries from Sudan, Saudi Arabia, and Egypt joined them. Money, arms, and combatants poured into the battle as fast as refugees staggered out. Fired by faith and hate, the Mujahideen ripped open the belly of the Soviet war machine. Kabul became an open-air morgue displaying the corpse of the Red Army for the entire world to see. By the time the tired, dispirited Red Army limped out of Afghanistan in February of 1989 thirteen thousand Soviet soldiers had died futile deaths."

"One would think after a victory like that, Afghanistan would become a truly united country. Just like we did after we kicked out the British," Tracy had observed.

"Unfortunately, that isn't what happened," her mentors noted. "As the last Soviet soldier sought the solace of his homeland, the Mujahedeen turned their weapons and animus on each other with a vengeance. The country was ravaged, rent asunder. Out of the resulting turmoil came religious fundamentalism and terrorism. All kinds of terrorism. Including bioterrorism."

It was bioterrorism that had caught Tracy in its tangled web. She was still dazed by the sequence of events, but the end result of it was very clear.

She turned out the light. The laboratory became quiet and dark.

Chapter 1

On a quiet and dark night at the beginning of May 1997, Dr. Tariq Bukhari struck. He silently entered the restricted P3 unit of Mayo Clinic's Microbiology Department at 11:00 pm.

"Deserted on Sunday night. Just as I expected," he muttered. "Now the difficult part."

A clumsiness which had afflicted him since childhood usually caused the doctor to move as though perpetually inebriated. During his post-doctoral research at the clinic, for three years Bukhari had orbited between his desk and the P3 room hundreds of thousands of times, inevitably crashing or bumping into anyone or anything within six feet of his path.

"Had too much of a good thing last night?" his colleagues would jokingly ask. In return, Bukhari would curse, blaming everyone else for his ataxic behavior.

At first, his colleagues tried their best to make sense of his pugnacity. However, Bukhari's outbursts of temper, matched only by his inability to handle any piece of equipment without threatening its immediate ruin and, by extension, the health and safety of anyone near him, led to his isolation. By his third year, the faculty and students of the entire Microbiology Department avoided all contact with him, with the sole exception of Dr. Dan Howard, his sponsor, and staunchest supporter.

But this night was different. Like a cardiac surgeon operating on coronary arteries, Bukhari was a study in concentration, though none of his colleagues were privy to this superlative performance.

Slow and easy does it, Bukhari reminded himself.

He strode toward the door to the P3 facility, where work on dangerous bacteria and viruses were performed, stopping briefly at his desk for the necessary keys. Surreal blue rays from a UV lamp burned within the P3 room as a constant warning of great danger.

Urgently, as though possessed, Bukhari proceeded through the P3 room's outer door. In the antechamber, he stopped to don his blue laboratory coat, a filtration mask, and two pairs of latex gloves. Confidently flinging open the interior door, he stepped into the heart of the P3 facility, a space barely large enough for one person to work in.

Bathed in the eerie blue light, a bacterial incubator stood to his left.

To the right was a small, 4° C refrigerator, reserved for storing reagents. Next the refrigerator, a humming liquid nitrogen-cooled freezer stored bacteria and temperature-sensitive chemicals at a frigid minus 70° C. Before him was a tissue culture hood, where experiments with bacteria and viruses were conducted under sterile conditions. A fan blew air through the hood to ensure neither the hood's air nor the room's air contaminated each other. A small stool facing the hood provided the only place to sit.

With a degree of skill he had never exhibited to his American colleagues, Bukhari rubbed down the hood's interior with the laboratory antiseptic, seventy percent alcohol, to reduce the possibility of inadvertent contamination. He then turned off the UV light and switched on an overhead incandescent lamp.

The sense of history, greatness, and total power, which had guided him since his earliest school days, now shaped his thoughts with overwhelming force and intensity.

"Where so many have failed, I -- Tariq Bukhari -- have succeeded. The weapon that so many have dreamed of, I have created! A few years from now, crowned with the thanks and praise of a grateful nation, I will be the brightest star of a new, eternal empire."

Turning around slowly in a tight circle, Bukhari surveyed the assorted racks, shelves, and equipment within the P3 room the way a conductor inspects his orchestra before raising his baton to signal the first note. As Bukhari began assembling his materials, every vial he touched leaped into his grasp. Every step he took landed securely upon the floor. His torso and limbs kept plumb to each other, instead of akimbo.

As he initiated preparations for testing his toxin, Bukhari allowed himself to enjoy the full rapture of his imagination. A sense of poetic speculation came over him as he withdrew a vial, known as an Eppendorf tube, from the minus 70° C refrigerator. The vial contained his invention, harmless in its frozen form. His mind played with numbers inside his head.

"The volume of the vial is…One milliliter of the toxin can slay... Therefore, the contents of the vial can kill.."

With great care, Bukhari placed the frozen Eppendorf tube to thaw in a rack inside the tissue culture hood, the metallic hum of the hood's fan providing a soundtrack as the doctor marveled at the pure beauty he perceived in his creation.

The superbug should come to life after twenty-five minutes.

At exactly the thirty-minute mark, he poked a small hole into the cap of the Eppendorf tube and connected it to a lyophilizer, a small machine designed to powderize liquids. The lyophilizer transformed the liquid medium, with swarming bacteria and its swirling cesspool of toxins, into a seemingly innocuous dry white powder, no different in appearance from table salt. Bukhari looked at his creation like a proud father looking at his newborn son. He quickly transferred the weapon, as he now preferred to think of it, unequally into two other vials with intact caps. He wrapped parafilm, a scientific version of Saran Wrap, around each one. Then he placed each vial within a larger vial and sealed the larger vial again with parafilm.

This insured no organism would escape from either vial unless he intended it. One tube, carrying less than a tenth of the initial powder, would be used tonight. The other, carrying the remainder, would return to Pakistan with him. He instinctively looked out the grilled window to see if anything or anyone was stirring. All was quiet.

Bukhari congratulated himself on his cleverness in the final phase of the experiment. A few weeks earlier, he had tested the concoction on guinea pigs and watched as the unfortunate rodents drowned in their own lungs. But that had not been enough.

"It's great it worked on guinea pigs, but will it work on humans? That's the question I want answered," Ghazni, his mentor, demanded. The head of the bioweapons project for Pakistan's secret service, the ISI, Ghazni was a perfectionist. Bukhari had wracked his brain for weeks trying to perfect such a human test.

With an innate gift for software manipulation, Bukhari had reconfigured his personal computer at home to penetrate every department of Mayo Clinic and its affiliated hospitals. From his off-campus apartment, he spent many late-night hours painstakingly scanning the illegally accessed in-patient registers of Methodist and St. Mary's Hospitals.

"Only airborne agents, Bukhari. Only those that can be disseminated by air," Ghazni had commanded.

To test such a pathogen, Bukhari would need a victim breathing through a ventilator and suffering from only one malady with no biological connection to his weapon. The doctor-agent would have only one chance to test this toxin in the measured confines of Mayo Clinic. According to the plan, Bukhari would place a telephone call to Ziad, his ISI control agent.

"When you start, say the journey has begun. If the test is successful, call again and say the end is near." Ziad had instructed.

Within a few hours of the second call, Ziad would meet Bukhari in his apartment, and the two would proceed to the laboratory to pick up the vial. They would then leave via the first flight to Pakistan from Chicago's O'Hare international airport.

Fate had finally delivered a suitable subject to St. Mary's on Saturday night. A sudden, severe asthma attack had afflicted Dr. Neil Kavesh, an otherwise healthy, middle-aged attending physician, with such sudden force he had been admitted to his own hospital's Medical Intensive Care Unit or MICU. In the course of treatment, the hospital staff had placed their ailing colleague on a ventilator, commonly known as a breathing machine.

Bukhari had made it a habit to scan the in-patient registers online as soon as he returned to his apartment each night.

Seeing a new admission, he cried out in excitement, "That's it! It's got to be him."

His heart began pounding as he recognized Kavesh's name. Though he did not know the doctor personally, he knew the staff would spare no effort to save him, especially since he was one of their own. However, should Kavesh perish, Bukhari doubted an autopsy would be performed, out of fear of its results and the potential backlash within the facility and the medical community. Thus, his tracks would never be uncovered.

With extraordinary enthusiasm, Bukhari prepared himself for both the experiment and his imminent return to Pakistan. After the successful tests of the toxin on guinea pigs, he had purged all personal effects and information from his apartment and a travel kit stood at the ready. Earlier in the day, as calmly as possible, Bukhari had called Ziad, who was masquerading as a taxicab driver and dropped the necessary code words into a conversation, signaling the experiment would soon take place.

Usually, students and faculty could be found working late into the evening every night of the week. Except for Sunday. No one, Bukhari was sure, had seen him enter the building, take the elevator up to the fifth floor, get the keys from his desk, or prepare the toxin in the P3 room.

The triumphant doctor cleaned up the P3 room with great fastidiousness. He discarded both layers of his gloves, stripped off his blue laboratory coat, and washed his hands thoroughly. He stepped out from the P3 room's outer section very slowly, carefully scanning the corridor ahead of him, and headed for the elevator, clutching the vial of poison tightly.

It was almost midnight.

Chapter 2

It was midnight.

"You're early, Josephine," Martha, the departing head nurse at St. Mary's MICU smiled at her replacement. "We've been taxed to the limit since Friday night. A miniature epidemic of bacterial sepsis, kidney failures, and congestive heart failures seems to have erupted in the city of Rochester." The head nurse continued, "You know Dr. Neil Kavesh? He collapsed during rounds on Saturday morning with a severe asthma attack and ended up being admitted as well. Finally, a patient in hepatic coma arrived late yesterday afternoon. He was patient number 12. We're full up. At least you won't have to worry about new admissions."

Josephine Gibson, the head nurse on the graveyard shift, listened as Martha gave further updates. The unit was now as slow as it had been busy during the day. The patients remained stable and had not overtaxed Sunday's second shift. Josephine looked forward to a quiet night and early morning. She also had a new face starting tonight, a Sarah Davidson, just out of nursing college in St. Louis and it would be nice to introduce her to the MICU on an uneventful night.

"A piece of bad news. Romero is on call," Martha apologetically added.

A look of disgust darkened Nurse Gibson's face. It would not be an overstatement to say Dr. Calixto Romero was the most unpopular resident at St. Mary's. Although he was a second-year trainee, the MICU staff despised him for his incompetence and his refusal to listen to anything they said, be it advice or information about a case. On many occasions when he was on call, only the experience and determination of the nursing staff had saved the life of a patient, though Dr. Romero always did everything possible to claim credit for it.

The mishandling of a simple case of unstable angina the previous week had placed Romero on probation; his next mistake would be his last. The program director and residency committee had removed him from duty for several days while they debated his future. But, as fate would have it, Philip Scott, the resident on call for the MICU, had a family emergency, forcing him to take the night off. Desperate for a back-up, the program director had called Romero back to duty thinking even an incompetent resident could do little harm on the traditionally quiet

Sunday graveyard shift. The director consoled himself that the presence of Nurse Gibson would mitigate any potential of error as he made the call.

Through successive waves of technology, administrators, and staff, Head Nurse Josephine Gibson had proven to be the most important factor in the success of St. Mary's MICU. She had made her presence felt for almost thirty years, transforming the MICU into her personal domain for the betterment of all. She was also a superb judge of character and could tell in a few minutes whether someone would become a good medical professional. Through the years, many doctors had admitted earning her approval equaled passing the medical boards.

Calixto Romero had not earned her approval. She hated the very notion of his being assigned to the MICU. However, the thought of Romero being there without her to guard the unit disturbed her even more.

Seeing Sarah Davidson approach, Nurse Gibson smiled and said, "Hello and welcome to the MICU, Sarah." After a few introductory pleasantries, she explained the workings of the MICU to Sarah Davidson.

"I'm sure this is very similar to the hospitals you trained at. However, there are a few important differences. The entrance is special." She pointed to a double door. "Its two-door airlock mechanism governs the MICU's only entrance in order to keep the area as sterile as possible. The rest is somewhat standard. As you can see, brick walls divide the twelve cubicles, arranged in a semi-circle. Each patient has a cubicle. The walls retard sound, keeping the cubicles quiet. Glass partitions seal off their open end, and a curtain can be drawn across each partition for privacy.

"The nurses' station is at the hub of the semi-circle. This allows the staff to view all patients simultaneously. To the station's far side, those enormous banks of computers and flashing monitors," pointing in their general direction, "record the vital signs of all patients."

Sarah observed the readings of blood pressure, EKG, pulse, and oxygenation status as they ran across the screens like the ticker tape at Wall Street.

"On the station's near side is the chart rack, and then the doctor's table." Gibson continued.

The soft blue light illuminating the MICU gave the room a magical quality and the nurses' blue scrubs blended with the light. Sarah noticed her four new colleagues at work at computer stations, entering patient data, and four other nurses checking on patients.

"Excuse me for a moment," Nurse Gibson whispered. Sarah watched

Josephine leave her side and exchange words with a figure in a white lab coat Sarah assumed to be an attending physician. There was so much to take in. Sarah Davidson noticed the time.

12:05 am.

Chapter 3

12:10 am. Good, Bukhari noted with satisfaction. Spoiling his mood, though, was this accursed peasant who kept bantering inanely as though they had been the best of friends for decades.

"So, ya got some troubles tonight, Doc?"

Act! Act! He could hear Ziad constantly remonstrating him with those words, years, months, and weeks ago.

"Nothing can jeopardize the mission, nothing. Not your temper or your driving. Ghazni or not, no one will be able to save you if I report your foolishness endangered the mission," Ziad had reminded Bukhari. Act? Now, for once, Bukhari would engage Ziad's advice.

"Yes," Bukhari replied with a forced smile. He was certain no one had seen him exit the Microbiology Department or the research division of Mayo clinic, the Guggenheim Building. He had made his way quickly through a stairwell door out to the parking lot. His black Dodge Viper awaited him.

How everybody hated him for that car! Except for Dr. Howard, the faculty considered it inappropriate and distasteful for a post-doctoral researcher to drive a luxurious, flashy car. The speculation was his family was loaded.

However, since Bukhari maintained only the most venomous and distant relations with his fellow researchers, they could only speculate. Though no one thought Bukhari was street-smart or savvy enough to be a drug dealer, the speculations soon became vicious.

"I bet he's trafficking in stolen cadavers or something just as gruesome," one of the technicians in the laboratory hypothesized.

However, the doctor's colleagues never even got close to the real story. Years ago, after formally enlisting in the ISI, Bukhari had demanded a sports car as a condition of his accepting the American assignment. From years of watching American soaps, he thought all successful young Americans drove brand-new sports cars.

"If you want me to carry out this mission successfully, then I have to have a new sports car. If you won't provide such a car, I won't go." His arrogant demand enraged the senior figures within ISI. They demanded Bukhari's summary beheading. But his audacity only seemed to increase the affection Ghazni felt for his protégé. Surely, he lobbied his colleagues, if the success of the mission required a car, it would be foolish not to agree to such a bargain.

When Bukhari departed to the United States, many jealous officers had attempted to cajole and bribe Ziad to ensure a humiliating end for the young doctor. However, the wily control agent was gambling Bukhari's success would mean Ziad's luxurious retirement. Still, Ziad had winced and prepared for the worst every time Bukhari drove his infamous vehicle in Rochester.

On Sunday night, Bukhari carefully set the tube containing his superbug on the front passenger's seat and gunned the car to life. With a whine, the engine shrugged away the idleness of the night. Ordinarily, the drive between Mayo Clinic and St Mary's could be covered in less than five minutes, but daring fate, Bukhari arrived in less than sixty seconds.

Embraced by the dimness of St Mary's parking lot, Bukhari changed his appearance. He donned a white lab coat with 'Dr. M. Bazzini' embroidered in blue across the coat's left breast. A few weeks earlier, as his Guinea pig experiments began to bear fruit, Bukhari told Ziad to begin planning for the final experiment.

"It's your job to get my disguise. I've more important things to do," he demanded of his control officer.

"What? Are you crazy?" Ziad had expostulated.

"You have a lot of time. I don't. Don't you want this mission to succeed?" With the possibility of success so close at hand, Ziad acquiesced, noting it as another affront to be avenged in the future. It had been a relatively easy task to burgle Mayo Clinic's laundry facility and select the right-sized coat to fit Bukhari's slim, stooped frame.

Bukhari snapped a stethoscope around his neck and slipped the vial into one of the coat's deep pockets. As he ambled towards the MICU's entrance, he began to wonder if the real Dr. Bazzini had any known connection or relationship to Dr. Kavesh. He began to feel the tingle of excitement as he approached the lobby doors.

The guard, his white hair standing out, hailed the approaching figure. "How ya doin' this mornin', Doc?"

Bukhari stared at the bored old man, incredulous and amused.

This rheumy old guard in front of me is responsible for the security of the hospital! And all he wants is a conversation, not identification. It's amazing! Wear a white apron and a stethoscope, and become an instant MD. Why bother with medical school?

"What?"

The old guard flinched at the sudden, harsh bark of Bukhari's response. "I asked how you was doin' tonight, Doctor--." He leaned forward to squint at the laboratory coat. "Buzzardini?"

Bukhari forced himself to laugh aloud. He shifted so the scripted name was obscured. "I'm sorry. It's been quite a long night."

"Emergency?"

"Always an emergency. You know how it is."

"Yup. Sure do. So, then you got some troubles tonight?"

Bukhari felt like breaking the seal of the vial into the man's face. He smiled instead.

"Well, you take care, Dr. Buzzardini--"

"Thanks."

Bukhari continued to the MICU. Going through its double doors, he felt as if he were entering the vault of a bank. He had not been inside the intensive care unit since the courtesy introductory tour he had taken three weeks earlier.

The soft blue lights inside the unit surprised him. Instinctively, he wanted to turn them off and turn on white incandescent lights. Nevertheless, he approached the nurse's station, knowing from his illegal computer connection Kavesh could be found in cubicle four.

Head Nurse Josephine Gibson observed a figure enter the MICU, and she quickly moved to intercept him. She did not recognize his silhouette.

"Good morning, Doctor--"

Bukhari looked into Nurse Gibson's unapologetic gaze and felt uneasy. She had Ziad's eyes. She knew. She had to know! How could he escape?

"--Bazzini."

"Good morning," he croaked.

Nurse Davidson hesitantly approached the two, and Bukhari turned to face her.

"Hi! I'm Dr. Bazzini from Pulmonary and Critical Care Medicine," he said as cordially as he could.

"Hi, I'm Sarah Davidson."

Nurse Gibson could not identify the physician standing before her. She recognized the name Bazzini but could not link it to the face before her. An unending stream of doctors flowed in and out of the MICU and it was impossible for her to even keep track of everyone.

"You're here to see--" she interjected, interrupting the bonhomie.

"Dr. Kavesh. I'm here to see Dr. Kavesh," Bukhari answered quickly.

Why would he want to see Dr. Kavesh, the head nurse wondered, intrigued? "He's doing fine. We expect to extubate him tomorrow morning. He did very well in his T-piece trial today," she informed the imposter Dr. Bazzini.

"Yes, so I heard. They asked me to come down and do one last check on him. Make sure he's still fine," Bukhari recited these imaginary instructions with a pout, as though ordered to the MICU against his deepest wishes.

Nurse Gibson recognized that pout. Perhaps this Dr. Bazzini had spent his first year in research and was only now beginning his clinical rotations.

"Dr. Kavesh is in number four, Dr. Bazzini. Sarah's his nurse. She can give you an update."

Sarah Davidson faced Bukhari, eager to deliver her first official MICU report. Bukhari, conscious of the time, dismissed the rookie with a quick wave of his hands.

"No need, thanks! I just need to do a quick check and then get back to the wards to see a consultation request."

The two nurses watched Bukhari scuttle towards cubicle four.

"You've got to feel sorry for junior physicians." Nurse Gibson observed.

"What do you mean?" asked Sarah.

"They always do the dirty jobs, coming around late at night, keeping ungodly hours. If things go well, some senior attending physician will take credit for it. However, whenever something goes wrong, well, I don't envy them. Ah, but that's the way it works in medicine. Always has, and probably always will."

Joys of medicine, Sarah muttered to herself as she observed Bukhari close the curtain around cubicle four.

Chapter 4

Tracy Hopkins was closing a chapter of her life.

Late Sunday night, she furtively stole into the communal office designated for graduate students and postdoctoral fellows in Mayo Clinic's Microbiology Department. Habitually, she glanced up at the ancient, buzzing wall clock hanging above her desk.

12:15 am.

She had forced herself to stay up this late in order to begin her escape from the program that had consumed her with frustration and disappointment. The position of the clock's hands relieved her. Tracy had figured no one would be in the department this late on Sunday or this early on Monday.

She carried a letter addressed to Dr. Dan Howard, her committee chairman - a man who, for all purposes, controlled her professional life and future in his hands. In the dim office, partially lit by an overhead lamp, Tracy glanced down at his name, printed neatly on the envelope containing her formal letter of resignation from Mayo Clinic's combined MD/Ph.D. program. She had sought the advice of her parents and Rory on the best way to present her resignation.

Her father, who had terminated his own career in the Navy in protest over what he considered a dishonorable course of events during the 1980s, advised her to get the act over and done with as quickly and painlessly as possible.

"Write a polite letter, stick it in the mail, and leave. End of story." He didn't think it would be worthwhile going into the details of her decision.

Rory, in what Tracy called one of his "frontier moods", had suggested otherwise.

"Why don't to confront Dr. Howard in person and tell him what you really think of him. Let him know why his attitude and behavior suck. Tell him he is a complete jerk."

Her instinct had been to get out as fast and silently as possible. The naked viciousness of Dr. Howard scared the otherwise resolute Tracy, and after two years of him, she considered it enough of a triumph never to see his long, skeletal face again.

Tracy elected to combine the approaches. She deposited her formal letter of resignation addressed to the Microbiology Department's chairman, Dr. Robert Webster, with a copy to the Dean of Mayo Clinic's Medical School, in the inter-office mail on Friday, confident of a Monday morning delivery. She offered no reasons for her decision, not wanting to offer anything in writing that could possibly complicate her plan to transfer to the University of Utah's Medical School. However, she elected to write a personal letter to Dr. Howard, confident should he even open it, its contents would never be disclosed to anyone else by the secretive, insular man.

Tracy originally thought her words would convey more gravity if her thoughts were handwritten. However, her emotions proved to be too strong. Her pen had shaken so violently she could not read her own handwriting. Forced to the word-processor, Tracy poured out every ounce of her previously camouflaged animosity towards Dr. Howard.

Two years of grievances had translated into many pages. As she deposited the thick envelope into Dr. Howard's inter-office mail slot located just outside the graduate student's office, she congratulated herself for delivering the letter in person. Tracy hated the thought of what the postage would cost for something almost the size of a parcel. As she returned to her desk for the last time, an enormous feeling of release blossomed within her. Confident of her solitude, Tracy sat on top of her desk, swinging her legs, reliving the past few years as a gesture of finality.

The wall clock's buzzing compelled Tracy to look up at its face.

12.20 am.

It's getting late. Better move on.

She swung her feet down back to the floor. Originally, Tracy had planned to carefully separate what possessions could be immediately disposed of and what needed to be saved. However, urgency bordering on desperation seized her the moment she unfolded a plastic garbage bag. Indiscriminately, she began stuffing assorted knickknacks and papers inside it. The bag soon bulged. As she tied up the bag's neck, she noted its appropriate symbolism.

Four years, all of it, garbage!

Tracy recalled her high school and college years with great fondness. The family had relocated to Ogden from Virginia within a month of her father's resignation from the navy at the end of 1983. A homebody at heart, Tracy had elected to attend the University of Utah in nearby Provo. Pursuing her natural gift for science, she majored in biology, graduating with both awards and academic distinction. In her senior year, several prestigious programs had extended offers to her to participate in a combined MD/Ph.D. program. Her mother, Doris, had been overjoyed. Her younger brother, Andrew, was ambivalent, lost in the cyber world. Her father, Bill Hopkins, a retired admiral, had been the only dissenter.

"Too bad you didn't go for nautical engineering. Perhaps your younger brother will do something to extend our family's traditional link to the sea," he sighed.

Excited by the challenge and prestige of earning two advanced degrees, she accepted an offer from Mayo Clinic, Rochester, Minnesota. She looked forward to Rochester's congenial small-town atmosphere. But Tracy also felt very hesitant about living more than two hours away by car from her parents, and the comforts of home. She was also mildly concerned about her relationship with her fiancé, Rory.

As it turned out, those misgivings were insignificant compared to what was to come.

The joint MD/Ph.D. program began with two years of medical school, followed by three years of research to earn the Ph.D., then back to medical school for the remaining two clinical years. Her first two years of study had gone exceedingly well.

"Well, it's challenging but engaging. Nothing I can't manage." Is how she had described the studies to her parents. The course work had been relentlessly heavy, but she had held her own and remained in the upper ten percent of her class. At the end of her second year, the standard protocol required her to select a research laboratory and undertake her own project. Unsure of her direction and running out of time, she elected to join the Department of Microbiology.

It turned out to be the worst decision she had made in her life. The department had a peculiar and antagonistic nature. Her problems had started at the very beginning. The program director, Dr. James Delmez, had informed her she would be expected to repeat the vast majority of the course-work she had already completed in order to satisfy the department's requirements.

"We can't let you do less course work than other graduate students, can we?" His monotonous, nasal voice droned. "Even if you did take those courses in medical school, you still have to show your knowledge is up to the standards of graduate school."

Tracy refused and decided to take proficiency tests, which she passed successfully. Dr. Delmez, his authority challenged, became Tracy's first professional enemy.

Tracy long suspected Dr. Delmez's hand in deliberately assigning her to the laboratory of Dr. Dan Howard as a retaliatory action. Though possessing the worst reputation of anyone in the entire clinic, no one could say for sure why, or how, Dr. Howard survived at Mayo Clinic as a researcher. Rumors circulated of his filching supplies, and even scientific data, from other laboratories. The research Dr. Howard produced was shoddy and unexceptional, to say the least. The animus generated against him was so great it was a testament to the civility in Rochester no one had arranged for his dismissal.

The legend of Dr. Howard had taken a rather interesting turn four years earlier. A new foundation, the International Society for the Interdiction of Pathogens, or I.S.I.P., had awarded Dr. Howard a grant, the size of which dwarfed any other award in Mayo Clinic's history. Howard's colleagues were simultaneously baffled and jealous; jealous the worst member of their faculty had been so rewarded, baffled because of a nagging insecurity that perhaps - just perhaps - they had been mistaken about their microcephalic colleague's scientific abilities all along.

Dr. Howard gloated over his new status. In the space of a week, he went from ruling over a laboratory with the prestige and facilities of an unused broom closet to one that was the envy of the entire Clinic. Yet, the entire Microbiology Department continued to debate what Howard had done to obtain such a grant. He still maintained the shortest hours of any tenured faculty member, and his work continued to be opaque as ever in its originality.

Even as a medical student, Tracy had heard unforgiving rumblings about Dr. Howard. After being assigned to work with him, she worried she was in for some tough times. However, during the introductory tour of his laboratory, she was consoled by its well-stocked opulence, not a trifling matter in times of dwindling funds. Alas, it was not long before she discovered the rumors she had heard about Dr. Howard were, if anything, far too charitable. Soon Tracy found a striking similarity between Dr. Howard and a rabid dog. Unlike any other human being she had ever encountered, he tended to literally foam at the mouth if confronted by anything he could not immediately dismiss. She found he did not operate with much of a knowledge base, so most of her questions were in fact met with foamy, sneering retorts.

Tracy had fallen into despair. Initially, she had tried to gain the assistance of the department's chairman, Dr. Robert Webster. A leader who did not know how to lead and a back-stabber to boot, he had been intimidated by Dr. Howard when he tried to raise the issue of Tracy's complaints.

Howard had used his grant to confront Webster. "I'll write to the Dean and let him know I'll move my grant and laboratory to another university. I've had enough of your petty interference."

Webster backed off, advising Tracy any problems she had with Howard were her own fault, given it was not her place as a graduate student to criticize a successful senior faculty member.

By the end of her first six months in the Microbiology Department, Tracy began to wonder if she would physically survive the three years demanded by the program. Despite her problems, she made progress with her own research project and impressed the other four members of her faculty committee. However, she dreaded the prospect of the qualifying oral exams. If just one member of the examining faculty committee decided to fail her, the others would most likely follow suit, for the sake of appearing unanimous. With his constant criticism and rumor mongering, Tracy was certain Howard would never let her pass. Tracy began to think of Dr. Howard's laboratory as a kind of a furnace, a machine designed to consume those who worked there. In the end, some would prove to be relatively fireproof, while others would allow the flames stoked by Dr. Howard to destroy them entirely. Most merely baked in the heat, and suffered, as she did.

Remembering the personal bitterness that had consumed her father after he resigned his commission, Tracy had resolved to survive Howard's laboratory. A creature like Howard would not destroy her or her future. The laboratory could be as mean, chaotic and sloppy as possible, but she, Tracy Hopkins, would overcome every obstacle with a graceful tenacity she had learned from her mother. She refused to contribute to the bedlam and disorder raging through the opulent, fraudulent laboratory by letting it affect her.

Over the ensuing school terms, her mother applauded her decision to quietly see things through. Her father could not understand why she did not just fight fire with fire. Tracy told him to do so would be to mimic Bukhari far too closely.

Just the thought of Dr. Tariq Bukhari made Tracy shudder violently. Except for the local car burglar who plied his trade every six months or so, Bukhari was perhaps the single most feared person in the entire Guggenheim Building. At the very worst, Howard could be dismissed as a lucky, nasty buffoon. Bukhari was as an altogether different animal.

Bukhari scared Tracy even more than Howard did. She often wondered if he suffered from some undiagnosed nervous disorder, which would explain the combination of his clumsiness and his vile temper. She associated loudness with Bukhari. If he was not knocking something off a table, he was screaming at the top of his voice at someone about some terrible crime they had just deliberately committed against him.

It was none other than Bukhari who had delivered the final blow. Earlier in the week, on Wednesday, Bukhari had accidentally swept some vials and assorted reagents off his desk. At the exact moment Tracy entered the communal office she shared with him and other students. Bukhari wheeled around to face her.

"You're jealous of me! You are trying to sabotage my work." He screamed at her.

During the entire two years Tracy had sat near Bukhari, he had never uttered so much as a "good morning". Though he had unleashed this sort of unwarranted, even insane, attack on countless occasions before, it affected her particularly strongly that day. In tears, she had run out of the communal office.

She had called in sick on Thursday morning. By Thursday afternoon, she had been in contact with the admissions office at the University of Utah Medical School. By Friday, they had promised to welcome her. She made her decision to withdraw from Mayo Clinic, informing both Rory and her parents the same day. She told her mother to expect her at the end of the upcoming week. Doris volunteered to fly up and assist her, but Tracy declined: she wanted some time alone. With a mixture of anger and regret, she devoted most of Sunday to the composition of her letter to Dr. Howard.

Footsteps from the corridor outside the communal graduate student office suddenly snapped Tracy out of her thoughts. She glanced at the clock.

12:30 am.

Damn! Anyone walking in will clearly see what I'm doing. Too late to pretend now.

Anyone showing up this late would have to be a fellow student.

Just as long as it's not Bukhari, though it wouldn't be surprising if it was him.

The doctor was known to keep strange hours, and to be very secretive about his work. However, despite his obnoxious behavior, she doubted he would even bother to ask her anything.

The footsteps grow louder.

Nervously, almost without noticing it, Tracy opened her desk drawer and withdrew an enormous pouch of pink bubble gum. Tracy had always been fastidious. Alcohol and drugs held little allure for her. However, she had begun chewing gum with a vengeance after joining the sordid world of the Microbiology Department. She had grown quite accustomed to depositing an enormous wad of the stuff in her mouth and chewing away like a cow for hours. By the end, it had become her only means of retaliating against her vile colleague. She could drive Bukhari crazy with the constant popping of balloon-sized bubbles.

The footsteps stopped at the front door.

Tracy discerned a certain hesitation in the sound. Whoever stood on the other side of the door was thinking twice about entering. Finally, the office door opened. In horror, she saw the sweat drenched Dr. Dan Howard eyeing her with a bizarre combination of incomprehension and relief.

Chapter 5

Bukhari heard the hissing ventilator even before he laid eyes on his victim.

After entering cubicle four, he immediately turned around to draw its curtains closed. In this confined space, the MICU's soft blue light felt especially eerie. Bukhari fought to contain the shudder slithering up and down his spine. He turned to see the supine body of Dr. Kavesh, breathing only through the mechanical efforts and grace of the ventilator. Bukhari steadied himself and shuffled towards the bedside.

The stricken, over-weight, middle-aged doctor was asleep. The sound and the rhythm of the ventilator set Bukhari's imagination to work.

What if nurse whats-her-name comes through the door? What if my creation fails? What if? What if? What if?

The worried assassin quickly drew his gaze towards the array of lights blinking above the patient's bed. Constantly updated readings of blood pressure, pulse, EKG, and oxygenation status were broadcast like a personalized television network.

Bukhari turned to look at the dials and gauges governing the ventilator's functions and settings. The breathing machine featured a special aperture through which medications could be administered to the patient. A scalpel, alcohol swabs, hypodermic needles, syringes, saline for injection and bandages lay neatly arranged on a stainless-steel table beside the ventilator.

Bukhari wondered if he should say something, a blessing or an imprecation, before injecting the superbug. He elected to mutter the name of his sponsor, his protector, the man who controlled his life near or far - Ghazni - and, of course, the Almighty Allah. Bukhari expended a second, imagining the pleasure it would give his mentor to hear such praise from his devoted protégé. Casting a quick glance at cubicle four's drawn curtains, he set to work.

With shaking hands, he quickly donned a facemask and two pairs of latex gloves, as he had done earlier in the P3 room. In contrast to the laboratory room's stillness, the noise within cubicle four became deafening to Bukhari's nervous ears. As he prepared to rehydrate the toxin, the sound of Kavesh mechanically breathing became that of an accuser in the ears of the assassin. The doctor's hands began to shake more violently with each passing moment.

Through sheer willpower, Bukhari steadied himself enough to take the scalpel off the stainless-steel table and slice through the tough layer of parafilm. Dropping the scalpel on top of the stainless-steel table, he connected a hypodermic needle to a syringe and filled it with two milliliters of sterile saline solution. The needle shaking in Bukhari's hand threatened to hypnotize him with its constant, rapid motion. Years seemed to pass before the needle found its way to the inner Eppendorf tube packed with the dehydrated toxin. Bukhari squirted one milliliter of the solution into the vial. He allowed his trembling hands to shake it for a few seconds. Setting the vial down on the freestanding instrument table, Bukhari watched it settle for a moment, like a pie cooling on a kitchen windowsill.

Like minute rice, the re-hydrated contents of the vial came to life.

A strange sense of calm descended upon Bukhari, as though he was a bomber pilot about to release lethal cargo on his victims. With a steady hand, Bukhari re-inserted the needle into the vial and began withdrawing the toxin.

Kavesh, though intubated and asleep, turned in his bed and made a moaning sound. To Bukhari's high-strung mind, the ailing doctor's ghost was already coming to haunt him.

The needle snapped in two and the vial fell to cubicle four's floor.

Damn, damn, damn!

Ziad's endless tutorials paid-off. Bukhari stifled the scream bursting within him. Bukhari knew he had just spilled an airborne toxin that could slaughter him and everyone else in the MICU.

He held his breath and injected a few drops of toxin into the ventilator's aperture. With his head and chest beginning to pound from his last un-exhaled breath, Bukhari quickly collected all the materials he had used and deposited them in a biohazard bag lying close by the bedside. It did not occur to him, in view of the spilled toxin, the act was redundant. He did it out of habit, and after concluding, albeit sub-consciously, in order for him to escape, everything had to appear as normal as possible. Knowing one breath of air could kill him, Bukhari struggled to force a smile as he yanked open the curtains and stampeded out of the cubicle.

The nurses sitting at the station could see something was wrong with Bazzini. Very wrong. Head Nurse Gibson quickly checked cubicle four's vital signs on her monitor. Everything appeared unchanged. She leaped out from behind her desk to intercept the strangely unsteady Dr. Bazzini. As she came close to him, she saw... he was holding his breath!

Pushing her aside with one arm, Bukhari staggered past the nurse station and finally exhaled. A flock of nurses gathered around him.

Straightening himself up and breathing as rapidly as a sprinter, he quickly began marching towards the MICU's airlock.

"Everything's fine. Extubation will be just fine. See you all tomorrow. Yes, yes, tomorrow morning will be just fine."

Head Nurse Gibson considered pursuing the departing figure of Dr. Bazzini. She decided to phone Floyd, the guard at the hospital's main entrance. Perhaps something much more serious had gone wrong? As she cradled the red telephone between her chin and shoulder, Sarah Davidson approached her at the nurse's station.

"Everything seems to be okay, Jo-"

She stopped as her supervisor raised a finger.

"Floyd, wait, just a minute - "She turned to Sarah. "Everything's okay in four?"

Sarah nodded.

"Never mind Floyd. Sorry to bother you. No, we don't have a situation. Thanks." Josephine Gibson set the telephone back onto its plastic cradle.

"Well, Sarah Davidson, welcome to the action-packed world of modern medicine. They don't show things like that on TV."

The surrounding staff began to giggle and snigger.

"Some bedside manner," interjected Sarah.

"Hope he found a bucket in time," suggested a voice.

"Somebody call the mop brigade!" offered another.

The laughter continued. Josephine Gibson thought to herself, this new nurse was going to fit in just fine. She smiled at Sarah.

Chapter 6

Dr. Dan Howard smiled at Tracy Hopkins. It was an insincere smile and the first one she had seen in their two-year acquaintance. He unfolded his stained, yellow handkerchief and mopped his perspiring pate. Horrified, Tracy watched the tall, spindly scientist move closer to her.

"Good... morning, Tracy," he croaked.

"Doctor Howard," she replied hesitantly.

"Ah..." Howard looked around the empty communal office and noticed the time. "Working late, I see?"

"I've got a lot to do."

"Good, good. Well, don't let me get in your way."

Tracy and Howard eyed each other like a mongoose and a cobra.

"I'll be on my way," Howard mumbled.

"Good night, Dr. Howard." Tracy panicked as she watched her tormentor slowly back away from her desk.

The letter! He must have read the letter! But when?

She had put it there only a few minutes ago.

He looked demented. His eyes had a peculiar gleam to them.

"Good night, Tracy." Backing out through the office door.

Unnerved, Tracy began stuffing her belongings into the garbage bag as fast as her hands would allow. She kept glancing at the clock. Just a few more minutes. The clock's electronic buzzing kept growing louder and louder within her ears. She chewed her enormous wad of gum as quickly as her heart pounded. Finally, for all practical purposes, the desk was empty. Whatever remained was not worth one extra second of being in the same building as Dr. Dan Howard.

Tracy struggled under the weight of the stuffed garbage bag as she attempted to sling it over her shoulder, her slim frame barely able to support it. Ultimately, the bag proved too heavy, and some of its contents spilled out onto the floor. Kneeling, she quickly stuffed the scattered contents back into the bag and started dragging it. It slid smoothly on the waxed tile floor. Tracy paused for a moment before the door, straining to hear any sound of Howard on the other side.

There was complete silence. Satisfied Howard had left, she opened the door.

Tracy immediately recognized the gun's make and model: the Walther

PPK - the 'James Bond' pistol. Her father and her younger brother loved James Bond movies. Though not terribly fond of them herself, she had been forced to sit through 'Dr. No' enough times to recognize the daunting piece of hardware. Dr. Howard was as unoriginal in his firearm selection as he was in his scientific research.

He's going to kill me!

She dropped the neck of the garbage bag and began backing her way into the office.

I will be the first graduate student in the history of science to be killed by a distraught mentor!

In the dim light, Tracy could see the gun was steady and aimed directly at her. The man holding it, though, looked like a geyser, ready to erupt.

"I'm not going to hurt you, Tracy," he intoned softly, though shakily.

My God, he's going to try and rape me!

"Let me go, Dr. Howard! I won't tell anyone about this. Honest!"

"I need your help, Tracy."

The gun was almost within his arm's length of her face.

"You don't want me, Dr. Howard."

"I need you, Tracy." He sounded as though he was trying to convince himself.

Bill Hopkins had made sure his daughter knew how to defend herself as effectively as any female marine fresh out of Parris Island. Tracy aimed a perfect kick at Howard's groin and struck her mark with full fury. However, she was horrified when Howard emitted only a small grunt, as though he had banged himself on a table corner in the manner of his protégé Bukhari.

Losing the last of her composure, Tracy tried to break past her seemingly impervious tormentor. Howard, betraying his physical viciousness, caught Tracy's cascading hair and yanked it as he jammed the gun into her cheek.

"I told you, I need your help! Your help!"

Tracy could feel his heart beat with the force of a jackhammer through the dingy cloth of his blazer.

That's it! He's hopped up on some drug! Something strong enough to desensitize him to pain! Methamphetamines?

Maintaining her cool as best she could with the pistol now directly behind her right ear, she decided to play for time.

"I don't know."

"This is important! Do as I say!"

Howard marched her through the corridor to the P3 room. He spun her around and threw her against the laboratory's double-doors, leveling the pistol at her as she struggled to stand still.

"Tracy, I'm so sorry. But I need your help! It's very important you help me!" His voice was becoming increasingly shrill.

"No."

Howard stared at her dumbly. The various chemicals cruising in his circulation fought with each other to provide an artificial sensation of courage, and in the process dimmed his comprehension. He could not believe she had refused him. Who could refuse an order when looking down the barrel of a gun?

"Do you want to die?"

Howard jerked her away from the P3 room's entrance violently. He cocked the pistol's hammer and pushed the firearm into her open mouth.

"I want you to get something for me. If you won't - you will die, right here, right now!"

Tracy remembered what her father had taught her: play for time; give your adversaries enough rope to hang themselves. Whatever Howard wanted, it was not worth dying for on the fifth floor of the Guggenheim Building.

"What do you want?" she managed to ask.

"P3 room, in the minus 70 freezer, Bukhari's rack - there'll be a vial. Get it."

He released the shocked young woman from his grip, taking care to keep the gun leveled on her. Tracy never removed her eyes from his, another of her father's self-defense instructions. Looking away meant fear. She must not show Howard any fear. Tracy could see the bloodshot condition of Howard's eyes through the darkness. She thought about screaming and realized she would be dead before the first second passed. She felt Howard's hatred; whatever he wanted, he would not shy away from an opportunity to execute her in cold blood. Slowly, she began to open the P3 room's door behind her back.

Like dancers, Howard matched Tracy step for step as they entered the special laboratory's outer room together. She broke eye contact for a moment while reaching for a box of latex gloves.

"No prep," shouted Howard, "just get in."

Why doesn't he get it himself? He obviously knows where it is, whatever it is! And why doesn't he want me to wear gloves?

Hypothetically, anything that could contaminate the P3 room and kill a human was either frozen, diligently sealed or both. However, as any good scientist knows, such assumptions are easily broken by the reality of having to work and share space with the sloppy likes of Bukhari. Tracy again decided to play for time. Whatever Howard wanted, whatever stray microbes might be floating around the inner chamber of the P3 room, they were less immediately life-threatening than the Walther PPK aimed directly at her.

Tracy entered the inner P3 chamber, welcomed by its blue light. As soon as she was inside, Howard slammed the door shut behind her, making her flinch. Regaining her composure, Tracy made straight for the freezer. Opening it, she quickly found Bukhari's labeled shelf space.

It was strange. There was only one vial in his space. She expected to see many vials, considering how much time he spent in the room.

So where did all his vials go?

Perplexed, afraid, Tracy began to chew her gum faster and faster. Using a pair of sterile tongs, she began to examine the vial. Another surprise was in store for her. A larger vial hid a smaller one within, and they were both sealed with parafilm.

Stretching out her arm, she turned around slowly to show the vial to Dr. Howard, who was looking intently through the inner chamber's small, shatterproof window. Despite her problems, Tracy could not help smirking at the ludicrous sight of Howard pressing his face into the glass with all his might.

He looks like a gorilla wanting a banana!

Her eyes fell on a small clock placed high up on a shelf overlooking the tissue culture hood.

12:35 am.

My God, this has been one quarter-hour never to forget.

Gingerly holding the vial by the tongs, she walked to the door. In slow motion, she saw Howard give a broad, insincere smile. Then he locked the door.

Tracy stood with the vial in her hands for a few minutes, staring into space uncomprehendingly. Then, with horror, she realized what Howard was doing.

He was going to kill her by exposing her to Bukhari's pathogen. The one she held in her hand. She was the canary in a coal mine. Tracy slumped on the floor, still clutching the vial, eyes fixed balefully on Howard, too dazed and stunned to do anything.

Howard stared at her coldly, his smile now a full-fledged sneer.

Chapter 7

The MICU staff sneered at the inglorious exit of the imitation Dr. M Bazzini. His bizarre behavior had provided the only disturbance in an otherwise unusually quiet shift. Head Nurse Gibson surveyed her domain with pride. All required tasks had been performed on schedule. All patients slept soundly within their healing pods. She decided to spend some time getting Sarah Davidson acquainted with her new colleagues and brought coffee and juice to the desk at the central station. Soon a jovial but quiet office party atmosphere was underway. Sarah made her first social rounds beneath the blue glow of the MICU's lights.

Meanwhile, Bukhari was experiencing a very real, acute fear of his spilled bioweapon. If his calculations were correct, the contents on the floor of cubicle four were enough to wipe out the human population of North America, let alone the intensive care unit. By the time Bukhari's eyes had found the vial on the floor, he knew the MICU was surely doomed - if the superbug worked.

His creation, his superbug, could only kill when inhaled.

Bukhari thought of his creation as a deeply intoxicated and heavily armed vagrant, asleep on a park bench. A police officer comes along to rouse him and taps the edge of his nightstick against the hard side of the bench. Through his stupor, the tramp hears the officer, perhaps he even feels the club tapping. Slowly, he wakes up and incrementally realizes where he is and what is being asked of him. Any police officer knows one of law enforcement's most dangerous tasks is interacting with intoxicated addicts, given how one can never anticipate with certainty how they will react.

Bukhari's superbug cast off its initial drowsiness rapidly. The portion of the superbug injected into Dr. Kavesh's ventilator got to work somewhat faster than its brethren scattered across the floor of cubicle four. The mechanical lung surely and swiftly transported the biological agent directly into the stricken doctor's respiratory system.

More human forces disseminated the spilled portion. Had Bukhari knocked the vial to the steel table, the pathogen would still have spread. However, it moved much faster at the floor level, where it was stirred up by the air currents generated by the ventilation system and assorted nurses circulating in and out of the cubicle on their rounds.

Slowness is seldom a desirable feature of a weapon, conventional or otherwise. No sane military commander or leader would request his ordinance department to design the slowest possible weapon, even if it possessed enormous killing potential.

The superbug was not slow in waking up and producing its lethal toxins. Its efficiency was no accident. Bukhari had been the best and brightest of Ghazni's students. He had created the perfect bioweapon.

Now the deadly superbug was circulating freely through the ventilation system of St Mary's MICU. Within its antiseptic, airtight confines, the superbug multiplied with a speed that was peerless. Bukhari's dream was to become a nightmare.

Chapter 8

Dr. Dan Howard peered through the small, grated window of the P3 room, staring at the fixed figure of Tracy Hopkins. He peeled his face away from the shatterproof pane to look at his wristwatch.

2:35 am.

Still not dead. She's still not dead!

Howard returned to pressing his face into the grated window. He inadvertently pushed both hands against the room's door, above the window's line of sight. The loaded pistol slipped out from his left, shooting hand, and clattered to the floor. Howard dropped as though Tracy had just taken a shot at him from her seated position behind the airtight door. Quickly, on all fours, he found the gun and returned it to his dominant hand. As he raced the few feet back to the door, its heavy bolts collided with his belt buckle. He returned the pistol to its shoulder holster and went back to gaze dumbly at Tracy. He quizzed himself.

What's her name? What was the girl's name?

The assorted collection of chemicals circulating in his system did little to provide clarity to his thought process.

Though he had always been a poor scientist, Dan Howard had been blessed with an innate instinct for politics on par with Boss Tweed or any of the other legendary Gilded Age Tammany Hall politicians. He had the ability to transform himself into anything anybody wanted at an instant's notice, so long as the expected performance ultimately rewarded him.

From the very beginning of his career at Mayo Clinic, Howard knew he did not belong there. On reflection, Howard had been amazed by a small clinic established in 1889 by the Mayo brothers in response to a tornado had grown to such a proportion. Not only had the clinic grown over the years in providing clinical care, but it also undertook basic research. In fact, it had received the Nobel Prize in Medicine in 1950 when Dr.'s. Kendall and Hench elucidated the structure and function of steroids. To take advantage of its Nobel Prize laurels, the clinic had aggressively hired researchers and given away tenure. Howard had been one of the astute ones to avail himself of the opportunity.

He had hitched his fortune to the once-brilliant, now stale, Dr. Robert Webster. Webster had valued the political support and perceived friendship of Howard. In turn, Webster and his once-considerable reputation shielded Howard. The senior authorities in the department considered Howard the equivalent of Webster's pet; to keep Webster, they would have to keep Howard. Initially, the investment had paid off well for all concerned.

During the mid-1990s, the traditional sources of funding for scientific research in America began to evaporate. The most established and distinguished scientists had to hustle as hard as the humblest graduate student for money. After the turn of the decade, Webster, now promoted to the Microbiology Department's chair, simply could not afford Howard's friendship any longer. To make matters worse, Webster's assumption of power had also changed him. Charged with a newfound sense of authority, Webster told Howard exactly how little he thought of him and of his abilities.

"Like everyone else, you will have to fund your own research. The clinic also expects your research to lead to several publications in peer-reviewed journals every year. If these criteria are not met, your tenure here will be jeopardized."

At first, Howard was shocked by the change brought on by promotion of his once-close friend. True to form, he resolved to roll with the changes posed by Webster's new attitude. If he was the worst member of the department, then he would behave accordingly. Howard allowed his laboratory to become the most disgraceful in the entire Mayo Clinic. If he could lose influence with someone like Webster, nothing mattered anymore. He could do no worse; he could do no better. He occupied his time waiting for the inevitable - a formal end to his career, as researchers far better than he succumbed to the economics of a new age.

Salvation had come from the least likely of sources. At first, he had nearly thrown away the letter, assuming it was a practical joke. However, he noticed his name had been typed, not printed, on the gold embossed envelope. His hands shook with excitement as his eyes skipped down to the page's bottom.

"Due to your distinguished reputation as a brilliant scientist in the field of microbiology research," the letter figuratively read, "you, Dr. Dan Howard have been recommended for a major, multi-year grant to be offered by the newly founded International Society for the Interdiction of Pathogens, or I.S.I.P."

Howard had never heard of such an organization. He assumed he never would again. Nevertheless, in the hope the letter was not the result of someone's perverted imagination, he wrote a thank-you letter to the foundation, setting a new record for obsequiousness. Several weeks passed. The Society called. Would Dr. Howard allow members of I.S.I.P. the pleasure of a tour of his laboratory to announce the award? Shock overwhelmed the scientist upon learning this news, and especially the amount of money involved. He could now literally buy everyone working on the Guggenheim Building's fifth floor. Dr. Dan Howard, the least distinguished member of the faculty, had suddenly become the most endowed researcher in the history of Mayo Clinic.

The weeks following the announcement passed joyously for the previously unaccomplished scientist. Howard greatly enjoyed all the media attention, especially the enormous private luncheon hosted by the CEO of Mayo Clinic in his honor. He loved being quickly reassigned a parking space right next to the main entrance, besting Robert Webster. He loved the looks of jealousy shot at him by his colleagues as he passed them in the halls or in the parking lot.

Howard, the modern scientist, cherished every moment of his new status. Howard the political animal wondered what the catch was. Very quickly, he saw I.S.I.P. did things differently than any other known scientific foundation: much like Dr. Howard, they did nothing. They asked for no accounting, no explanation of expenditures, no plans, and no results. The language in all of their formal paperwork deferred to Howard's presumed expertise the administration and use of the grant to its fullest potential.

The first year had been a dream come true, and Howard un-bottled all his pent-up desires. He spent money lavishly, attracting a better crop of researchers. With the added prestige emboldening him more than usual, he pilfered the interesting work of his charges. The I.S.I.P. Foundation considered the work superb and gave him even more money.

The latter part of the year had seen the arrival of Dr. Tariq Bukhari, from Lahore Medical School, Pakistan. Bukhari's arrival and installation had, if anything, been choreographed even more smoothly than the announcement of his award. The foundation had basically presented it as a fait accompli. At the time, Howard could hardly have cared less. One more post-doctoral fellow? Go stand in line.

But the normally distant and disinterested Howard could not help but notice this Dr. Bukhari. With great frequency, I.S.I.P. would call to check on Dr. Bukhari's status, 'for visa purposes.'

"We hope you're helping him and making sure he does well." Subtle hints were made, ensuring Bukhari's progress and preferential treatment.

The political calculator quickly summed up that somehow, Dr. Bukhari and I.S.I.P. were connected. This did not bother Howard in the slightest. He correctly deduced his grant depended on staying out of Dr. Tariq Bukhari's way as much as possible.

For three years, the arrangement had proved to be quite fruitful for Dr. Howard. He did not ask about whatever Dr. Bukhari seemed to be working on. In fact, Howard expended great effort in protecting the post-doctoral fellow.

Several months ago, in the continuing process of collecting physical chits to demonstrate his considerable financial prestige, Howard elected to buy a gun. Completely ignorant about guns, he recognized the Walther-PPK at a local gun shop. He liked the association. Dr. Dan Howard - like James Bond, a man who needs to carry a gun. Soon enough, he realized carrying a gun was far more of an effort than simply owning one. The small pistol eventually found its way into the bottom left-hand drawer of his desk.

Around the same time Dr. Howard began to exercise his constitutional right to bear arms, Bukhari's assorted experiments began to work. Dr. James Delmez, the program director, now working for Howard after losing his grants, mentioned even for all their freewheeling ways and Tariq Bukhari's carte blanche, they had significant expenses.

"You know, we are consuming more animals than the rest of the department put together" He observed. Not that he cared about the animals. He only wanted to know what they were being used for.

"Maybe he is reselling them to pay for gas. And car insurance." Howard made one of his rare jokes.

What they did not know was that Bukhari had to make certain - had to be sure without the slightest possibility for error - that he had created the superbug to fulfill his mission. Ghazni had repeatedly told him that he, Bukhari, was the fittest one to go abroad. He would develop the very weapon that would be the West's destruction right under its nose. He could take as long as he wanted. He could have as much as he wanted. The only proviso was when the time came, he and his invention could not fail, for the repercussions of failure would be swift and certain.

Week after week, wave after wave of Guinea pigs succumbed to his invention. Soon, Bukhari had given the appropriate signals to let his control officer Ziad Ghazni know the final test was about to begin.

At this point, Ziad received some highly unusual instructions directly from Ghazni which were without precedent. The leader of the ISI's bioweapon program wanted Dr. Howard to ask Bukhari specific questions about the superbug, to be recorded on tape. In simple code, a list of questions in Pushto was sent to him, which Ziad translated into English.

Ziad was perplexed.

Ghazni's a brilliant scientist. Why did he want someone else to answer these questions? Why did he want Howard to ask them? Why record the answers?

Slowly, the answers to his own questions became apparent to Ziad. This was to be a backup plan to ensure Howard's eternal silence.

Ziad had been living in the US for a few years before Bukhari showed up. As part of his job, he had learned English and had familiarized himself with American culture. He realized, though, his lack of scientific training eliminated any chance of his identifying whether Howard was lying. Now, Ziad, the ex-Mujahedeen fighter who had spent more hours in combat than out of it, decided to summon some help.

In late April, a few weeks before the fateful night of the superbug's deployment, Dr. Howard received a call from I.S.I.P.'s main office. Apparently, two auditors would be paying an immediate visit to Dr. Howard and his laboratory. Nothing urgent. After four years of ever-increasing funding, the Foundation's board merely wanted a first-hand report of what transpired in the laboratory. A late-night meeting time had been requested, owing to 'travel difficulties.'

Dan Howard had worked his way through college as a biochemistry major synthesizing assorted recreational chemicals for sale to his fellow students. In the slow hours leading up to the auditing team's arrival, Howard began gobbling amphetamines he had made.

Courage, I must face them with courage!

As the assorted chemicals began bolstering his system, he felt confident these inspectors would be as laissez-faire as the philanthropic organization who employed them.

At 10.30 pm, a burly, short dark man sporting an enormous mustache knocked at the door of Howard's office. Marching in, he identified himself as Zulfikar Qutaybah Khalaaq. Ziad had run across the name while reading a report on fraudulent medical practices and had loved it for its complexity. No American would ever remember a name like that. A blonde giant followed him, introducing himself as Kirk Lesh. Silently, the two men circled Howard, blocking the terrified scientist's path back to his desk.

Despite the enormous quantity of amphetamines cruising through Howard's circulatory system, his heart nearly stopped as Tariq Bukhari entered the office, banging his hip loudly on the doorknob. Uncharacteristically, though, Bukhari failed to unleash his usual invective against anyone present. The visibly agitated post-doctoral fellow sat down on his special chair, placed against the wall near Howard's desk. Howard saw Bukhari acknowledge the other two with the slightest of nods. It was the first time in over three years Howard had seen Bukhari offer a hint of courtesy to anyone else.

"Dr. Howard," began the fellow with the mustache. Howard focused his increasingly constricted attention upon him. "...It is my great pleasure to report the I.S.I.P. Board of Directors finds your work to be of invaluable service to the future health and prosperity of the human race."

The egomaniac in Howard began to glow.

From the corner of his vision, Howard watched the gigantic blonde set up some kind of device.

"However, in accordance with the terms and conditions stipulated in the award notice of your grant, we ask your assistance in a small project of ours."

A video camera? On a tripod?

Howard wondered what the giant had in mind as he directed Bukhari to reposition his chair so the post-doctoral fellow and the faculty member would appear close together. Lesh proceeded to set up a small but powerful light tower and suspend a boom mike from another tripod placed on the desk.

"We would like you to ask Dr. Bukhari a few questions concerning his work here in your laboratory."

Howard turned to focus on his bellicose protégé. To his surprise, Bukhari had dressed himself up to the nines, as though he were about to attend a black-tie-optional awards banquet. Howard found himself gaping at Bukhari's candy-striped bow tie.

"We trust you have no objections to this small inconvenience."

Howard returned his gaze to Ziad, masquerading as Zulfikar. The short burly agent sat in his chair with enough authority to transform it into a throne.

"It will be my pleasure. My work would have been discontinued were it not for the extreme kindness and generosity of the I.S.I.P... "

"Thank you, Dr. Howard," interrupted the suddenly acid-tongued blonde giant, "we are aware of your sincere, eternal gratitude towards our mutual employer. However, for our little project, we need to ask that you remain a pure, uncorrupted man of science. Ask the following as though you were administering Dr. Bukhari an oral doctoral examination."

Ziad slipped a package over the smooth desktop to Howard. Howard opened it with trembling hands. The list of questions made him feel no better. Cholera? Toxins? The old scientist's jaw dropped. What had

Bukhari been doing, experimenting with these?

"Dr. Howard, please be aware that my colleagues who want the answers to these questions have extensive scientific training. It would be most disappointing if you soft-pedaled any of these questions or if, in any way, you failed to exhibit your usually rigorous standards in questioning Dr. Bukhari."

With a jerk, Howard returned to the present. Though he sported a wristwatch more suited to the income of an investment banker, Howard forced himself to gaze at the clock hung above Tracy's head.

3.15 am.

Not dead yet. What's her name? Whoever she is, she's not dead yet.

Her slight frame and short stature had allowed Tracy to prop her feet up onto the counter. She had put the vial back in the rack and sat with her eyes closed. Howard saw her breathing normally. Apparently, she was napping!

How can this girl sleep at a time like this!

The chemicals inside his brain returned Howard to his nightmare two weeks ago, when he learned the truth behind his protégé's research through his forced 'examination' of Bukhari.

"Smile for the camera," the blonde giant had instructed him. Instinctively, Howard attempted to do exactly that. The scientist felt the light's strong heat against his face. The small one said something in a language Howard could not place. Bukhari responded with the same pattern of sounds. Apparently, Khalaaq and Bukhari were compatriots!

"Dr. Howard, please begin," intoned the voice from the other side of his desk. The actor in Howard delivered a bravura performance as if his life depended on it. He began to read the questions.

"Ah, ctb is..."

"The sum of all my work," answered Bukhari quickly. The small video camera captured everything without emitting a sound.

HOWARD: Dr. Bukhari, how did you isolate the cholera toxin gene, which produces the toxin in ctb?

BUKHARI: I followed the standard procedure by first isolating the cholera toxin gene from vibrio cholerae, the cholera bacteria. I used the RE bgl II—

LESH: RE?

HOWARD: What?

LESH: Why don't you ask our candidate what a RE is?

HOWARD: Why? Everybody knows what REs are.

LESH: Don't assume the entire world is as smart as you are Dr. Howard.

Howard simultaneously felt elated at the compliment and terrified at its implications. Who exactly would be viewing this tape? Howard the actor continued to rescue Howard the scientist.

HOWARD: Could you tell us what REs are, Dr. Bukhari?

BUKHARI: Restriction enzymes are special enzymes that cut out specific DNA sequences from total cellular DNA.

LESCH: Could you simplify that a bit?

BUKHARI: They are programmed enzymes, birds of prey in the microbiological world. If you want a particular gene cut out from the total cellular DNA, you get the appropriate RE. It dives into the tangled web of DNA strands, and, like laser-guided bombs, knows exactly where to go. It locks in right away onto the specific DNA sequence that binds the genes in place. Once it reaches its target area, it destroys everything locking that particular gene in a frame. The gene you want is liberated, floating up in a cosmic cesspool, while the native DNA is left behind like a bombed-out bridge.

HOWARD: And what was the gene you isolated?

BUKHARI: The cholera toxin gene, ctx.

HOWARD: And you used?

BUKHARI: A RE called bgl II.

HOWARD: What did you do with the gene?

BUKHARI: I introduced it into the plasmid pLRT-

LESH: And a plasmid is-

BUKHARI: Special carrier DNA that moves genes from one cell to another-

HOWARD: Like carrier pigeons!

The men masquerading as Lesh and Khalaaq exchanged smiles over Howard's new enthusiasm. So, this was the other reason why Ghazni wanted Howard involved, thought Ziad. He knew Howard would become scientifically interested, and genuinely quiz Bukhari, thus inadvertently giving a scientific second opinion.

BUKHARI: I cut pLRT with the RE bgl II so the edges of the cut plasmid were identical to that of ctx also cut with the RE bgl II. Then I added the cut ctx gene into the cut pLRT suspension. To complete the process, I added DNA Ligase.

Howard opened his mouth to ask for further clarification. As though irritated, Bukhari beat him to the punch by responding.

BUKHARI...DNA Ligase, of course, is the opposite of a RE. It, much like a surgeon, sutures wounds, the wounds, in this case, being in the plasmid and ctx gene. The application of Ligase healed the cuts placed into the plasmid and the ctx gene. This new pLRT was now ready for the next act, carrying the ctx gene within it.

LESH: Like a kangaroo in its mother's pouch?

KHALAAQ (stifling laughter): Although we appreciate your spontaneous analogy, Dr. Howard is asking the questions here tonight. Please continue, Dr. Howard.

HOWARD: And what was the next step?

BUKHARI: I transferred the gene to a receptive bacterium, mtb.

HOWARD: Mtb?

BUKHARI: Mycobacterium tuberculosis.

HOWARD: Dr. Bukhari, how did you introduce the gene into the mtb?

BUKHARI: I used the technique of electroporation - the new pLRT was placed into a culture of mtb. To facilitate the DNA transfer, an electric current was passed through the mixture. This introduced the plasmid into the mtb, creating what I call ctb.

HOWARD: Dr. Bukhari, what evidence do you have to show the ctx gene produces the cholera toxin in its new host?

BUKHARI: I conducted several experiments whereby I grew ctb in culture dishes and recovered the medium. I carried out immunoprecipitation assays on the medium, wherein I placed antibodies against the toxin and ran it on a gel.

HOWARD: And your results were?

BUKHARI: The antibody bound the toxin every time, and the combination could be seen on the gels.

HOWARD: Have you performed tests for biological activity and, if so, what experimental animal did you use?

BUKHARI: Ctb has been tested on Guinea pigs. These animals, if infected with a regular strain of mtb, survive for months. However, they die within half an hour when placed in direct contact with minuscule amounts of ctb.

HOWARD: Could you describe the manner of death for these animals.

BUKHARI: Their lungs became filled with fluid. Apparently, ctb made the toxin that induced the lungs to secrete copious amounts of fluid.

In silence, Howard gaped at the three men surrounding him. He could not believe the next question he was going to ask.

HOWARD: Dr. Bukhari, is this manner of death what we can expect for humans exposed to ctb?

BUKHARI: Absolutely.

HOWARD: Drowning in one's own secretions. How terrible! What...

BUKHARI (interrupting): For your information, I made a recombinant tubercle bacillus with the cholera toxin gene in it which, when inhaled by a human, would cause acute pulmonary edema.

At last, the normally pugnacious Bukhari had decided to make an appearance from behind his striped bow tie.

Howard was too shocked to respond for a while. Dimly, he was aware Bukhari and the mustached man were looking at him intently. He glanced at the giant, who was frowning and appeared to have lost some of his composure. He left the room quietly. Howard the actor continued to read the script.

HOWARD: What was the purpose of creating this recombinant bacterium?

Bukhari's two-word answer knocked him down flat.

BUKHARI: Biological warfare.

'Biological warfare,' uttered in Bukhari's voice, cycled endlessly through Howard's mind as he recalled the interview. The rest of the interview was an even bigger disaster. At the end of it, he recalled vaguely, the blonde had returned and stowed away all of the video gear. The two men had shaken Howard's hand, thanking the busy scientist profusely for his valuable time on such short notice. With that, they had walked out through the door of his office, like two salespersons who had dropped by to leave their latest catalogs. Bukhari had left the office with a smug, contemptuous look on his face.

Howard had returned to sit behind his desk, dumbfounded. An ambush. That's right, an ambush - just the way it always happened in spy movies. He, Dan Howard, had been set up. Was it real? Did it actually happen? Was this an elaborate joke? Howard could not decide what had happened. If it had been real, then he was dead. They would not let him live: he knew too much. For the next week, Howard refused to leave his office, sleeping under the desk, cradling his beloved James Bond handgun, ready for action even though he had never fired a single shot with intent to kill.

Strangely enough, Bukhari had become exceedingly cordial towards him after that night, almost friendly in the conventional sense of the word. It was as if the young doctor had shared some great secret with his entrapped sponsor. Responding to this strange new course of events,

Howard's innate admiration for Bukhari's ingenious creation allowed him to ask more questions about the project.

However, Bukhari proved coy in giving direct answers. Still, for the first time, Howard began to fear Bukhari's laboratory habits. The knowledge of Bukhari's work habits scared the old scientist more than the events of the week before had. The only thing more dangerous than a functional biological weapon was a functional biological weapon running loose in his P3 facility.

The political animal in Dan Howard correctly realized his life, as he knew it, was over. It did not matter if this meant his outright murder, or simply having to live with the fact a toxin could wipe out the whole of North America had been developed in his laboratory, under his auspices.

Still alive. She's still alive. Maybe Bukhari didn't contaminate the area after all!

3:45 am.

Howard brought the butt of his pistol to bear against the shatterproof pane of the P3 room, waking Tracy with a start. She shook herself, groggily hoping someone had come to rescue her. Through her hazy vision, she saw Dr. Howard and his unblinking eyes on the other side of the window. She heard his muffled shouting.

Tracy forced herself to retain her aloof posture, casually straightening herself and looking at the small clock mounted above the tissue culture hood.

Howard had begun unbolting the chamber's inner door, pointing his gun at Tracy.

He's coming to kill me!

Tracy spat out the gum in her mouth and let out a loud scream.

Chapter 9

Dr. Neil Kavesh was dying to yank the tube out of his mouth and take a natural, deep breath.

At 3:45 am on Monday morning, he began to drown. The bacteria, forced into his lungs by the ventilator, had quickly got to work. Five liters of fluid had rapidly entered the doctor's lungs. None of the sophisticated equipment attached to him diagnosed the internal flooding, reporting only his oxygenation status was deteriorating.

Dr. Kavesh awoke, choking and fighting for his life. The ventilator could not assist him in breathing anymore. Identical alarms sounded inside both cubicle four and at the centrally located nurses' station. Nurses Gibson and Davidson quickly absorbed the information from the silently screaming monitors: a pulse over 100; blood oxygenation of less than 80 percent and falling rapidly. Oblivious to Nurse Davidson's sudden appearance by his side, Kavesh began to panic. His eyes snapped open. Sweat began to drench his brow as he tried to suck in more air than the ventilator would allow.

Immediately, Nurse Davidson realized an emergency existed, one that had to be handled by the doctor on call. With equal measures of trepidation and urgency, she lifted the telephone by the patient's bedside and made a call to the on-call doctor. A sense of frustration rose inside her as several rings passed before she heard the irritated voice of Dr. Calixto Romero.

"Dr. Romero here," he finally answered.

"This is Sarah. Dr. Kavesh in number four is having trouble breathing. His pulse is 110 and his pulse oxygenation is down to 80 percent. The ventilator alarm is going crazy!"

Romero gave a long, melodramatic sigh. He cursed this nurse's gross incompetence. Obviously, the patient's asthma was reactivating.

"What's his inspired oxygen?" he drawled.

"Sixty percent," she replied.

"Increase it to 100 percent. Also, give him 80 milligrams of Solumedrol." Nothing steroids cannot fix, he thought with satisfaction. Good thing they were discovered at Mayo Clinic.

"Will you come and take a look?"

Romero really hated this attitude some nurses had. It was as if they had to see the doctor stand by the bedside and wave a magic wand over the patient to ward off whatever evil spirits brought them down in the first place. It did not seem to matter if the situation could be handled over the telephone.

"No. If he doesn't improve, call me back."

Nurse Davidson slammed the telephone down and rushed off to carry out his instructions.

For a brief time, the increased oxygen arrested the speed of Kavesh's demise. The doctor even managed to fall asleep for a few moments, as more oxygen was able to penetrate the dense mass of fluid occupying his lungs. His respite was short-lived.

Within ten minutes of the ventilator changes, the ventilator's assorted alarms began sounding again as Dr. Kavesh began to succumb to the inundation of his lungs. Viewing the monitors with increasing alarm, Head Nurse Gibson rushed to call Dr. Romero, waking him again.

"Dr. Kavesh cannot breathe and all of the alarms are going off. Get here right away!" She hung up before the startled doctor could reply.

Romero leaped to his feet and stormed into the MICU proper. How dare that insolent cow order him around! He swept aside the curtains of cubicle four.

"What the... "

Kavesh's dying eyes convinced the resentful doctor of the situation's legitimacy. Dr. Romero glanced at the ventilator to verify the settings. He saw appropriate rates for inspired oxygen, pressure, and volume. He pulled on his stethoscope and listened to Kavesh's chest, expecting to hear loud wheezes of asthma exacerbation. Instead, Romero heard nothing, nothing at all. He listened harder - bubbling! The sound of fluid bubbling in Kavesh's chest.

Impossible! Asthma exacerbation does not produce fluid. Moreover, Kavesh had no history of heart failure.

Romero silently begged an answer from Kavesh's wide, terrorized eyes. The two men panicked simultaneously.

"Blood count, arterial blood gasses, and electrolytes! Stat! Twelve-lead EKG now!"

Cubicle four became a hive of activity as every nurse jumped in to help. Blood was drawn, an EKG performed.

Kavesh's oxygen saturation continued its rapid decline... eighty.... seventy-nine.... seventy-eight.

The EKG monitor showed an increasingly irregular heartbeat.

Beep... beep.... beep-beep.... beep-beep.

"Give him a double dose of nebulizer!"

Romero remained convinced asthma exacerbation was at the root of the breathing problems. The fluid would be an enigma to solve later. The nebulizer would have helped if it had indeed been an asthma exacerbation. Five minutes went by. The nebulizer achieved nothing.

The oxygen level in Kavesh' bloodstream accelerated its free-fall.... seventy.... sixty-nine.... sixty-eight.

Kavesh's heart began to beat even more erratically!

Beep... beep-beep... beepbeepbeepbeep.

Kavesh lost consciousness.

"Get a chest X-ray!" Gibson half suggested, half ordered.

A digital X-ray was quickly taken.

The results of the arterial blood gas test were the first to come back. Romero looked at them uncomprehendingly. Carbon dioxide normal, oxygen low; entirely inconsistent with a severe asthma attack. In desperation, Romero increased the volume and pressure of the inspired air, hoping an increase in airflow would somehow remedy the situation. The breathing machine pushed a greater volume of air with a stronger force into the small, remaining lung tissue. It was like blowing air into an over-inflated balloon. The balloon burst.

Oxygen saturation fell into the forties and sank to thirty-nine... thirty-eight.

The heart began to go crazy. It did not like this overabundance of carbon dioxide and lack of oxygen. The rate shot up to two hundred twenty.

Beepbeepbeepbeep.

"He's in V-tach! Call a code! Cardiovert him with 360 joules now!" Gibson shouted.

The cardiac arrest crash cart burst into cubicle four. Romero hurriedly activated the cardioverter to charge it. Once ready, he placed its two paddles on Kavesh's chest.

"All clear!" he warned.

Everyone else stepped back from the doctor and patient. The charge lifted the increasingly lifeless Kavesh clear off the bed's surface with his arms flailing, like a man drowning at sea. Romero looked optimistically at the monitors. The patient's signs did not improve.

"Again," ordered Romero. The procedure was repeated several times.

No effect.

Romero called out in desperation, "Any other laboratory results back?"

"All electrolytes normal, blood counts normal," was the quick, anonymous reply.

The answer so baffled Romero he stood away from the patient's chest to ponder the situation. Kavesh was not internally bleeding into his chest. Abnormal sodium or potassium levels were not causing his heart to beat irregularly. So, what was it?!

"Give him an ampoule of bicarbonate! Give him lidocaine!" In desperation, Romero threw everything in his armamentarium at the near-dead Kavesh, hoping something would work. Nothing did.

The heart had had enough. The entire staff looked up simultaneously at the EKG monitor as it registered a flatline.

"External pacemakers! Quick!"

Romero tried pacing the heart externally, hoping it would respond. It did not. It was like flogging a dead horse.

The X-rays, developed from a scanned image and processed within the MICU, were thrust before Romero's eyes. He refused to believe the evidence before him. Two-thirds of Kavesh's chest cavity had filled with fluid. His lungs looked as though they were two sponges left exposed outdoors to soak up rainwater. The pathetically small nubs of unsubmerged lung on top could not supply the oxygen demanded by Kavesh's body.

By failing to consider anything other than asthma exacerbation, by failing to get a chest X-ray sooner, and by failing to remove the fluid in Kavesh's chest, Romero had sealed his professional ruin.

The ubiquitous, steady tone of the EKG machine doubled as Kavesh's funeral march. Romero called off the code and officially pronounced Dr. Neil Kavesh dead.

It was 4:15 am.

Chapter 10

The dashboard clock read 4:15 am when Bukhari rejoiced by driving his car out of the apartment complex.

He spat into the river with contempt. Tariq Bukhari discarded the white laboratory coat that had served him so well and dumped it into the Rochester River, four miles from Mayo Clinic. The stethoscope followed quickly. He now had to get back to his apartment for his rendezvous with Ziad.

Just a few hours had passed since he had sped out of St Mary's MICU with bursting lungs. He had anticipated the possibility of becoming infected by his own creation while administering the toxin to Dr. Kavesh. For that eventuality, he had obtained a bottle of ctb's antidote, specially sent from Pakistan. He took out the bottle and fingered it for a while, unsure whether to take a few capsules or not. He decided not to.

"Allah ordained that I perform this deed tonight, and Allah wouldn't command me to do so unless it is intended that I live. If I don't live, that, too, is Allah's will. Ghazni has promised me eternal glory for developing ctb. Glory will be mine, dead or alive!"

After leaving the medical intensive care unit, Bukhari had hurried back to his apartment and turned the computer on. Connecting to St Mary's mainframe, he accessed Kavesh's monitors. He had watched with breathless excitement as his victim's oxygenation status plummeted. His heart had raced as he watched Kavesh go into cardiac arrest. Racing out of his apartment in a state of giddy excitement, he drove straight out of Rochester. The car was his only friend, and it was with the car he would celebrate accomplishing his goal.

He stayed out a little while longer before turning the Dodge Viper around and heading back. He was due to rendezvous with Ziad in another half-hour.

Bukhari hated America and everything politically and culturally American. He hated America as much as he secretly yearned to love it. Subconsciously, he managed to separate the economic benefits of residing in the US from the political and religious aspects. The one American passion he indulged in was a love affair with automobiles. He had not hesitated to share his love of driving with Ziad, who happened to share the same interest. Driving the wide spacious streets of Rochester and the interstates of the Midwest became paradisiacal experiences for the two men.

However, unlike Ziad, Bukhari held no romantic views of the physical condition of American roads. Only the cars. Though driving an American car on American roads always reminded him of the terrible poverty and hardship into which he had been born, it was also proof that he had overcome the arrows life had thrown his way. Those who shared his native village joked that God had only completed half of his work in creating their village. Mechanical vehicles had no reason to attempt using the dirt paths that passed for streets in the village of Parachimar in Pakistan.

The village was as ancient as it was poor. No one could remember why anyone had settled there in the first place. Through the succession of centuries, many different aristocratic families had laid claim to the small village and its surrounding lands. Some had even fought each other over its possession. None had visited it for more than a few hours.

The villagers toiled in the barren fields all-day and slept a few fitful hours each night. They had only one form of recreation - one with a significant side effect. As a result, the village had more children than it could possibly provide for. Most of them perished at an early age from malnutrition and disease. Tariq Bukhari was the twelfth child of a landless farm laborer.

When he was seven, someone in his family sold the young boy into slavery. Bukhari was never certain who it was. All he knew was that one day an elder sister delivered him into the care of a man who marched him from his village to the frontier city of Peshawar on foot. Like most of his fellow villagers, Bukhari had never been more than a few miles away from the earthen hut that had always been his home. For his first few moments in Peshawar, the young Bukhari enjoyed the innocent sensation of being a child and experiencing the wonders of urban civilization. He marveled at the opulent dress of the townspeople and the strange, loud moving carts that flowed haltingly throughout the densely packed, paved streets without any beasts of burden to draw them forward.

His wonder was short-lived. The man he was with had been introduced to him as a family friend who would take him to a better life. In truth, the man was a slave procurer for a factory that made soccer, cricket, and baseballs for export to the US and Europe. Children in the US and Europe played with the balls that children in Pakistan slaved over. The factory depended on child labor for the manufacture of these cheap sporting goods.

Mentally and psychologically, Bukhari never left the brutal, prison-like atmosphere of that factory. Had hatred for that part of his life not blinded him to his past, he would have connected his lifelong physical clumsiness to the years he had spent working there. The ceaseless weaving, poor food and lodging, lack of ventilation, and the harsh and arbitrary nature of discipline meted out by the overseers - all this destroyed what natural co-ordination he once possessed. After a year of such existence, Bukhari began to walk like an old, arthritic man. His work, such as it was, began to suffer. The overseers constantly threatened him with expulsion onto the streets of Peshawar and certain death from starvation or exposure, whichever came first.

However, one of the overseers, Hamid Gul, saw something in the rapidly fading boy that gave him cause for consideration. Indeed, it was an idea no one else in the factory had ever heard of before, much less implemented. The child workers usually came and went like sparrows. Some managed to escape back home. Others managed to reach adulthood for a while before dying. Most simply disappeared one day, never to return to their workstation, to be replaced by someone new and painfully younger.

Hamid Gul observed that young Tariq refused to be broken. Though he kept falling farther and farther behind as his body weakened, his spirit remained strong.

"Why not turn the boy into a junior overseer? Let him handle the stick. Why not put such talent to use?" Gul suggested to his fellow overseers.

At the age of nine, not even able to spell his name or count beyond simple numbers, Tariq Bukhari became the master of his fellow children, berating and admonishing them.

His viciousness surprised and relieved the adult overseers. With young Tariq in charge, they had more time for playing cards or carrying on with their other businesses, legitimate or otherwise. The young Tariq, in turn, unleashed all his fury and hatred, day after day, month after month, on other children.

Two years after his 'promotion,' the sharp blaring of police whistles roused the children. Most of the little workers had no idea who policemen were, or what they were supposed to do. A swarm of strange, brown-uniformed men wearing berets showed up outside their quarters one day.

"Outside, in a line!" They yelled.

In a concession to Western concerns about child labor, many years before Iqbal Masih was to address the US Congress and be executed in

Pakistan for his speech, the Pakistani national government had elected to make a show of shutting down a few factories around the country. The Peshawar sports factory had a reputation for foulness that had reached all the way to the United Nations. Its closure was hailed by the Western world as a victory in the cause of human rights. As with all of the other children, eleven-year-old Tariq Bukhari suddenly found himself unemployed and without the simplest of means for survival.

The children from the factory were first assigned to the state orphanage. That institution's director soon begged, then bribed the local government to remove the children as quickly as possible. Hard beyond their years, unaccustomed to having time of their own, the children ran riot as a pack. Bukhari was, by far, the worst case. He had become used to being unquestioningly obeyed and having the complete authority to punish all who failed to comply.

The local authorities, looking for assistance, contacted an American Methodist missionary society who ran an orphanage in Lahore. The conduct of the newly manumitted kids shocked even the well-experienced missionaries. Reverend Karl Knisely, the leader, agreed to take all the children en-masse back to Lahore. Shrewdly, he recognized the kids only knew brutality and each other. To split them apart at this point would only guarantee their individual destruction. Perfectly fluent in Pushto, Reverend Knisely enlisted Bukhari's help in keeping the children settled and together for the long journey to Lahore.

"Remember young Tariq, we all depend on you. Make sure all children stay together till we reach Lahore."

Formally empowered once again, Bukhari acted as a ruthless guard dog. Not one child was lost on the journey.

Many of the children never grew accustomed to the sudden new world of food, steady shelter, and personal care. Bukhari, on the other hand, took to it as though he had never known anything else. After several months had passed, Knisely began the process of educating the still-illiterate Bukhari as his own personal project. Even Knisely was surprised by his intuition in this case. Tariq Bukhari was a bonafide, raw, natural genius.

The adolescent boy absorbed knowledge the way a desert seed soaks up water. Within a few years, the boy had reached his expected level of education and was even beginning to master foreign languages such as English. Knisely had also invested a considerable effort in instructing Bukhari morally. The pastor never failed to tell Bukhari he had extraordinary gifts and it was his responsibility to use those gifts to help others as he himself had been helped.

Under the kindly man's protection and guidance, Bukhari began to shed much of the cruelty that had been his nature early on. He even apologized to those who had worked under him at the factory. As he grew older, his past excesses bothered him increasingly. For months he pondered how he could atone for the great volume of injuries he had inflicted on those just as wretched as he?

One day, a new volunteer began to teach a first aid class at the orphanage. As with every bit of knowledge he was exposed to, Bukhari quickly mastered what the instructor had to offer. Till that day, he had never considered the human body as anything other than a vehicle to inflict, receive, or endure pain. An idea began to take shape in the young man's mind, but he could not find the means or the words to express it.

A large fountain erected by the British Empire in honor of an English nobleman who had helped colonize that land spouted near the entrance of the Methodist orphanage. Except as a repository of bird droppings, the statue itself had long since lost its relevance. However, the fountain served as a local gathering point. One morning before the start of school, as the young Bukhari walked from his dorm to the schoolyard, cries began to fill the air.

"Help! Help!"

Rushing outside the gate, he saw an older man lying in the street, blue in the face. The word was that thieves had robbed the man and tried to drown him in the fountain. Young Tariq rushed through the buzzing crowd and administered resuscitation to the battered man until the local paramedics arrived. As the crowd roared its approval, Tariq Bukhari realized what his life's goal would be: to become a doctor.

His adolescent years passed quickly. He elected to attend the medical school in Lahore, sponsored by the mission. It turned out to be a fateful and difficult choice, but Bukhari's inner discipline saw him through it. When his determination faltered, he only had to go for a walk to become re-enthused about his goals. Poverty, with its dire consequences, surrounded him and warned him of his fate should he succumb to laziness.

In America, time after time, Bukhari recklessly drove through the streets of Rochester, looking for any shanty, any typical urban filth - any sign that kindred impoverished souls had staked out habitation within the city's boundaries. After each expedition, he returned disappointed. Everyone in the Midwestern town appeared superficially happy, or at least content. Prosperity seemed to be the rule. He often found himself driving to Minneapolis to see the homeless and the destitute, the boarded-up windows and abandoned buildings, to reassure himself that poverty did, in fact, exist in America. However, each trip to the twin cities only magnified the relative richness of Rochester, and his fury grew. The local news reported nothing amiss besides the typically inhospitable arctic winters and the occasionally poor boating conditions on the innumerable little lakes that dotted the countryside.

The fury still burnt brightly as Bukhari turned his car around. He had an appointment to keep. Suddenly tired, Bukhari drove slowly to his apartment.

Time mattered little to him now.

Chapter 11

By the time Howard got to Tracy, she had let out a couple of loud screams. There was no one there to hear them.

It had taken the drug-addled Dr. Howard several attempts to unbolt the P3 room's inner door. Watching his attempts, Tracy espied a hand-held parafilm cutter. She quickly snatched it from the work shelf and prepared to meet her tormentor with a weapon of her own.

As the door opened, Howard tried to focus his strained eyes simultaneously on Tracy and on the vial containing Bukhari's ctb. Tracy thought she saw him favor the vial. However, Howard had merely thrown a false glance at the counter-top. As she tried to run past him, he grabbed her wrist and wrenched the sharp cutter from her weakened grasp. In anger, Howard began to shake her - as much to jog his own memory as to disable her efforts at resistance.

Tracy!

He looked at the scared, increasingly limp, petite woman crushed between his hands.

Tracy Hopkins!

Tracy Hopkins, his graduate student. Howard began to search his mind for his strategy in locking her in the P3 room.

Bukhari.

He remembered now. Bukhari had called to inform him the final test would take place in an hour from the time of the call.

"Dr. Howard, I am also pleased to tell you that you will receive a cash reward for your efforts. Could you be available at 5:00 am on Monday morning at the office?"

"At 5 am? In the office?" Howard asked incredulously.

"Yes, at 5 in the morning. You see, ISIP was extremely impressed by the videotape and they want to demonstrate their appreciation of your interviewing skills with this gratuity." Bukhari replied with uncharacteristic charm.

Howard was sure the commendation would be delivered in the form of lead currency. Nonetheless, he agreed to meet his protégé in his office.

In reality, Howard planned to be long gone by the time Bukhari showed up at the Microbiology Department. But he realized he feared Bukhari's slovenly laboratory habits more than he feared the prospect of his own murder within the walls of the very laboratory he had connived for so long to sustain. He was convinced, despite all possible safeguards and precautions, Bukhari had managed to infect the P3 room with his own terrible ctb weapon.

From his car, he had watched Bukhari enter and exit the parking lot. Howard had wasted precious time debating whether or not he should enter the P3 room himself to grab the other bioweapon vial, the existence of which Bukhari had implied when he had let his guard down. It was not by purloining the vial he planned to save humanity. It was his skin he wanted to save, and purloining the vial was the only way of doing it. If he didn't, he was sure he was a dead man. Whoever was behind the I.S.I.P. would surely come after him two minutes after Bukhari completed his test, the details of which Howard was unaware of. Still, the thought of walking into a cloud of bacteria held as much appeal as being mown down by Bukhari and his friendly neighborhood assassins.

After gulping down a handful of his pills, Howard had checked his gun as best he could, and had gone up to the fifth floor. He panicked upon discovering Tracy Hopkins in the communal office. She was a non-entity to him – quite expendable It occurred to him in a flash of brilliance to send her into the P3 room to fetch the vial. The fact that she was still breathing normally after several hours only reconfirmed the brilliance of his reasoning.

As his gaze returned to the struggling woman he held unmercifully in his arms, he realized she had become his problem. A very, very big problem. His hand had slipped over her mouth to muffle her screams when he felt her bite him, or rather heard his dulled brain tell him her teeth were piercing the flesh of his hand. Unblinking, he studied her flushed face and realized he had to kill her. The thought nearly made him throw up, for despite the chemicals cruising through his system, he could not bring himself to kill another human being with a gun. He had not felt these pangs of conscience when he had locked Tracy in the P3 room, because if she had died then, it would have been by Bukhari's hand, however indirectly. That moral buffer would not exist if he killed her with his gun.

Howard stole a glance at the heavily wrapped, unlabeled vial standing in the defrosting rack on the counter-top. Perhaps, he thought through the haze of the endlessly cycling chemicals, Tracy could be of more service to him alive than dead? Keeping one hand firmly pressed over her mouth, he reached over to the cabinet and grasped a bottle of chloroform. Using his free hand, he awkwardly unscrewed the bottle's cap, withdrew the heavily frayed handkerchief from his trouser pocket, knocked the bottle to its side, and allowed the chemical to pour onto the waiting cloth. Howard then tried to reproduce what he had seen countless times in movies and on television. He moved his hand from Tracy's mouth to the bottom of her chin in order to keep her mouth closed while quickly jamming the lightly soaked cloth against her mouth and nose.

Almost immediately, Howard felt Tracy go limp in his arms. He dropped her to the floor, satisfied she would be unconscious long enough for him to re-pack the toxin. Under no circumstances would Howard trust Bukhari's work with anything. Stepping over the supine Tracy, he put on a pair of gloves and picked up the vial when he realized he would require a special, larger tube to ensure additional safety, a tube found only in the main laboratory on the other side of the department. He set the ctb vial back onto the defrosting rack and left the P3 room.

Howard felt all would be well. No one was in the building. Even if someone was, the noise of his wrestling match with Tracy would be considered something not to get involved in. In a matter of hours, he would be in protective custody and well rewarded for the service he had just provided. Tracy, well, they could deal with her.

The doors of the P3 room closed. Tracy counted to twenty and opened her eyes.

Chapter 12

The doors of death had never been far away for Abolhassan Ziad, but death, in its own peculiar way, had been very kind to him. It had spared him as a young child when typhoid epidemics raged through his village on more than one occasion. Death avoided him repeatedly when he was a young conscript in the Pakistani Army fighting with the Afghani *Mujahedeen* against the Soviet Red Army. And death had spared him during the constant internal struggles within the ISI that sometimes rewarded success more harshly than it punished failure.

Ziad had learned to respect death, which is why he found Bukhari's behavior, the childish way in which he was celebrating the demise of his victim, so offensive. The doctor loudly cheered in his native Pushto, toasting his own intellectual acumen as though he had just scored the winning goal and won the World Cup for Pakistan.

"We did it, we did it!"

Ziad felt an enormous contempt for this brash maniac who had no reverence for the power of his own weapon.

When Ziad was a junior field officer serving with the *Mujahedeen*, he had become acquainted with Sahabuddin. One day, the feared and revered commander of the ISI had asked Ziad to see him for a personal meeting. The junior officer feared for his life as he entered Sahabuddin's huge office, which resembled their countless makeshift field headquarters.

"At ease soldier. Have a seat" Sahabuddin reassured him.

His superior bade him to sit on the portable canvas folding chair, and after inquiring about his health, Sahabuddin came to the point.

"You have used many weapons and fought with many them. Which one do you fear the most?"

While Ziad was pondering an answer, his commander interrupted him.

"Do you know much about biological weapons?"

"No, not much," Ziad admitted.

"What do you think of biological weapons in war? Give me a truthful answer."

"Quite frankly, Sir, I think they are dishonorable weapons. Only cowards would resort to using such weapons."

"Why?" Sahabuddin queried.

Ziad was at a loss. He instinctively did not like them but could not put his feelings in words.

"Are you scared of such weapons? Weapons you cannot see, smell, or hear? Can't touch and feel? A weapon you don't even know is around you till it kills you?" Sahabuddin persisted.

After a moment of silence, Ziad reluctantly nodded.

Sahabuddin had let out a long, resounding laugh at his junior's response.

"If I may ask, Sir, why is that funny?" Ziad sullenly asked.

Sahabuddin only smiled and replied Ziad had fought among the *Mujahedeen* for too long. It was then he had been told to leave for America and establish his cover in anticipation of future needs. With that, Sahabuddin had wished Ziad luck in America and dismissed him.

Ziad's assignment in America had proved to be enjoyable. He especially relished his cover as a taxi-cab driver initially in New York and later in Rochester since he enjoyed driving. Ziad had invested more than a decade negotiating the clogged, mined, and Red Army-laden footpaths and trails of Afghanistan's mountain ranges. Most of the vehicles he had seen over the course of those ten-plus years had been of Soviet origin, burning or disabled through his efforts. The few command cars and trucks he and his group of *Mujahedeen* had been able to capture intact were of such shoddy construction and workmanship they could only be sold or traded to Western military collectors in the surplus weapons bazaar around the Khyber Pass. Like all soldiers who had tasted combat, he considered it luxury beyond measure to drive in the calm, well-maintained streets of Rochester without fear of rocket attack or roadblock ambush.

However enjoyable the driving had been, Ziad found Bukhari and his ultimate mission to develop biological weapons loathsome. The sight of Bukhari dancing and gloating bothered him tremendously.

It's fine to dance around after murdering a man in his sleep but try slitting a heavily armed Siberian muzhik's throat while he's dangerous, drunk, and on guard duty!

Ziad gazed around Bukhari's emptied apartment with disgust. He flinched as the increasingly jubilant Bukhari grabbed him by the shoulders and forced him to look at the computer monitor terminals.

"Look, just look. He's dead! The mission has succeeded. We are heroes!"

All the computer readings were either a succession of zeros or flat lines. As if to convince himself, Bukhari explained how each individual reading proved Kavesh was truly dead.

Bukhari seemed to have completely forgotten he had spilled most of the ctb on the floor, and the consequences of his actions remained to be seen.

"You have only one hour to collect any remaining items." Ziad reminded Bukhari.

"Only one hour to take care of Howard."

Chapter 13

As Howard walked away from the P3 room, Tracy, still lying on the floor, listened carefully.

Perhaps, in his addled mental fog, he has forgotten about me or thought he has killed me.

The few drops of chloroform that had landed on Howard's filthy handkerchief had failed to make much of an impression on Tracy's central nervous system. She counted to twenty again.

No footsteps.

Realizing the importance of the vial, Tracy made up her mind neither Howard nor Bukhari would get it. The young woman seized the ctb vial and wrapped it in several more layers of parafilm. She looked at the centrifuge resting on the counter to the left side of the tissue culture hood. In it, she found a pink Eppendorf tube filled with purified water, used for balancing other vials. With fast, fleet fingers, she placed the pink balancing tube inside a larger Eppendorf tube and wrapped it tightly. Except for the color, the fake and the biological weapon vials were indistinguishable.

Tracy dropped to all fours and looked around the corner of the still-open door. There was no sign of Howard. Quickly, she scuttled across the floor out of the P3 room and then ran to the secretary's desk down the hall. Crouching behind the secretary's table, she grabbed an Express mail envelope and mailing label. Furiously scribbling an address, jamming the colorless vial inside the well-padded mailing envelope, she stopped only to scrawl a brief note. She stapled and taped the envelope shut and set it face down on the 'Out' tray. The Express mail service would pick it up by 9:00 am.

With the real vial out of way, Tracy decided to make a run for it. Should Howard return to the office, he would see the open P3 room door and the imitation pink vial exhibited prominently. Hopefully, in his muddled state, he would not notice the color difference. She was counting on the vial to distract him long enough for her to reach the stairwell.

Tracy scuttled on all fours to the office's solitary door. As she pressed her ear to the door, she heard nothing. She reasoned it would probably be safer to crawl out from behind the door as she opened it, in case Howard had his gun leveled and ready to fire. Sitting on her haunches, Tracy pushed open the office door with her hands, catching it as it swung back on its taut hydraulic pump. Not seeing her assailant, she stood up and decided to run.

Her footsteps boomed down the empty hallway. She sprinted toward the stairwell located at the end of the hallway where the members of the faculty had their offices. Tracy ran faster than she ever had before, passing door after door on either side. Finally, only one door remained: that of Dr. Robert Webster, the Microbiology Department's chairman. With a giddy feeling of triumph, Tracy put her hand on the stairwell door's knob and bade Dr. Webster and his department farewell. Panting, she pushed open the door with her shoulder.

Tracy never saw Dr. Dan Howard standing to the side of the door, one hand holding the pink vial, the other holding the gun. She never saw him bring the butt of his gun down on her head.

Chapter 14

Dr. Romero sat with his head in his hands. He was tired and humiliated, and his chest felt as if a ton of bricks lay on it. The dejected resident returned to the call room next to the nurse's station, turned off the light, and sat in deep darkness, musing about the end of his medical career.

Maybe the hospital will exonerate me and salvage something of my professional career?

Not likely. The death of Dr. Neil Kavesh during his watch would overrule any sympathy for him. The opportunity to save Dr. Kavesh could have been his greatest moment. Instead, it was his most damning failure.

Why is my chest feeling so tight?

Like a constantly replaying tape, the scenario refused to leave his mind.

I did everything right. I acted every inch the medical professional. Didn't I do every procedure correctly? Weren't my answers always correct in class? Hasn't my laboratory work always been perfect? All right, maybe I could have gone in to investigate the situation a little earlier, but that damned Nurse Davidson didn't convey the level of the emergency adequately. How was I supposed to know what was going on in cubicle four? Doctors don't have magic antennae, sweeping all the beds in all the wards constantly. Isn't that why St Mary's employed nurses, so they can help doctors do their job properly?

Romero began to cough.

"Beyond any doubt, the death of Dr. Neil Kavesh is the fault of Nurse Sarah Davidson. Had that incompetent novice done her job properly and given me all the information I needed, I could have saved Kavesh's life. Instead, due to her rash blurring of issues, my career has been destroyed." Romero muttered.

Why am I having so much trouble breathing?

Romero knew exactly how much the staff hated him.

Oh, I ignored their disrespect and insults behind my back. Now, now that it is all over I, Dr. Calixto Romero, will go out fighting like a man. I have nothing to lose. Chief Nurse Gibson will still have a job tomorrow morning. I will have wasted ten years on a profession that will soon have nothing to do with me.

The infuriated doctor, coughing and short of breath, staggered out of the small call room and returned into the cerulean blue of the MICU. He noticed Dr. Kavesh's cadaver had not yet been wheeled away to the morgue.

"Where's Nurse Gibson?" He gasped.

He wanted to vent his opinion of her and her shoddy abilities to her face. Romero noticed the illuminated clock in the main console of the nurse's station.

4:56 am.

The graveyard shift's secretary was lethargically attending to the requisite paperwork to declare Kavesh legally dead. Unable or unwilling to speak, she waved Romero over to her table to sign the death certificate. A wistful, if unoriginal, thought came to Romero as he signed the document.

A man can't even die without generating paperwork.

Romero signed with increasing tiredness. Aside from his resignation, he expected this to be his last official act as a physician. He saw a nurse he did not recognize patting Chief Nurse Gibson gently on the back. The older woman was bent over a chair, coughing uncontrollably.

The petulant doctor came to hover over the agonized nurse. He figured he would wait until she finished coughing and then he would give her a piece of his mind. Suddenly, Sarah Davidson came into view.

"Dr., I—"

Romero peered into the confused eyes of the new nurse. She, too, was coughing violently. Losing all strength, she suddenly sank into his arms.

Unnerved, the resident lay the shaking woman down on the floor, stood up, and looked in vain for someone to aid. Unmistakably, every staff member in the MICU was coughing violently or struggling to breathe. The monitors of all remaining patients began screaming their alarms. Valiantly, the few nurses still capable of standing tried to respond, but to no avail. Except for a few already in position, none were able to reach their patients, all of who were dying in their private cubicles.

Choking! I'm choking!

Romero quickly undid his tie, unbuttoned the top of his shirt, to no avail. The heaviness in his chest was becoming unbearable. Quick screams, imprecations, and sobs began to fill the air, competing with the seemingly louder shrieks and alarms from eleven monitors. Increasingly short of breath, he fell on the floor.

Escape! I must escape!

With every ounce of strength in his body, Romero crawled on all fours toward the airlock door. As his strength left him, he resorted to crawling on his elbows and knees. He noticed he was clambering over bodies and he cursed them for not making way for him.

Throughout her more than thirty years as a nurse, Josephine Gibson had always felt she had what it took to be a doctor. She sometimes allowed herself to regret not having been born in a different time, where the notion of women practicing medicine would not have been met with such scorn and resistance. Josephine Gibson had always thrived on the special tension, the life and death decisions she had to make in split seconds.

Head Nurse Josephine Gibson assessed that whatever killed Dr. Kavesh was busy killing her and everyone else in the MICU. The sloshing that idiot Romero had heard in Kavesh's lungs was the hallmark for whatever was afflicting them now. With the last ounce of strength in her oxygen-deprived body, she forced herself to crawl toward the main console of the nurses' central station. An enormous red button, the size of a small cake, blinked next to the red telephone.

According to protocol, if possible, the doctor on call had the responsibility for depressing the HAZMAT alert button during an emergency situation. This signal caused everyone inside the MICU to be trapped with whatever it was that had caused the alert. The outer airlock would seal and would be operable only from the outside. The Rochester Police and Fire Departments would be notified and come prepared to decontaminate the entire facility. A loud air raid klaxon would sound, alerting the hospital of the development.

Through the blackness slowly enveloping her vision, Head Nurse Gibson saw Doctor Romero attempting to exit the MICU. With her last gasp, she pressed the HAZMAT warning button and collapsed to the floor, drowning steadily within her own lungs.

Romero found himself using the last of his strength tapping on the interior door of the airlock. He found himself reminiscing about a vacation with his family at one of Minnesota's ten thousand lakes. How had he wound up on a ship that had just been torpedoed? Who would do this to him? A siren started wailing; the deep blue of the MICU's lights became a volcanic red.

Dr. Calixto Romero died with his face down and his right palm pressed flat against the unresponsive interior panel of the airlock's inner door. The red light was extinguished.

Chapter 15

The red light of false dawn filtered into the interior of the fifth-floor offices and corridors of Mayo Clinic's Department of Microbiology. Dr. Tariq Bukhari and Abolhassan Ziad boldly entered the department's offices.

"Go get the vial, I'll look out for Dr. Howard," Ziad ordered Bukhari.

The senior ISI agent now realized he had been far too hasty in asking the rotten old researcher to rendezvous with them at the laboratory. When he had given the instructions to Bukhari to relay to Howard, it had seemed like the least obvious place to ask him to go to be murdered. Now it struck him as a bad idea. Ziad looked glumly down the hallways and identified different rooms, calculating Howard's possible escape routes.

"Where is he?" He whispered to himself.

Bukhari's enraged roar lead Ziad to withdraw his .45 from its holster. He followed the bellow until he came upon the doctor, hollering from the center of the P3 room's inner chamber. Running out of the P3 room, Bukhari was shouting threats and curses in a mixture of every language he knew.

"It's gone! It's gone!"

"What's gone?"

"The vial! My superbug! It's gone!"

"What do you mean gone?"

"It's not there anymore! It's not where I left it. It's gone!"

"Are you sure? Are you sure you didn't misplace it?"

"No! I put it here only a few hours ago! It was here!"

Ziad could only think of one explanation.

"Howard, that hyena must have taken it!"

"No, not him." Struggling to overcome his temper, Bukhari pointed to the sole of one shoe: Ziad noticed it was smeared with a very peculiar, stringy form of bubble gum.

"What's this?"

"Bubble gum! She chews it like a cow. She's the one who must have taken it!"

"Who's she? Who are you talking about?"

"Tracy Hopkins! A graduate student in the department!"

"But why would she take the vial?"

"She has always hated me, been jealous of my talents. She's been spying on me, she knew all along about my superbug. She waited until I left for St Mary's, and then she took it!"

"Why do you say she took it simply because there is gum on your shoe?"

"The gum wasn't there when I left just a few hours ago. It's here now. So, she must have been here, and must have taken the vial!"

Accustomed as he was to Bukhari's ways, Ziad refused to believe a word he was saying. Obviously, he had only made one vial of the toxin. Alternatively, he had given the other one to that dog Howard. It did not matter. He had had enough of this biological weapons business and Bukhari. They were bound for Pakistan on a flight leaving Chicago's O'Hare Airport at 11 am. Let Bukhari plead his case directly with Ghazni back at ISI headquarters in Islamabad.

"Let's leave quickly. We have a long trip ahead of us!"

Bukhari froze. He knew what Ziad meant, what the words implied. He would go back to Pakistan empty-handed, a failure. He would go back to face his mentor, his savior, betraying the trust that had been placed in him. The trust that dated back to his dark days in medical school.

Medical school had been a shock to Bukhari. Though located not far from the Methodist orphanage, it may as well have been situated on a distant planet. Except for the unique, gentle respite of the orphanage, the young Bukhari had only known the brutality of his home village of Parachimar and the Peshawar factory. However, in none of these places had he felt inferior. Just abused.

In medical school, for the first time in his life, Bukhari felt looked down upon. Most of his fellow students were the sons and daughters of Pakistan's landed elite or wealthy merchant class. Those whom he met and tried to befriend cared little of his struggles or his background. Many of them came from families whose wealth stemmed from the operation of factories dependent upon child labor. Only the steady guidance of Reverend Knisely kept Tariq Bukhari from succumbing to his inner rage, newly reactivated in the midst of those who profited from the system oppressing him since birth. The clumsy condition of his body and the low regard of his peers tore at him relentlessly from within.

One day in his first year, he had gone to visit Reverend Knisely after dinner, as he often did. The kindly man looked distraught.

"I have to go back to America. The synod has asked me to return." He told Bukhari.

"For a couple of weeks or months?" The young student thought this meant the reverend would be away for a short vacation.

"Hopefully, it will be for a brief time." Reverend Knisely assented.

A few days later, the Methodist minister left Lahore. Though he kept in touch with his young charge for the next few weeks, the old minister never returned to his adopted Pakistan. He died in a car accident outside St Louis, Missouri, a couple of weeks after his arrival.

The news devastated Bukhari. As was his habit, he took it personally. One of Reverend Knisely's great gifts had been to calm the young man down and make him realize that despite what had happened to him in the past, the world was not out to destroy him. Without the steadying influence of the reverend, Bukhari lost his moorings.

He began reacting to his fellow students differently. Despite the copious awards and citations he earned, his peers had continued to look down on him, considering him a lucky street urchin. In the depths of his subconscious, Bukhari began to wonder if they were right. This nagging suspicion began to prick at him like the stiff collar of an ill-fitting shirt. Gradually he developed a defensive, arrogant attitude that made him even less acceptable to his fellow students. He had begun medical school with hope and a desire for service. Now he felt nothing but resentment and hatred. Only his savagely honed sense of inner discipline kept him going.

In his second year of medical school, the angry, lonely, and scorned Bukhari met Ghazni. Not directly, though. Someone introduced him to someone who introduced him to someone until finally, he met the Rasputin-like plenipotentiary ISI official. For all that had happened in his troubled childhood and youth, Bukhari had remained very apolitical and irreligious. Religion and politics implied a larger world, a world that did not interest the furious, self-absorbed student. Ghazni changed that.

"You are without a doubt the most gifted student I've come across". The senior ISI man flattered Bukhari endlessly, complimenting him about his remarkable success as a student.

For the first time since Reverend Knisely's departure, Bukhari heard kind words spoken to him.

"Mark my words, you will change the world," Ghazni remarked on innumerable occasions their nation would be better off because of Bukhari, and how bright the future was for him.

"Pakistan was founded on Islam, yet there is no respect for it. Islam tells very clearly wealth has to be shared. Yet, the wealthy keep getting wealthier, while they torment and subjugate the poor. Islam forbids class distinctions since we are all the same before God. But in Pakistan, the wealthy landowners' lord over the peasants and workers. Where is the adherence to Islam?" Ghazni spoke of all the great evils forced upon the poor people of Pakistan by their own brethren.

The wily man knew more about Bukhari than Bukhari knew about himself.

"These rich people who used you, Bukhari, are the same ones who look down on you today in your class." Ghazni linked every episode of Bukhari's life to the actions of the infidel propertied class, masking their tricks with the pretensions of democracy. The rage ruling Bukhari hung him high on every word spoken by the deviously clever ISI man. All the kindness and humanity Reverend Knisley had taught him was erased, replaced by hatred and hunger for heavenly retribution.

"If you want revenge my boy, you shall have it. Obey my instructions and revenge will be yours." The ISI official offered the stricken young student a chance to get back at everyone who had ever harmed him.

The temptation of Ghazni's world proved to be too strong for Bukhari to resist. It was as though he had never met Reverend Knisely.

"Just tell me what to do, and I'll do it." The young medical student vowed.

"Your time will come soon." Ghazni smiled.

That summer, Bukhari discovered he had been accepted and enrolled in the University's new joint MD/Ph.D. program. His natural inclinations, mixed with subtle hints from Ghazni, led him to do research in microbiology. He wrote an excellent thesis on the natural history of tuberculosis, which Ghazni refused to publish, fearing his prized agent-to-be would be discovered, and maybe usurped for genuine scientific research.

With two years remaining in medical school, Ghazni began preparing Bukhari for life in America.

"Speaking English is not enough, you have to learn to use American idioms. You must learn how to wear Western clothes and wear them appropriately. Finally, you must learn how to drive a car. Without a car, you will be lost in America."

Bukhari's stipend was increased. Through the last years of medical school, Ghazni had carefully shaped the young doctor's mind with religious and patriotic fanaticism, and with the idea of the ISI as the only logical recourse and means of expression of patriotism. Ghazni's plan was to implant the seeds thoroughly in Bukhari as he grew older, those seeds would germinate and take over his thoughts and actions. However, the older Bukhari got, the more his boyhood came to dominate him. At the age of thirty-two, when he departed Lahore, he might as well have been a twelve-year-old.

In the plentiful, nominally benign Eden of Rochester, Minnesota, Dr. Tariq Bukhari allowed the invective of his ISI patron to constantly stoke the fury that filled him. Daily observations of prosperity confirmed his warped reasoning the wealthy, in America as in Pakistan, were robbing the poor, and the situation had to be remedied. His weapon would change all that. Only now, his weapon was lost.

No! The evidence is too clear. Tracy Hopkins has stolen the vial. I will find her and punish her horribly.

The doctor ran toward the stairwell, located at the far end of the department near the faculty offices. Bukhari was elated upon reaching the stairwell. He had outrun Ziad! Fear had given him the speed of an Olympic sprinter. He ran down the stairs, reached the ground level and immediately raced down to the parking lot.

Bukhari had no idea what hit him as he was running through the parking lot. He felt nothing as two men carried his prostrate body to a waiting car.

Chapter 16

In the two years of their formal acquaintance, Dr. Dan Howard had never really paid much attention to Tracy Hopkins. He recognized she was one of his students who always seemed to be upset over one thing or another and expected him to do something about it

She wanted me to spoon-feed her a dissertation topic. Oh, and she also did not like Tariq Bukhari and had gone to see Webster about him.

Webster had tried to use her complaint as a burr to throw under Howard's golden saddle. As had become his custom, Howard threatened to leave over the issue of Tracy's complaint.

"If the Microbiology Department values a mere graduate student more than someone like me, the mega-grant magnet, then I can find some other notable institution who knows how to treat its rainmakers well." Howard threatened.

Webster dropped the issue and remonstrated Tracy for wasting his time with trivia. Howard remembered retaliating by savaging one of her experiments and threatening to bring her up for dismissal. In reality, he remembered her work as being quite good. He plagiarized most of her data for a paper he wrote, with himself as the sole author.

As he saw her sprawled on the dirty stairwell floor, Howard noticed Tracy was on the tiny side of petite. Five feet one or two, 100 pounds at the most. An easy package for an old man like him to carry. He slipped her a couple of knockout chemicals he kept in his office, and then drove to Minneapolis/Saint Paul International Airport. Had a survey been conducted on people who had noticed them, the majority would have said they had seen a father taking his sick daughter to Washington, D.C.

Recalling what little experience he had in medicine, Howard determined the blow he had administered to Tracy had hurt her, but not enough to cause her a cerebral hemorrhage. Fortunately for him, she had remained groggy throughout the first stages of their trip to the airport and had conveniently slumped asleep on his shoulder after take-off.

It had been years since a woman had done that with Howard, even involuntarily. Though he was not particularly attracted to her, he appreciated the sense of humanity it gave him. It inspired him to reflect, rather than automatically ingest more pills. Something approaching a nascent sense of compassion began to well up in him.

Perhaps - perhaps Tracy did not have to die after all. Maybe she will co-operate?

His thoughts turned to what lay ahead of them in the nation's capital.

A few days after the video deposition incident, a man named David had approached Howard. Flashing impressive badges and naming well-known figures in the government and secret services, he had impressed on Howard the gravity of his situation.

"You have three choices. Die by Bukhari's germ, die by Bukhari's gun, or live by co-operating with us." Howard could not figure out how David knew so much about Bukhari. He realized he was being given a way out by a branch of the U.S. government, and he was going to grab that chance.

Someone's coughing broke his thoughts. He turned his head to look for the source of the annoying interruption.

It was Tracy. Still asleep, she was coughing and breathing heavily.

Chapter 17

Bill Hopkins took a deep breath and stretched, his head almost touching the top of the doorway. The retired Admiral still carried himself as though on the Annapolis parade ground.

Though physically fit, Bill Hopkins felt he was not making a meaningful difference. That lack of productivity caused him a great deal of dissatisfaction. Between rising in the morning at 5:30 am and hitting the deck at 10:00 pm, he re-lived on an hourly basis the sequence of events leading him to resign his commission. He still took immense pride in having voluntarily ended his starry ascent in the nation's military as a gesture of protest. Still, with each passing day, he felt less certain he would ever have the opportunity to serve his country again and to do what he did best: anticipate the tactical and strategic movements of the enemy.

Originally, the Navy had wanted to place Bill in their nuclear engineering program. That had not suited the young man.

"I want to fight, not sit around waiting for an order to blow things up" Hopkins had protested.

The navy, realizing its error, reassigned him to an operations unit. Bill Hopkins first saw action in Korea, but it was in Vietnam he came into his own. On the Mekong Fleet, Bill Hopkins became a legend, serving three tours until the scrapping of the river interdiction system, and with it the navy's role in that aspect of the war. Eager to keep fighting, Bill switched to intelligence and became something of a roving analyst, working with whichever government branch needed his services the most. After the war, he continued his work with military intelligence, often in liaison with the CIA.

Ronald Reagan's election filled him with great hope. The post-Vietnam honor and prestige of the entire United States military stood a chance of being rehabilitated with him in charge. Instead, one fateful day under an unforgiving Mediterranean sun, there was an incident..........

Bill had decided to move as far away as possible from Washington, D.C., without winding up in American Samoa. As a Boy Scout, he had once passed through Ogden, Utah, on his way to a jamboree in the Grand Tetons. The distant memory of it proved to be good enough for him. The reality of Ogden in the 1980s did not disappoint him either. He and Doris built their dream house on a large wooded lot high up on a hill but close to the outskirts of town. It was spacious but not excessive. Doris had enough room for her ever-expanding library and Bill had enough space to build a separate garage for his hobby, restoring classic cars. Hardly the occupation he had anticipated after graduating from the Academy, but not as bad as some others he could have chosen.

Still, at his age, Bill felt as though he was losing more and more battles. All he had left was his family. He missed his daughter Tracy, of whom he was extremely fond. Except she was going to be married to that ultimate pretender, the fake rebel, Rory. Bill worried Rory would ultimately turn out to be a pretend husband to his daughter and a pretend father to his grandchildren.

Rory had been the only issue ever to drive a wedge between Bill and Tracy. Bill Hopkins had been a combat veteran, a master in the game of international espionage, and had developed the automatic prejudices which often accompany such occupations. With the vitriol of those who have undergone the rigors of combat experience, Bill Hopkins hated Rory.

"I can't stand his tangled hair, pleated into locks, his casual dress and manners, and his disdain for the military. I'm sure if Rory had lived a few decades earlier, he would have been a hippie protesting against the Vietnam War. I have a hard time understanding why you socialize with someone like him " Bill had angrily shouted at Tracy during one of their arguments.

The elder Hopkins also hated Rory's insistence of facts over faith. Perhaps what bothered Bill Hopkins, a self-made man, the most, was Rory's enormous trust fund. A trust fund which had allowed Rory to quit college at the age of twenty and open his own white-water rafting and skiing business. Admiral Hopkins had risen through the ranks in the military and could not stand anyone who attained his goals without working long and hard for them.

Bill never understood why Tracy cared for Rory, and Tracy was unable to explain it to him in a way he understood.

"The institution that hurt you so much, one that I completely distrust but you still swear by, is what attracted me to Rory. Rory is a peacenik, and in my own way, so am I. I cannot accept killing people or destroying their lives for the sake of pompous pretensions of power and politics. I find Rory genuine, simple, and without hang-ups. Rory is a breath of fresh air."

As much as she loved her father, Tracy felt people like him first formed opinions, then looked for the facts to back them up. Rory, in contrast, spent a great deal of time looking at all angles of a situation and often even then chose not to take a firm stance.

"Sorry, don't have enough information" he would shrug.

Tracy supported Rory's decision to quit college and start his own business. She had realized his options were especially limited as a 'Post-Gulf-War Marxist Theory' major. His business ventures had prospered over the next four years. During the spring and summer months, he would guide river-rafting expeditions down the Snake River from a base in Jackson, Wyoming. During the winter ski season, he ran an upscale ski shop in Salt Lake City, displaying a commercial sense that impressed even Bill Hopkins on the one occasion he had visited, with the intention of forcibly persuading Rory to abandon his daughter. Instead, Bill Hopkins had returned home that night to Ogden, the new and proud owner of a $1,000 all-weather sleeping bag - approved by NASA and the National Geographic Society. When Doris mentioned the price, Bill responded he had received the 'family discount'. He then hated Rory even more.

Bill's thoughts swung to Andrew, his son - almost six years younger than Tracy. Extremely bright, Andrew never even played with toy soldiers as a young boy. Bill had accepted his son would rather fiddle with his computer than help him fix cars or go hunting. He had always wanted a child who enjoyed the same sort of roughhousing he had loved and couldn't help feeling disappointed Andrew had not turned out to be that child.

After decades of marriage, he still felt very close to Doris. A Ph.D. in romance philology, she had tired of the bleak career prospects in the academic world and was quite happy to be Mrs. Doris Hopkins, just so long as she could maintain her large personal library.

Bill had begun his Monday by assessing what was necessary to rehabilitate an extremely mauled '68 Shelby Mustang, a personal favorite. He did not need his tools at this phase of the project; he simply allowed his mind to wander over the car the way a sculptor examines an uncut block of stone. It was his favorite phase of each project. The wee hours of the morning had flown past quickly. Before he knew it, a grumbling in his stomach signaled breakfast time. Cleaning up in the bathroom attached to his work garage, he headed for the kitchen with lightness in his step.

The sight of his next-door neighbor and tormentor Charlotte Kennedy chatting with his wife made Bill want to run out of the house and grab a bunch of doughnuts at some roadside shop. The senior Hopkins had deliberately selected a remote plot for his house so his neighbors would be a considerable distance away. Both Bill and Doris considered themselves social and hospitable people, but they just did not want anyone living within whispering distance.

Bill disliked Charlotte Kennedy about as much as he disliked Rory. Sometimes one would lurch ahead of the other, but then events would transpire to even them out. A widow, Kennedy owned a home far larger and with more extensive grounds than the Hopkins home. Allegedly, she had a family, but Bill had his doubts, given that she seemed to spend every waking moment over at their place. He was sure his food and beverage expenses would be cut in half if the annoying woman would stay away from his house for more than an hour. Every time he saw her, it seemed like she had cake, ice cream, or a can of pop in her mouth or her head stuck in the refrigerator looking for something to munch on. Mostly it bothered Bill that the large and ungainly woman was always offering her advice and opinions on everyone else's personal business. Charlotte Kennedy also seemed to possess an unholy ability to get Doris anxious over trivial things.

Unlike Bill, Doris loved her company and disagreed with him over the nature and length of her visits. In an attempt to get rid of her, Bill had tried quite a few tactics, including winking and making kissing sounds when he saw her. However, in addition to forming some erroneous ideas about her own physical attractiveness, Kennedy had held her ground and kept coming back for more. Bill had given up that mode of attack and was trying to come up with a new strategy.

The two women caught sight of Bill entering the family room adjacent the kitchen. Too late to escape now, Bill grumbled to himself. At that point, an idea occurred to Bill. Maybe he could annoy his neighbor by turning up the radio loud enough to make conversation impossible. He quickly hopped over to a small radio Doris kept on a shelf above the kitchen sink and turned it on.

" ....Rochester, Minnesota." The radio said.

Bill turned the volume up some more.

The news came over, loud and clear for all to hear.

"A tragedy has occurred today on the grounds of the world-famous Mayo Clinic. Two dozen people are feared dead from a possible case of carbon monoxide poisoning. Early this morning, Rochester police and fire units responded to a special alarm in the medical intensive care unit of St Mary's Hospital. The emergency services haven't entered the unit yet, though they have been able to see the interior on video camera. The exact cause has not been ascertained at this point. All they know is that it's most probably chemical or carbon monoxide-related. Authorities feared the worst as telephone calls placed to the MICU went unanswered. A small robot, armed with chemical detectors and sensors, was sent into the sealed facility. Results from the probe are expected to be released shortly. This is Tim Johnson reporting from Rochester for..."

"Oh my God, Doris?"

"Yes, Tina?"

"Tracy's in Rochester, isn't she? Oh, my goodness, all those people dead, you've talked to Tracy, of course, haven't you?"

Doris burst into tears, immediately imagining somehow, for some reason, her daughter was among those killed.

"Get out," Bill roared at Charlotte as though still the officer on deck watch, "get out!"

He escorted Kennedy to the door at a trot and slammed it resoundingly behind her. For once, Doris did not remonstrate his outburst of rudeness towards their destabilizing neighbor.

"Bill, you don't think she could have... "

"Not unless she decided to work as a paramedic on the side. You know she's not doing any clinical rotations right now."

"I'm so worried. With all those horrible people in her department... "

"You call her, I'll call Rory." Bill practically choked on the name as it tumbled out of his mouth. In the years the two of them had known each other, he had called Rory only once, and that was to ask for directions to the ski shop.

Both calls were fruitless. Rory was up in Jackson, Wyoming, scouting out the Snake River in anticipation of the first crush of tourists due in the upcoming week. Doris was only able to reach Tracy's answering machine. She tried calling the laboratory, only to be told Tracy had not been seen earlier in the morning.

Bill tried his best to comfort his wife.

"This is the day she formally quit the MD/Ph.D. program. She's probably all right, just not in the mood to talk to anyone. Remember she didn't speak to any of us the week Rory proposed to her?"

Neither of them heard the remaining news filtering in from Minnesota.

Chapter 18

The senior Senator from the state of Minnesota, David Dockhorn had gone about transforming the land of ten thousand lakes into his personal fiefdom. Several prominent political pundits asserted David Dockhorn had revolutionized the way politics was played in the Midwest.

"Minnesota has never seen anything like him. He's more like a freewheeling Louisiana-style politician rather than a conservative Midwestern one." A talking head on ABC's Sunday program once commented.

However, despite his unsavory edges, the state loved his large heart, which was evident by the wide margins by which he won re-elections. In turn, he took the time and effort to cultivate and care for his constituents. Highways got built, bridges were repaired, daycare was subsidized, and health care was made affordable. Charities benefited from his largesse, and he made sure the donations were well-publicized. There was no doubt Senator Dockhorn felt the average citizen's pain and took measures to rectify it, or at least give the appearance of doing so.

"Scandals follow Dockhorn like odor follows a skunk. There have been sex scandals, campaign contribution scandals, scandals about his political appointees, and scandals about his attempts to conceal his scandals. However, none of this seems to matter to his constituents. So long as he does not get indicted, they forgive him." ABC's talking head continued the show about senate races in the upcoming elections.

Masterfully, opaquely, Dockhorn constructed a network of informants to cover the state at every level of law enforcement and government. Soon the entire state became like his personal fiefdom. Dockhorn became the master of what he called the Minnesota shadow cabinet. Even the Governor was beholden to him.

After a couple of successful senatorial terms, Dockhorn had realized he was getting too busy to handle all his affairs on his own. He needed an unscrupulous but capable man, one whom he could trust to keep the gears spinning in his favor, both in Washington and in Minnesota.

Fate had determined David Dockhorn would meet and employ Thor Martin. Dockhorn stood apart from his senatorial colleagues in that he enjoyed a good night out on the town and was not ashamed to admit it. Sometimes he appreciated a refined, uptown kind of night; other times he did not mind standing knee-deep in honky-tonk sawdust. What's more, he expected anyone working for him to share in his extra-curricular tastes and not complain about either his pace or choices.

The Thor Martin case had caused quite a sensation when it broke in the national media several summers ago. Martin had received a commission as an officer and was stationed in an experimental chemical weapons rescue unit at Fort Blizzard, high in the Minnesota lake country. Martin had begun a rather public affair with a buxom officer who had just ended an affair with the base commander. Unfortunately for all concerned, the base commander was a certified alcoholic. The sight of his shapely ex-love openly squiring around the base proved to be too much for him. After several weeks of inner torment, he committed suicide in a drunken stupor, holding Martin responsible for his death in a melodramatic suicide note.

The Army elected to press charges. Martin hired an aggressive civilian civil rights attorney.

"Your honor, since the dead officer's problems manifested themselves long before Martin's relationship began, he should not be held accountable." The lawyer argued to the judge.

At the same time, the lawyer advised Martin to use non-violent techniques to attract sympathy and attention. Thus, while in the stockade, Martin began a hunger strike a la Mohandas Gandhi, protesting the institutional hypocrisy of the military, and calling on no one to enlist for fear of losing their lives and careers over personal matters. It was not that Martin had a high regard for Gandhi; in fact, he privately considered the latter a coward masquerading as a saint. It was just he had no other option but to emulate someone whose tactic of appeasement and pacifism he had little respect for.

It was easy to go on a hunger strike against the Queen of England. She didn't shoot or hang the people who opposed her. How successful would hunger strikes be against Mao or Hitler? How many dead hunger-striking Chinese peasants or Jews would it have taken to change the Red Guards or the SS? Thirty million hadn't made a difference to Mao, and six million hadn't even touched Hitler's conscience.

Luckily for Martin, the tactic worked, just as it had for Gandhi five decades earlier. With military sex scandals blooming all over, the Court elected to let Martin's case slide, punishing him with a dishonorable discharge, but allowing his paramour to remain in the service with only a slight reprimand. Always something of an iconoclast, and embittered by the experience, Martin resolved to stay away from anything approaching a normal career or lifestyle from then on.

One year after Martin's public ordeal, Senator Dockhorn happened to cross paths with him at the St Gothard County Fair. While making the rounds of the beer and sausage tents, Dockhorn noticed two security guards struggling to drag a huge blonde handcuffed male to their makeshift holding area.

"What's going on there?" An intrigued Dockhorn wondered aloud to one of his aides.

Soon the aide returned. "The man arrested is a Thor Martin. Mr. Martin was arrested after he punched an off-duty marine." The aide barely could contain his smirk. "The soldier apparently stated marine women were prettier than army women."

Dockhorn remembered Martin and, at that moment, realized the ex-military man was just the person he had been looking for, his man Friday. Martin got involved in peccadilloes, just like him. Martin's regard for the law extended only so far as how it could be gainfully used, also like him. Finally, Martin seemed to have no direction in life. Dockhorn resolved to give Martin a purpose: to serve him.

With his trademark facile ease, the Senator sprung the unrepentant Martin out of jail and began to charm him.

"Hey soldier, I liked your left hook. If you have the time, why don't we have a drink?"

Always ready for a free drink, especially when offered by someone who had rescued him from jail, Martin was only too happy to partake of the brew. In a matter of hours, he had signed himself onto the Dockhorn bandwagon.

Martin discovered he enjoyed being Dockhorn's eminent factotum. The Senator being as corrupt as a Third World military despot did not bother him at all. In fact, it tended to make his job more interesting, given that the Senator would offer his services to the highest bidder. In a way, the Senator was the true Machiavellian prince: if x paid him more than y, then he would support x until y could pay him more. His natural, charming ebullience and easy, self-deprecating ways made him a favorite with everyone he came in contact with. The national media, starved for genuine personalities to cover in Washington, never failed to ignore his considerable indiscretions so long as he would say something amusing. The running scuttlebutt considered Dockhorn to be the most interesting man inside the Beltway. The real crime would be to lock him away.

The two men made a strange pair. Martin looked as though no piece of furniture had yet been constructed that could support his enormous frame. In contrast, what struck anyone meeting the Senator for the first time was his smooth silky voice, folksy and completely disarming, but thoroughly in control. No one seemed to notice his slicked-back hairstyle, and a demeanor as though he had just arrived from four consecutive days of gambling in a backwoods casino.

The Middle East had long intrigued Dockhorn because of the well-known deep pockets of those who contested the territory. Like so many other American public figures, Dockhorn realized the Arabic countries of the world would always be, per capita, the most prolific spenders on military equipment and technology. With one of his first flashes of brilliance, early in his career while in the House of Representatives, Dockhorn had set himself up as a key link between Congress, American arms manufacturers, and those nations in the Arab world wanted American weapons. The past twenty years Dockhorn had devoted to public service had been extremely prosperous. He had played the Afghan Mujahideen resistance against the Soviet Union the way a sharp and unscrupulous broker plays Wall Street with illicitly acquired insider information. Like a dog who could only smell one scent, all Dockhorn saw, all he cared about, were the numbers to the left of the decimal point. As the post-Soviet world grew more complex, the lines of the Senator's allegiances began to become hopelessly tangled. Dockhorn assigned Martin the job of keeping all of his foreign suitors in order, ready to do business.

The Senator had his main in-state headquarters in a large St Paul office tower he had nicknamed "Fort Independence." Deep within his full floor's worth of office space, next to his main office, he kept a small, carefully secured chamber for his most sensitive discussions and negotiations.

Dockhorn had been woken up early Monday morning with the news of the St Mary's disaster.

"Why don't you head off to Rochester. See what's going on and let me know as soon as possible. Use my private plane - probably the fastest way". He ordered Martin. Although he was not certain of the specifics, Dockhorn wanted to ensure he had nothing to do with it, and if he was, he wanted to become uninvolved as quickly as possible.

When Martin returned, he found the Senator waiting for him in the private conference room. Dockhorn bade the emotionally drained Martin to have a seat.

"Looks like you've seen a ghost," Dockhorn opened with deliberately bad taste.

"Two-dozen, to be precise," Martin replied.

"Bad?"

"Terrible!"

"Who's responsible?"

"I.S.I.P."

"I don't recall them being a sponsor of anything that kills dozens of people."

"Not in so many words, but they are."

"Thor, I need a drink. Maybe two. So do you. Start from the beginning."

"I arrived early in the morning. The first person I ran into was Rochester Police Department's senior detective, Satch Rusk. Remember him?"

Dockhorn nodded. Rusk was a twenty-year Chicago Police veteran who wanted to cruise into retirement investigating not more than one lost cat a month. His new employers in Rochester had not disappointed him. His caseload over six months in the small city equaled what he had to contend within one week in the big city. Still, he occasionally found himself missing the old thrill of crime scenes.

A few years earlier, Rusk had had some problems with a developer who wanted to run a huge highway through the middle of Rusk's small farm at the city's outskirts using a federal transportation grant. In a rage, Rusk had driven his pickup truck to the developer's site and had shot the tires of all their vehicles. Rochester's police department had had to arrest one of their own.

Dockhorn had heard about the case and decided to get involved. He knew the developer and did not like him because the developer would not play the game by Dockhorn's rules. With a few calls, Dockhorn had canceled the federal road-building grant, canceled the re-zoning of the land designated for the developer's proposed mall, and had all charges dropped against Rusk. Martin had spent some time in Rochester making sure the Senator's wishes had been carried out.

"As I was picking my way through the assorted television trucks and emergency vehicles parked outside St Mary's, Rusk came over and offered the latest news."

"The FBI's taken charge of the investigation. They've got one of their robots ready to go in through the airlock. Feds want to see what's in the air before authorizing anyone to go in for the bodies."

"Not quite the standard procedure, is it?" queried Martin.

"Not quite a standard situation," replied Rusk.

Conferring in hushed voices, the two men had made their way to the FBI's command truck. Martin and the FBI chief, Dick Abbott, recognized each other and exchanged terse greetings. Based out of Minneapolis, the FBI chief knew the Senator and Martin quite well and was one of the few government men the wily politician had not been able to corrupt. Abbott had tried on many occasions to find something to pin on the Senator, only to find the evasive politician elude him each time. Martin knew the FBI chief still kept a close eye on them and was waiting for an opportunity to strike.

With wires and antennae sprouting everywhere, the FBI command truck resembled a mobile NASA mission control center. An enormous bank of monitors received the small, radio-guided robot's multiple transmissions of audio-visual and air sampling data. More than a dozen officials, including those of local law enforcement agencies, huddled silently with St Mary's officials and watched the screen.

The small robot slowly made its way around the unit, gingerly avoiding the corpses blocking its path. The cadavers had looks of incomprehension frozen on their countenance, like a dog that had been disciplined by its master for chewing on the furniture. The color of their skin ranged from blue to gray, and their blood-red eyes were wide open. A few had their hands around their throats as if trying to dislodge some internal blockage. Head Nurse Gibson lay in the central nursing station, her hand still on the red button, her open unseeing eyes gazing fixedly at the door. Calixto Romero lay next to the air-lock doors, his fingers spread out like the talons of a vulture, clawing at the door. The MICU alarms still shrieked with uninhibited abandon, as angry flashes of red light bathed the corpses.

Martin saw even the most hardened law enforcement officials gasp in horror at the televised sight. Rusk put his hands to his ears in an attempt to block out the transmitted alarms. Martin tried very hard to retain his composure.

"All right Satch. I've seen all I want to. Call me if anything comes up. Anything at all." He quickly bade Rusk farewell and gave him his direct personal number. In a somber and reflective mood, he drove back to the airport.

"That's the sum of it, Senator. I journeyed to St Mary's hoping the deaths had been the work of some sleepless, overworked, underpaid, under-appreciated resident who had gone off the deep end. Or even a jilted nurse who had decided to insult the medical profession by killing instead of healing. But it doesn't look like that. Looks like we are in the thick of it."

Dockhorn pulled at his rubbery, blowzy face, sighed, and in his most helpless voice, pined, "Well, what do we need to do to get out of this one, Mr. Martin?"

While traveling back from Rochester, Thor Martin had made many plans. One of them involved their next step.

"We need time to let this thing play out some more, Senator, but we've also got to throw the Feds and the forensic guys off the trail for a while."

"How do you reckon we'll throw the Feds off the trail?"

"You've got to personally take charge of this investigation."

"Me? Take charge of the investigation? Come up with another plan, Thor. A better plan."

"No, Senator, I'm serious. Go make the rounds in Rochester, start tying knots in everything. Tonight, in time for the evening news, stage a live speech announcing you think this represents an outbreak of a dreaded drug-resistant pneumococcus bacteria. The medical community will laugh at you, argue with you, disagree with you, but don't worry about that. The point is to keep them debating, divided, distracted, and not find out the truth. The FBI and forensics guys will freak out when they hear your version. They'll figure they either missed the boat entirely or they've got a leak in the middle of their operations. That should confuse things for a few days at least. I'll draft the text for your speech."

"I guess that'll give us a few days. Then what?"

"I'll need some more time to come up with a plan for that. And some help. But let's play for time now."

"Well, you get the Lone Ranger award for saving the day once again, my boy. Thanks for coming through. You'll go a long way, you know. You can count on me for that.".

Thor wondered how exactly he was going to disentangle himself from the Senator.

Chapter 19

Dr. Dan Howard wished he could disentangle himself from Tracy Hopkins. Tiring of her coughing, Howard had slipped her another sedative, knocking her cold. With not much else to do except prevent the flight attendants from hitting his knee with their serving carts, he gradually returned to his fateful 'interview' of Bukhari. Bukhari's words 'biological warfare' rang in his ears, much like a schizophrenic hearing voices in his head.

Biological warfare? Biological warfare! Who had he been sleeping with all these years? The army? That would not explain Bukhari or the other man who spoke Bukhari's language. Who, then?

During the interview, Dr. Dan Howard had become agitated. For the first time in his life, he was overcome with fear. His mouth had gone completely dry, and his heart threatened to pound out of his chest. With great difficulty, he had continued to read.

HOWARD: Dr. Bukhari, why did you choose mtb?

BUKHARI: Mtb is a truly amazing bacterium. The cause of the oldest known disease, it can survive almost any environmental condition. It can even live inside the white blood cells which are supposed to kill it. Such hardy bacteria are perfect for biological warfare.

There is an additional reason. After tuberculosis dissipated as a public threat in the West, Europe, and the US lost interest in it. In contrast, Asia continued vaccinations against it. Therefore, the West is immunologically naive to mtb. See how quickly tuberculosis made a comeback on the coattails of AIDS? The situation is analogous to plague, the Black Death that invaded Europe from Central Asia five centuries ago. You know what happened then. Almost a third of the population of Europe perished!

HOWARD: You are, no doubt, aware that drugs exist to treat tuberculosis?

BUKHARI: Yes, such drugs do exist, but how good are they? They have to be taken in combination since the bacillus becomes resistant to the drug if taken alone. That shows how difficult it is to destroy mycobacterium. In addition, the best medications take months to act, even when taken as recommended, once again demonstrating the hardiness of the tubercle bacillus. Time is very important to the treatment of tuberculosis. That's where cholera toxin acts as the hammer to mtb's anvil. It does not give anyone the luxury of time.

Howard had put his sheet of paper down. He had to resolve this, make sure this was a ridiculous creation. That way, he desperately hoped, he could convince Bukhari to dump his insane project and move on to something else. Like Pakistan.

HOWARD: I'll get to cholera in a minute. Instead of mtb, why not go for something along the lines of pneumococcus, the causative agent of pneumonia? Or streptococcus, the flesh-eating bacteria? Alternatively, bacillus anthracis, of the anthrax fame?

BUKHARI: Because the Middle East and Central Asia have no immunological advantage with these organisms. We would be just as susceptible to these organisms as you would. In fact, taking into account easier access to superlative medical care, we would be at a greater disadvantage.

At that moment, Howard had realized it was us versus them. 'Them' was the West, and 'us' was Bukhari's lot. These were the beginnings of a biological war. His desperation, scientific and personal, increased exponentially. His gastrointestinal tract threatened to empty its contents through both orifices simultaneously.

Ziad sensed the changes taking place in Howard's mannerism and countenance. He had to counter Howard's anxiety before he did anything stupid.

KHALAAQ: This is a hypothetical situation, Dr. Howard. A potential biowar weapon. As you know, the I.S.I.P. Foundation is a purely philanthropic organization and seeks to engage in only those projects that will assist in saving the world, not destroying it. I do believe Dr. Bukhari's tongue slipped across an incorrect expression.

Ziad's eyes said more, with considerable violence, at the suddenly cowed Bukhari. Howard, partly assuaged by Ziad's words, saw an opportunity to hound his, apparently, homicidal protégé.

HOWARD: Why not use something more, ah, traditional, along the lines of yellow fever or malaria?

BUKHARI: It would not be practical. Their propagation would require specific vectors such as the correct species of mosquitoes which don't exist in America, or any Western country. While they could, in theory, be introduced, there is little likelihood they would survive.

HOWARD: But, Dr. Bukhari, again, for the classic reason of simplicity above all else, why not use a virus along the lines of Ebola or Smallpox?

BUKHARI: For the same reason I wouldn't advocate staphylococcus, pneumococcus or streptococcus. They cannot be controlled, and they cannot be manufactured easily. Why use something that cannot be controlled, or would be impossible to manufacture? One line of soldiers fighting against one line of skeletons works well. Two lines of skeletons facing each other--

HOWARD: Well, how can ctb be used without encountering the same lack of control you identify for other biowar agents?

BUKHARI: Because, a simple cure exists.

HOWARD: A simple cure?

BUKHARI: An antibiotic.

HOWARD: What?

BUKHARI: You heard me. An antibiotic.

As though their ranks had been reversed, Howard was wriggling in his perpetually sinking seat, an eager graduate student anxious above all else to follow the master's path of exploration.

BUKHARI (cont.): This is the other reason why I picked cholera. As you know, the causative agent of cholera, vibrio cholerae, secretes a toxin. The cells of the intestine internalize the toxin and the toxin then stimulates an intracellular enzyme, adenyl cyclase. Stimulation of this enzyme makes the intestine secrete copious amounts of fluid. In fact, five micrograms of the toxin can cause the release of five liters of fluid, enough to kill a human by dehydration.

HOWARD: Yes, I know all that. How does it relate to ctb?

BUKHARI: The ctb creation process leaves it susceptible to the antibiotic chloramphenicol and only to chloramphenicol. It remains resistant to all other known antibiotics.

HOWARD: Why is that?

BUKHARI: Like mtb, ctb can grow in either glucose or galactose. The cholera toxin stimulates adenyl cyclase, which in turn increases the intracellular molecule cAMP. This leads the bacteria to preferentially use galactose instead of glucose as a source of nutrition. Bacteria using galactose become very susceptible to chloramphenicol. Thus, ctb became susceptible to chloramphenicol. In my experiments, chloramphenicol sheathed the Guinea pigs and their lungs in impenetrable armor.

HOWARD: Chloramphenicol is hardly a state secret!

Bukhari, as though dismissing the lowliest of questions, had turned his eyes upward and sighed.

BUKHARI: Chloramphenicol is not a state secret, but it isn't used in the Western world. Since it was linked to bone marrow suppression a couple of decades ago, pharmacies here don't even stock it. In contrast, chloramphenicol is commonly used in my part of the world. Should this weapon be used here, in America, there would be very little time to undertake the tests necessary to discover, let alone manufacture and distribute, the antidote.

HOWARD: Is there any other reason you picked cholera? Why not diphtheria, botulism, tetanus? They make pretty potent toxins, too!

BUKHARI: I've already mentioned some reasons why I chose cholera. In addition, cholera acts locally and is, therefore, fast-acting. In contrast, the other toxins need to be absorbed before they can act. Therefore, they are relatively slow. For example, it takes anthrax days to become lethal. As you should know, Dr. Howard, cholera toxin is a remarkably small molecule; so many molecules can be made quickly. These advantages do not apply to the other toxins you mentioned.

Howard had not been willing to give up easily. Digging deep into his scientific background, he had struggled to come up with reasons why this would not work.

HOWARD: Talking about slowness, this wouldn't work as a biowar weapon. Tuberculosis is a slow-growing organism. Therefore, ctb will be slow-growing, too. It won't be able to replicate fast and make enough toxins to cause significant damage.

Bukhari had sensed Howard's weakness and desperation. He swung in for the kill.

BUKHARI: You obviously don't know much about their genetics. Mtb doesn't grow fast since it has only one copy of rRNA gene in it, unlike vibrio. It utilizes its cellular machinery to make new proteins, not replicate itself, again unlike vibrio. However, it doesn't have a gene that codes for toxins, and so cannot make use of its abilities. Given a gene that codes for toxins, it can make loads of the deadly protein.

There is an additional feature. Ctb has many, many copies of the ctx gene, in contrast to vibrio, which has only one. Therefore, a ctb bacterium produces a hundred thousand-fold more toxins than a vibrio bacterium. The rate of replication is completely irrelevant. This is the perfect biowar weapon. This is a superbug.

With a sudden thump, the plane landed, jolting Howard out of his reverie. He looked over and saw Tracy had awoken too, and she was groggily looking about. He quickly stuck his finger in his jacket and pushed the pointed finger into Tracy's midriff.

"Quiet! Just do as I tell you!"

Tracy, soporific, short of breath and weak, nodded. In her befuddled state, it did not occur to her that the chances of Howard being able to smuggle a gun into the airplane were very remote. More interested in self-preservation, especially when confronted with the maniacal and drugged Howard, Tracy complied. The drugs in her system began to attack her consciousness again, and she was barely able to walk, even with assistance. Leaning on Howard, the sickly graduate student made it out of the plane, and the strange couple made their way into the terminal.

Numerous newspapers and television monitors within the concourse exploded with news of St Mary's MICU deaths. The different branches of media seemed hell-bent on scaring their respective audiences. Was it an accident? Medical carelessness? Howard heard a TV newscaster report Senator David Dockhorn would be releasing a statement at 7:00 pm this evening. Confident of what lay ahead, Howard anticipated being done with business in time to see the Senator's speech.

A limousine driver met the pair at the main entrance. Howard possessed an intimate familiarity with Washington. One of his ex-wives hailed from it. The treacherous scientist assumed he was being taken to Rock Creek, Chevy Chase, or some other opulent, exclusive neighborhood within the Beltway. His expression turned to dismay when he realized the chauffeur was heading south. Trying to keep calm and not swallow another handful of pills, Dr. Howard watched with horror as the city around him began to exhibit the countenance of extreme decay.

Soon the limousine came to a halt before an abandoned luncheonette in the heart of Southeast's Anacostia district. The chauffeur got out and signaled his passengers to alight.

"Here you are. Your destination."

"Are you sure? This can't be. There has to be a mistake!" With great trepidation, Howard got out of the limousine.

"No mistake. This is it."

A more awake Tracy, gradually shaking off the effects of the chemicals, followed Howard. Graciously, the chauffeur waved his hand through, welcoming the pair to Ash-Sham's place of business.

There was no doubt the luncheonette had seen better days. A battered security door still somehow hung from its hinges. An enormous, intact plywood board covered what used to be a window looking out on the street, transforming the interior into a secure, sepulchral den. Howard hugged Tracy as he gazed around the squalor and attempted to pick his way through the wreckage without ruining his custom-made Italian shoes.

Tracy had no idea where she was, or how she got there. She was so taken aback by the surroundings she did not notice Howard holding her tightly. Had Tracy been fully aware Dr. Howard had his arm protectively around her, she would have preferred the company of the wild dervishes that slowly came to surround them.

Imran, the leader of Ash-Sham, approached Dr. Howard. Simultaneously, six members of his company, along with the chauffeur, muttered to themselves, fingered the long blades of their knives, and inspected Howard and Tracy as though they were examining meat hanging on hooks in a bazaar. A veteran of sectarian violence, Imran neither liked nor respected Howard. He knew Howard had neither the heart to be a soldier, a thief, or anything in between. With a nod, he ordered the well-dressed chauffeur to remove Tracy from Howard's grasp.

"Welcome to Washington, Dr. Howard," he mocked.

Howard was terrified. This was not the way it was supposed to be. He was supposed to meet the CIA, and hand them the vial. He was supposed to be feted and felicitated for his fearless act, not made fun of.

"Who are you? Why did you bring us here! This place is terrible!"

That was the wrong thing to say.

"I am Imran, Dr. Howard."

Chapter 20

Howard was at a loss for words and petrified by what he saw. His host was a young man who seemed to embody a combination of cruelty, sadness, wisdom, and cynicism. A scar running at an angle from his mouth to the corner of his right eye distorted his welcome smile. Even though his mouth smiled, his unblinking coal-black eyes intently watched him, much like a Cobra eyeing the flute of the snake charmer.

"Where are the government people?" Howard managed to whisper.

Imran rubbed his misshapen nose, a nose nature had designed well, but which had obviously been broken more than once. He was not in the mood to answer questions. He had some of is his own.

"Where's the vial, Dr. Howard?"

"What vial?" Howard bluffed.

Imran's men gathered around, guffawing. Imran pulled out a long knife from its hiding place within his trousers. Smiling and sneering, he approached the almost hysterical Howard. He placed the knife under Howard's chin, its sharp blade cutting into Howard's Adam's apple. As Howard swallowed, his Adam's apple bobbed, and a thin trickle of blood ran down the blade.

Blood had always frightened Howard, which is why he never went to medical school. The sight of his own blood almost made him faint. With Herculean effort, he pulled himself together. It was obvious if he wanted to live, he would have to give up the vial. He only hoped the vial would ensure his survival.

From a deep pocket inside the breast of his jacket, he removed a small, shielded HAZMAT carrying case containing the pink vial brimming with purified water.

Imran took the vial with the deference of a devout man holding rosary beads. He backed away from the scientist, his eyes fixated on him.

"Thank you. You'll have a special place in the history of humankind, Dr. Howard." Imran intoned softly.

Like a man gazing at the Koh-I-Noor diamond that had accidentally come into his possession, instantly making him a wealthy man, Imran gazed reverentially at the vial.

What would Omar do if he knew what I had in my hand?

Omar, my chief, my nightmare. Omar, the Saudi who wants to destroy the House of Saud!

Omar came from a wealthy and influential family. His father, like half of Saudi Arabia, was related to the House of Saud. A shrewd man, he had taken his share of petrochemical wealth and had husbanded it quite successfully. His son, originally named Aurangzeb, was a man born to scan ledgers and stock sheets. He took his father's fortune and nurtured it into the GNP of a small nation.

The death of the patriarch coincided with Omar's first brush with what Americans would call a 'mid-life crisis.' Omar could not comprehend how the possession of billions of dollars in assets strung throughout the world could feel so empty and provide such little amusement, personal comfort, or hope for the future.

While driving through the streets of Mecca on his way to the holy Kaaba, Omar realized what ailed his spirits. His stately chauffeur driven Mercedes was held up in traffic by an American military convoy that was passing through. Peering out to get a better view, he was shocked by the sight of a bare armed, unveiled woman driving an army jeep.

So this is what my country has denigrated to! Our rulers have allowed infidels to guard our most holy shrines! The Kaaba guarded by women! What does this say about our manhood? This must stop! The infidel Americans must be thrown out, and our country made to follow the true path revealed in the holy Koran!

Enraged, but wholly satisfied with this revelation, Omar immediately petitioned to meet the King, to personally remonstrate with him for his shortcomings and demand immediate rectification.

Omar, for all his intellectual gifts, had never served the House of Saud in any formal capacity. Neither had his father. Therefore, his request for an audience was answered by a mere Prince, who was stuck with the job of soothing distraught billionaire subjects who needed their ruffled feathers smoothed.

The words cordial or successful could not be used to describe their parlay.

"This government is full of cowards. You ask infidels to guard our holy sites. Mark my words, you will all be destroyed if you don't make amends very quickly!"

"There is nothing wrong with asking our American friends to help us with our defense. Actually, it's quite smart. They fight wars for us, they get killed. We stay safe and keep on making money." The prince slyly winked.

"So making money is more important than keeping kafirs away from the Kaaba? This is blasphemy! You'll all go to hell."

Had Omar stopped himself sooner, he could have walked away as someone who would never have the King's trust but was a free man.

"I promise to change all this. I promise to make Saudi Arabia the land of Islam. The land of the pure and fearless, where Allah's will rules. A land without the house of Saud."

Faced with such a direct threat from a man known to keep his word, the Prince had no choice on what to do next. As the guards led the angry billionaire away to be incarcerated, the interviewing Prince ordered all of Omar's assets frozen and his entire family to be placed under house arrest.

The matter did not conclude so easily. Though Omar could have purchased a comfortable prison existence for himself and lived out his days as a great imam counting down the hours of his martyrdom, this was not to be the case.

A few days after his interview with Omar, the Prince received an urgent message from his first cousin, the Finance Minister.

He learned if Omar remained imprisoned and out of sight, a gigantic portion of the Asian and Middle Eastern financial markets stood to collapse. It appeared Omar was a superb currency speculator. Thousands of investors, analysts, and the like tracked his daily actions like rainmakers checking their dowsing sticks. His disappearance and consequent lack of activity had mushroomed into a worldwide rumor the Saudi currency was worth speculating on, paving the way for financial panic. The severely weakened Middle Eastern currencies would be the first to suffer mortal blows. Asian currencies would be next, given the heavy volume and interdependence between the two.

Reluctantly, the Prince, in conjunction with the Interior Minister and several other wags in charge of departments designed to keep any disaffection within the Saudi super-rich contained, arranged a compromise. Omar would be allowed to go into exile, provided he forswore any intention to depose the royal house.

With a grand flourish, Omar gave his word, while also announcing his retirement from the financial world due to health reasons.

No one in the Exiles Department of the Foreign Ministry thought anything of Omar requesting Chad as his place of exile. The government of Chad expressed its delight over the prospect of granting non-tax-free sanctuary to one of the world's richest men. Omar made a great show of accepting their welcome and of pledging all of his powers to make Chad a better place to live.

In truth, he had selected Chad for the natural advantage of its long, almost unguarded border with Sudan. After a few months had passed, Omar exchanged addresses, taking up a rather public residence in Khartoum, Sudan, where he announced he would henceforth devote his time to studying Islamic history, and engineering the downfall of the House of Saud. It was there, within the cauldron of lawlessness, that Omar became Omar.

It was not that Omar's original name was in any way unworthy. However, he decided during his self-administered studies, all successful revolutionaries needed a good nickname for public consumption. Since he had resolved to emulate the great Caliph of the Ottoman Empire, he dubbed himself Omar.

In deference to his benefactors in Khartoum, Omar named his movement Ash-Sham, or 'the North,' in honor of the Northern, Muslim, Sudan, who had spent five decades attempting to extirpate the Southern, Christian, half of the nation through slavery and a seemingly ceaseless war of attrition. Lawlessness, however, works both ways. On the one hand, Omar experienced complete liberty to create, staff, and outfit his revolutionary army. Saudi intelligence, however, was also equally at liberty to stop him by any violent means it chose.

Those were heady, exciting days for the suddenly enthused man. Omar actually enjoyed the thrill of knowing someone, somewhere in the teeming city of Khartoum, was attempting to assassinate him. He also enjoyed playing the military man, recruiting veterans of Khartoum's expeditions against the South.

France's excursion into a neighboring country to quell a Sudanese-sponsored coup one summer moved him to reformulate his plans. All the bravado his forces displayed hunting down terrified, unarmed villagers living in mud huts vanished when faced with a small contingent of the French Foreign Legion, operating without any heavy weapons or air support.

"That's the problem," Omar explained to his deputy. "Operations along the Nile on unarmed civilians hardly provides the kind of action a crack army needs to train itself. We have to find a better training ground." This was true considering their ultimate goal would be to do Ibn Saud one better in the ultimate conquest of not only Mecca and Medina but the entire Islamic world.

Omar began considering other nations suitable for relocation. After visiting sites as diverse as Malaysia and Madagascar, he decided on Afghanistan. On paper, the decision made sense.

"You see, Saudi influence there is minimal. Mujahideen veterans can be secured to provide combat and survival training. Security can be easily maintained to keep Ash-Sham members in and all others out." As Omar explained to his deputy, he loved the sheer audacity of it. No one would ever think of looking for him East of the Arabian Peninsula.

It was in Afghanistan that kismet would decree that Omar and Imran would meet.

Howard watched Imran intently as the Ash-Sham leader stood transfixed before him, holding the vial in his hand. As the crooked scientist wondered what his fate would be, his eyes silently beseeched the man in front of him to spare his life.

Meanwhile, two men sneaked up behind him. One of them had a wire in his hand, which he swung around Howard's neck. Howard grunted and instinctively reached for the wire as it began to choke him. His efforts failed as the wire dug deeper into his flesh. Howard clawed at it desperately, hoping to insert his fingers and save his throat from the assault, but to no avail. With a jerk, the wire was pulled, and Howard's neck snapped. His brainstem rammed into his brain, leaving his lifeless body hanging from the wire.

The execution of Dr. Howard shook Tracy out of her torpor. She had just witnessed the gory end of her Microbiology Department nemesis. Ruthless men with expressions that could freeze water surrounded her. If she didn't act now, she probably would face Howard's fate. Or worse. She kicked the chauffeur holding her arm in the shins and again in the groin. As the chauffeur let her go with a grunt, she darted quickly through the crowd of thugs who were too busy laughing at the chauffeur's misfortune to take action to stop her.

"She is running away, you idiots!" Imran shouted after a while as his men stood around waiting for orders. "Get her!"

The men immediately began pursuing her. Imran was sure she would not get too far. Anyone who appeared well-housed, fed, clothed, and moneyed, was fair game in Anacostia. She would not get far.

Tracy threw herself out of the luncheonette through its hanging security door. Like animals gathering around the last watering hole during a time of drought, the Ash-Sham men began to swarm around her.

Without any bearing, Tracy ran into the middle of the car-less boulevard and spun around, trying desperately to either locate help or an escape route. Two of Imran's men continued the chase and were within feet of her. She took to the road, and though short of breath, the thought of an impending garroting gave wings to her feet. As one of the men lunged at her, she abruptly changed course, and he fell headlong into the street. The other, close behind, stumbled and fell on top of him.

That gave Tracy a few seconds, and she dashed off again. Just as the two fallen men were about to get up and resume the chase, they heard screeching tires. A van swung around the corner and headed straight for them.

Tracy dove for cover behind the burned-out hulk of a car on the opposite side of the boulevard. The two men pursuing Tracy halted, instinctively knowing somehow this van was meant for them - either to hunt or to be hunted by. They never stood a chance. The van did a quick half-spin, knocking them both into the sidewalk, their bodies as bent and broken as the car Tracy was hiding behind. The vehicle then backed up, opened its sliding door to reveal a heavy-caliber machine gun. The gun opened fire directly into the luncheonette.

Imran had stayed behind to evaluate the performance of his men, staying close to the corpse of Dr. Howard. The Ash-Sham leader used his dead victim's body for cover as bullets began flying through the room. The men around him were less lucky and were cut down as they initially ran toward the door, and then ran away from it. Within a few seconds, all five men were dead from acute lead intoxication. From the sound of the bullets ricocheting, Imran was sure these were safety bullets, designed to be used when firing inside a structure to reduce the risk of shooting anyone several rooms away. Still, he did not want to assume anything until he was certain the firing had stopped.

An engine roared, and with the squeal of tires, the van sped away. Slowly, Imran got up and looked around. There weren't any other survivors. His henchmen were sprawled all over the floor, blood pouring out of them as if they were leaky hoses. He looked outside. Tracy was nowhere to be seen. He looked at his watch. It was almost noon.

What perfect timing!

He smiled, caressing the vial.

Chapter 21

Where's the vial?

Thor Martin wondered where Tracy was, and why she had taken the vial. He did not buy the jealousy theory, though Bukhari was so sure of it. He had spoken to Ziad again, making sure Bukhari was staying out of sight and out of trouble. The news of the MICU deaths had altered Ziad's plans to depart for Pakistan.

"We can't leave now. We have to let things settle down before we escape." Ziad still had to contend with an angry and vengeful Bukhari. Martin wondered how Bukhari was adjusting to captivity in a gilded cage.

Tariq Bukhari occupied a special place in the mind and heart of Thor Martin. The political fixer was incredibly envious of the scientist-ISI agent. Thor wished he had had the determination to put his good brains to work in academics, as Bukhari had, and to become as accomplished. However, he had not been able to control his wild urges and was now stuck working as the glorified assistant of a morally challenged Senator. Martin could not help but think about Bukhari as he struggled with the text of the Senator's speech for the evening news announcing a *pneumococcus* epidemic. His mind wrestled with the medical science he had half-heartedly tried to learn a decade earlier.

Would Bukhari have found this easy? Would he have laughed at my efforts?

Thor Martin's appetite for rowdy life was as large as his physical frame. He did not go into a bar to start a fight. However, if one were offered, he never backed off, regardless of the odds. This call of the wild had always made schooling, and any form of formal education, a difficult experience. The prospect of being cramped indoor reading books all day smothered the spirit that burned so brightly in him.

Martin elected to leave home and travel after graduating from high school. He joined a trucking company and saw more of the US in a couple of years than many people did in their entire lives. Ironically, during his travels, he realized the value of education. Deciding to give it another try, he enrolled in a local junior college in Southern California. Surprisingly, he found himself attracted to the biological sciences and decided to major in molecular biology.

During that time, Thor Martin found himself in love for the first time.

Candace, a fellow biology major, grounded him and gave him a reason to do more with his life than carouse all the time. The two of them began to talk of a permanent life together.

One weekend during their senior year, Candace told Thor she was returning home to Ojai, deep within the spectacular California wilderness, to attend an old friend's bachelorette party. She never returned. While home, she ran into her ex-high school boyfriend, and the two eloped to Las Vegas. Except for a short note offering her deepest apologies, Martin never heard from her again.

At first, Martin felt too numb to do anything more than try to maintain his now normal, studious, and sedate routine. However, without Candace to balance him, the hellion in him exploded with an incredible vengeance, as though punishing him for losing so much time to sobriety.

Martin burned everything that belonged to or reminded him of his lost love in the Mojave Desert. Bidding college farewell, he began a bender that lasted several years. One morning he woke up in a jail cell in Solitary Tree, North Dakota. Apparently, in a drunken rage the night before, he had driven his motorcycle through the front window of a bar who had refused him service because of his profoundly intoxicated state. The judge, looking at his list of considerable offenses, gave him a blunt choice

"You have two choices, playboy. Either you go to jail or join the army and make something of your life."

Martin could not believe his ears. He had heard about such options being offered to juvenile delinquents back in the '50s and '60s, but this was a different era. The judge gave him five minutes to decide. Three minutes later the bailiff marched him to the local recruiting station, conveniently located in the same building.

The Army was good for, and to, Martin. He responded well to the physical exercise and strictly enforced discipline. With his almost completed degree, he was assigned to an experimental chemical warfare unit, designed to help decontaminate a battlefield as well as to serve in an offensive capability should the need ever arise. Subsequently, from a small pool of candidates, he had been selected to help form a new battalion from his old chemical weapons outfit and found himself stationed in Minnesota.

It was a strange post. During the day, every indication existed that his life and orientation belonged to the United States Army. By night, however, a terminal case of boredom settled over the post like a blanket of snow. The carryings-on there rivaled those of any unleashed college fraternity.

Sometimes, a terrible sense of 'what if' consumed Martin. In his late thirties, he still had not married and appeared unlikely to do so at any time in the foreseeable future. He wondered what would have happened if he and Candace had gotten married? He wondered what if he had gone ahead, completed his degree, and gone on to medical school? Would he be any happier? Would he have been a different man, a better man?

These questions slipped through his mind as he struggled to recast the threat of *pneumococcus* in a way that was both accurate and credible to the minds of the vast majority of Americans. Inadvertently, his thoughts returned Bukhari.

He remembered making arrangements for Bukhari's J1 visa and all the voluminous paperwork required for his work at Mayo Clinic. Though generally, his office did not deal with such issues, this had been an exception, prioritized by the Senator himself. Martin remembered perusing Bukhari's file years ago, realizing then he had been nothing but a handyman for Senator David Dockhorn.

Still, his life with the 'King of Independents' had been a lot of fun. The power he could exercise by way of his affiliation with the Senator amazed him. The access. The associations. The influence.

From Bukhari, Martin's thoughts turned to Ziad. Incredibly, he and Ziad had become friends, if that word could even be used to describe a relationship between a politician's henchman and a terrorist. Martin had also been responsible for all the documents and permits concerning the senior ISI agent's false residency in the United States. Their conversations often related to the army and war in general. On the one hand, Martin held Ziad in awe, having listened to his stories of combat over and over again as though he were a small boy reading about the Cat in the Hat. On the other hand, they were both men of action, of a kindred spirit transcending culture and geography. That he had socialized with a known agent of a hostile foreign power hardly bothered Martin.

A silent vibration alerted Martin to a call on the private, secure line - the Watergate line, as he and the Senator liked to call it. If ever tapped by any law enforcement agency, the line would provide enough evidence against both of them to imprison them for years. Martin quickly snatched up the ash-gray receiver. The caller-ID indicated the call originated from Rochester.

The voice of Detective Satch Rusk caught Martin's attention.

"Are you guys up to speed on what's going on here?"

The detective's question puzzled the normally aware aide.

"What did you find?"

"The FBI thinks the Rochester police department is full of dolts!"

"The Feds not letting you have any fun poking around with your mail-order detective kits?"

At significant crime scenes in which they became involved, the Feds knocked the local law enforcement officials away to direct traffic and fetch coffee, causing enormous resentment. Dockhorn had taught his aide the most important information from a crime scene often arrived courtesy of someone whose feelings had been hurt.

"Yunno, they shut down all non-essential services at Mayo around noon today. So, before everybody goes home, I ask who's called in sick and all the rest. They use an old, elementary school-style system, so the personnel office knows everything before first break.

"I set a couple of my boys on it, department by department. Lotta folks not accounted for in the Microbiology Department. Three, as a matter of fact, including one big time professor named Dan Howard. Also missing is a post-doc named Tariq Bukhari, and a student named Tracy Hopkins. My boys go up to check around. Nobody's seen a thing or heard a thing. Checked all the mail logs. One FedEx package left that department on the first mail run. Left on Howard's account number but was signed out by the student Hopkins. Something from his laboratory is going to be in Jackson, Wyoming, by tomorrow morning."

"Did you check to see if Howard or Hopkins have any forwarding addresses or known contacts in Jackson?" Much later, it occurred to Martin he never asked Rusk for the address in Jackson to which the package had been mailed.

"Sure did! What else do you expect from me? Hopkins is from nearby Utah. More interestingly, she resigned her position at Mayo Clinic on Friday! Howard has no connections in Jackson or nearby, at least none that we could find."

Martin thanked the diligent detective in his heartiest and most officially promising tones. He felt sick to his stomach as the full horror of the situation dawned on him.

Martin knew who was responsible for the MICU deaths. On his flight from St Paul to Rochester, Ziad had left an emergency code message on his personal voice mail.

"It is a stark and dark night."

The ISI man had used the word 'Stark,' a reference to the US ship struck by Iraqi missiles in 1987. They had selected this word as an urgent code word, never to be used lightly. If Ziad were ever in trouble, the plan had been for him to call, leave word within a larger context, and then head for Wildwood, the Senator's legendary opulent estate near St Paul. While in flight, Martin had immediately relayed authorization for Ziad to be admitted to the estate.

Martin had not wanted to know too much about I.S.I.P. when it had first come to his attention and decided to cut down his involvement that fateful night when Howard was set up. That way, he could quite honestly say he knew nothing about what had been going on. All roads would lead to Senator Dockhorn, and Martin would be out of it.

When Martin had told Dockhorn about the situation in Rochester and Ziad's admission of responsibility, Dockhorn had been unnerved for a few moments. It was the first time Martin had seen the wily Senator stammer or turn pale. But it didn't last long, and Dockhorn took charge again. On the secure line from his office, Dockhorn reached Ziad at Wildwood. Quickly, the ISI control agent related Bukhari's experiment, the lost second vial, and Bukhari's insistence that a Mayo Clinic graduate student named Tracy Hopkins had stolen the vial.

Dockhorn had ordered the ISI men to remain out of sight within the lush depths of Wildwood until ordered otherwise. He then sat on his mahogany desk, his head in his hands, pondering the whereabouts of the second vial.

"A small tube containing enough biological warfare material to exterminate all humans in North America! And we had something to do with it! They never mentioned that kind of a project to me. They promised it had something to do with specialized tuberculosis research." He complained to Martin.

Now, Martin put his head in his hands.

A biological weapon has killed people in Rochester. Tracy Hopkins, with or without Howard, has stolen the other vial. Why? And where's Howard? Could it be possible Howard and Hopkins are in cahoots, trying to sell the vial to someone else?

Although he had joined the Senator's staff well after the last fires of the Iran-Contra scandal had cooled, Martin soon learned of the Senator's deep devotion to Afghanistan's *Mujahideen*. He also learned the Senator's interest in all things connected to Central Asia and the Middle East stemmed from emotions less altruistic than the Senator's noble claim of assisting oppressed peoples of those regions. As soon as he had earned his employers trust, Martin found out Dockhorn had been milking these regions since the early 1970s, beginning with his support for the Kissinger Doctrine giving greater power and military support to Reza Pehlavi, Shah of Iran.

Dockhorn, along with several other junior congressional representatives, filled the vacuum separating America's weapons manufacturers and the governments of those nations. Surprised by his initial success, the Senator amazed himself even more at the number of decades for which he had kept the gravy train rolling. No circumstance, no condition, no detail proved to be too fatal for his avarice, or the means to satisfy it.

At first, the then Congressman Dockhorn threw his support behind any legislation or policy decision which would allow the Shah to purchase any American weapon, support which rewarded him handsomely. The Soviet invasion of Afghanistan dovetailed issues nicely for the new Senator's program, and his business actually increased, with all the *Mujahideen* forces and the entire Pakistani military requiring modernization, courtesy of the American taxpayer. As much as he allowed himself to think about his actions, Dockhorn could hardly wait for the Central Asian weapons market to be exploited, with oil flowing from behind every sand dune in an area almost two times the size of continental United States.

Martin discovered very quickly the Senator made no bones about whom he was especially fond of. The ISI. Dockhorn had been dealing with Sahabuddin since the Pakistani agent guarded his party during a fact-finding tour of Afghan refugee camps in 1980. The bonds that had formed then amid weapons and war had only grown stronger as the decade rolled by.

The evidence remained incontrovertible before Martin's consideration: Dockhorn did not care if Bukhari had built a hydrogen bomb on the grounds of Mayo Clinic. Nothing, but nothing could interrupt the flow of money and favors between Islamabad and Wildwood.

"You know, of course, I never want to hear about any of this nonsense again," he could hear the Senator say to him.

Martin closed his eyelids with the fingers of his free hand as he returned the receiver to its cradle with the other. He kept imagining he was back in Rochester, in the FBI's mobile command unit, watching the robot's transmission from inside the contaminated St Mary's MICU. Each corpse, male or female, sported a version of Bukhari's patented expression - a cross between the sneer of utter disdain and a choleric scowl - seen so clearly the night of the videotaping.

The image kept growing logarithmically in Martin's mind. Unable to suppress his emotions and frustrations any longer, a shocking wave of harsh laughter erupted from deep within the tense aide.

After years of washing countless tons of the Senator's dirty laundry, Martin cracked, albeit quietly. Years of experience dealing with emergencies eventually brought the distraught aide at least temporarily back to his senses. He began to hatch a plan.

He faxed the evening's speech to the Senator, who was preparing to go before the cameras set up in the parking lot of St Mary's Hospital in Rochester.

Then he made a telephone call with a sense of mission he had never felt before in his life.

Chapter 22

These men have a mission. Just what is their mission?

Even in her exhausted state, Tracy had no trouble figuring out her captors were unique. What she could not figure out was how she had gotten there in the first place, why, and who the three men were. Since being ambushed by Howard, everything was a blur. All she remembered was running down the street to escape Howard's killers, only to be kidnapped by these men.

An older man, about her father's age, seemed to be in charge. He patted his neatly combed hair in place as he addressed her. Tracy tried hard to remember the names of the three men but couldn't, though they had introduced themselves soon after picking her up. They seemed nice, but she had no idea who they actually were.

"Tracy, I know you may have a hard time believing this, but I remember your father planning you, yes planning you, counting down the days until your arrival. He had just met your mother while home on leave. Boy, before that nothing could get the mind of Fightin' Bill Hopkins out of the Mekong Delta," the older man was saying, his hands resting on his slightly protuberant belly.

A sense of disbelief overtook Tracy. No one had ever called her father 'Fighting Bill Hopkins' except for her mother, and that was only once, right around the time of his resignation from the Navy.

"We were catching up after he 'coptered back into Kiem Phong. Said he met your mother and knew she was going to be the one, told her he would be back in 250 days to marry her, and that you would be born 650 to 700 days into the marriage. He started making little scratch marks on the walls of his quarters."

Tracy fought between laughing and crying.

"We went through some of the worst fighting of the entire conflict over the next few months. Vietnamization? Hell, nobody told us, and nobody bothered to tell that to Charlie. They came after us with greater ferocity after '71 'cause they knew nobody would care or believe us."

In all her years, Tracy had never heard her father say anything about his tours of duty in Vietnam.

"Old Bill received a battlefield commission. A navy officer promoted to lead what was left of two marine companies after they had been ambushed. Of course, it's quite another story about how he even got into that situation... "

Tracy trained her attention on this man who was happily lecturing her on her father. She tried to figure out the color of his hair. It was white, but it had an additional quality to it, as though some force, other than age, had bleached all of the color out of it.

"I was the one who got your father interested in life outside combat. He hated to think he would never get in the thick of things again. Did you know he turned down promotions just so he could stay in the field?"

"He never once thought he wouldn't make it. He always said he had to make it back to your mother and you."

Tracy did not want this strange man who knew all about her family to see tears streaming down her cheeks. She shifted her gaze away to avoid looking at him and turned her attention to a young man whose shirt was making a desperate effort to contain his muscles. As he paced back and forth next to the windows, he smacked his hands with force against each other as if punching an imaginary object. Tracy briefly wondered how many hours he spent in a gym. For what seemed like the millionth time, she tried to make sense of the room they were in.

"The military was different in those days, for both good and bad reasons... "

Enough sunlight poured into the enormous, half-empty room to allow Tracy to guess it must be afternoon. She could see the outlines of two, perhaps three, doors leading to an outside balcony. Tracy surmised at some point, several decades ago, this room must have been the upstairs sun porch of an enormous mansion. The stench of mold and mildew suggested it had been unoccupied for decades. She was seated on a folding, portable canvas chair that was completely disagreeable.

"We were friends. Friends talk. You can do that sort of a thing if you have equal degrees of security clearance. Believe me, Tracy, your dad and I were, still are, I hope, friends... "

Unable to keep her mind focused on what he was saying, Tracy continued to survey her surroundings. The objects in the room had been arranged the way children arrange living room furniture to make forts in-order to play war games. Should attackers march up the sagging staircase, they would be cut down from the fortifications erected by these men. Obviously, they assumed no one would be able to fire up at them successfully from the streets of Anacostia, less than a hundred feet away, separated by the remains of a once grand lawn, now a heap of dirt and garbage.

"Tracy, I couldn't tell any of this to my own children... "

Tracy tried hard to pay attention to what he was saying but was unable to. The older man had started by asking for her help but had soon switched to telling family stories. His rambling style, along with the residual effects of the drugs, made concentration very difficult. She coughed a couple of times and looked around her again.

The young, muscular man continued to pace the perimeter of his hidden outpost, careful not to present his silhouette against the empty window frames. Every now and then, the third man would join him on his patrol, then ease back to hear the one-sided conversation. Tracy smiled a bit at the third man. Standing in between the other two, his slim build and height made him almost invisible. The elegance of his dress was particularly interesting, more fitting of an investment banker than someone who rode around in vans, shooting machine guns.

With a startle, Tracy felt the old man gently – paternally - grasp both of her hands between his.

"We need your help, kid. For our nation's security… "

She could not help but laugh. What was that saying about patriotism being the last resort?

"Al." the older man beckoned the dapper, middle-aged man.

Tracy watched as Al sat down in an old-fashioned office chair and rolled it over next to her. She recoiled as he leaned in towards her from the creaking, ancient chair.

"You're good. Uncle Sam spends a lot of money training agents to be as good as you!" Tracy squirmed away from his well-groomed but close countenance.

"My dear colleague and commanding officer, David, whom you have been speaking with, has failed in trying to persuade you with the family approach. Sorry, boss."

He winked at David, who waved back in jovial defeat. Her new lecturer pulled away from her slightly.

"I'm going to try with the truth about that little school you seem to be earning a degree from, Mayo Clinic. Here's the scoop. You heard it here first. Dr. Howard's a dirty man. He's a very nasty piece of work, mixed in with something very big and very ugly. Your buddy Bukhari's a branch of the same tree. We know he's an agent connected to Pakistan's secret service. They have a program dedicated to rustling up a biological warfare weapon, something really doomsday. We're pretty sure your young friend Bukhari succeeded in creating it. This is where you come in. We need your help. We've got to know what he was making. Can you tell us something, or help figure it out?"

"Mayo Clinic's not a little school... "

"She speaks!"

"Al, you're a genius."

"All it took was one good insult to her alma mater. Now that's the way the higher education system is supposed to work."

Tracy watched the older man reclaim his position before her.

"I think I'd better interrupt my learned friend here before he starts singing the old school song from whatever correspondence college he attended. No doubt ol' Al here forgot to mention that your Senator from Minnesota, David Dockhorn... "

"King of the Independents," chimed in the other two.

" ...promoted, protected, and did everything but the household chores for Doctors Howard and Bukhari. But, that is just to give a little background. To carry on with what Al was saying, we don't have much time - and we shouldn't stay here long. Just tell us anything you can so we can bring this terrible drama to an end."

Tracy coughed, cleared her throat, and looked at David before speaking.

"Don't mind me. You guys can go anytime you want."

David and Al groaned and began pacing in frustration. John, the young man on patrol, returned to the field of Tracy's vision. He carried an enormous, double-barreled sawed-off shotgun under the crook of one arm. In the other, he carried an ordinary videocassette. He shouted at Tracy, like a drill instructor yelling at raw recruits on a parade ground.

"Do you know what happened at Mayo last night?"

"No. I mean, yes, I know what happened to me, if that's what you're talking about." Tracy frowned.

"No, that's not what I'm talking about. Woman, I want you to watch this."

Forcefully, but with his weapon pointed wide, he pulled her to a spot before a television attached to a VCR, then crammed the tape into its slot. Meanwhile, Al took up the patrol, and David came to stand beside Tracy.

A network news program brightened the room. Tracy's heart began beating faster as she recognized the figure of Senator David Dockhorn, speaking from behind a podium. She heard him struggle over a word. Pneumococcus. Two dozen people, nurses, and patients had lost their lives in a matter of a few hours on Sunday night. The Senator was ascribing the deaths to a drug-resistant strain of the pneumococcus bacteria.

Tracy gasped in horror. Two dozen? Poor souls! Then, her scientific mind began to whirl. What was the Senator talking about? Pneumococcus, drug-resistant or not, can't kill so many people so fast.

John hit the rewind button and stood between the picture and Tracy.

"Woman, you've got to help us. This is what we're up against. This is what we've been up against for years. I'm gonna make you watch this over and over again until you see the light of day and tell us what we need to know so we can take these guys down."

Tracy shook her head, indicating she had seen enough. John hit the power button, and the screen went blank.

Chapter 23

Andrew's screen-saver counted down the time remaining until he began college at Massachusetts Institute of Technology. Brightly colored, it alternated between displaying the time in lightyears, Vulcan years, Klingon years, Romulan years, and Federation years. MIT had offered the junior Hopkins an early acceptance since Andrew had enough credits to graduate from high school in the winter term. At Christmas time, Andrew bought the subject up.

"Dad, why don't I finish school early?" He mentioned casually, his thin gangly body swallowed by the sofa.

"Why? Are you eager to start college? Or do you just want to leave home?"

"Neither. I wanted to have some free time before starting college." Andrew slipped further in the sofa, with his feet sticking out and his head abutting the armrest.

"Free time, I see. What do you plan to do with your free time?"

"I'd like you to teach me to ride a motorcycle so the two of us could take off on a four-month tour of America," Andrew replied with a straight face. Bill practically leaped out of his chair with joy.

"Way to go, man," Rory grunted his approval. Tracy looked at her mother, wondering how she would react.

"Before you get too carried away, Andrew, your father and I need to discuss this. In the meanwhile, help clear the table." Doris firmly stated.

In the ensuing parental discussion, Doris told her husband, under no circumstances would she allow her son to turn into some Hell's Angel, roaring around the country like an aimless delinquent. Bill's arguments and pleas were ignored. He was delighted his son had finally begun to show some of the Hopkins' family pluck. However, Doris forbade Andrew to miss so much as an hour of his childhood at home.

Doris loved her two children and would do anything in the world for them except letting them grow easily into adulthood. In her eyes, Andrew would always be the elementary school mommy's boy. His departure for the East Coast would not be easy for her, and she was in no hurry to hasten it. In truth, Andrew rather enjoyed Doris' mothering. Like most seventeen-year-olds, he enjoyed seeing just how far he could push his parents without getting into serious trouble.

Bill retired to the garage without responding to Rory's offer to take Andrew's place on such an expedition. To appease Andrew, Doris approved the extension of her son's night curfew till 11.30 pm.

'The last carefree days of youth' had not made much of an impression on Andrew. He struggled to stay awake in his classes and could hardly wait to study nothing but computer science at MIT. Though graduation ceremonies were over a month away, Andrew had already begun to feel the first pangs of realization that in a matter of weeks, he would be leaving the only home he ever knew, the only room he had ever called his own. The acoustically perfect room, the only room that was 'dad-proof.'

Bill Hopkins could not stand electronic noise. The sound of his power saw cutting through an engine block would not bother him in the slightest. The artificial sounds of a fantasy battle in space would drive him to distraction. The years had tamed Bill somewhat - he could now walk through a parking lot without going to pieces if he heard the beeping of a car alarm. His son's computer, though, was an entirely different matter.

Andrew had grown up with the '90s software revolution. To Bill, it sometimes looked like a contest between the software programmers of the world pitted against the aptitude of his son to see who could stump the other. So far the race remained in a dead heat. No program had been written which Andrew had not mastered in a couple of days and then written to the company on how it could be improved. Bill teased his son about being late and too old to write a program that would secure his fortune before the age of twenty.

Bill and Doris had allowed Andrew to move into the sub-basement of the house when he turned thirteen. A concrete cube beneath the house's foundation deep in the hillside, the room was every young boy's dream come true. It was soundproof, dark on demand, and out of parental audio-visual range. Andrew had perfected a cyber lifestyle by staying awake until the wee hours of the morning in pursuit of ever-expanding knowledge. Bill never complained about the noises Andrew's computer made anymore.

As he grew older, Andrew appreciated the solace his room offered. Like all boys his age, he sometimes found his parents bothersome. He knew his father was disappointed his only son had not elected to apply his science and math skills at Annapolis. Andrew did not enjoy hunting or fishing and showed no interest in politics or the military. Nevertheless, like most sons, he sought his father's approval. Though Andrew felt closer to Doris, he did not want to become a modern version of Travels with My

Aunt. The closer his high school graduation drew, the younger his mother seemed to think he was. He had not found any neighborhood kids who shared his interests, and the situation in school was not too different. His classmates could not talk about anything except what Michael Jordan's score was, or if they had scored the night before. Andrew had turned to computers and the cyber world, as it gave him intellectual stimulation and quenched his thirst for knowledge.

Especially on certain days, Andrew treasured the warm embrace of his room more than anything else in the world. Seated before his bright screen, flanked by opposing posters of Bill Gates and Steve Jobs, he lectured the monitor like a newscaster addressing the camera.

"News of the St Mary's deaths came while Andrew Hopkins was attending stupid school. Dad appears to have kept a level head. Mom automatically assumed Tracy's dead. Mrs. Kennedy makes things worse by pointing out the obvious. Dad boots Mrs. Kennedy out and tells her never to come back. Andrew wishes he could have seen that. Mom and Dad spend all Monday afternoon waiting for news or a call from Tracy. Andrew tries to help, but for the first time in years gets told to go to his room. Andrew sulks but figures the folks want to be left alone.

"Andrew goes to his room for a while. Much later, he learns Mrs. Kennedy had decided to brave Dad's blockade and show up with store-bought cookies. While exchanging heated words with Dad on the subject of manners, Mom takes a call from Rory. He had not heard from Tracy either. Rory tells the 'rents not to worry. Mrs. Kennedy tells mom Rory is being callous. Dad throws Mrs. Kennedy out and tells her again never to come back. End story."

The young man sighed. He gazed down at the small chronometer at the base of his monitor. 7.30 on a Monday night. Too early to do anything, too late to do anything. Maybe he would just surf the Internet. God, I love computers, he thought to himself.

Absorbed in his game, insulated in his den, he never heard the gunshots.

Chapter 24

Tracy's composure was shot to smithereens. She recognized some of the faces on the television as the gory sights from St. Mary's MICU were beamed to the world. She had traveled in the Mayo Clinic shuttle between Guggenheim Building and St Mary's with some of those killed. What affected her the most was Sarah. Sarah Davidson, who had moved in next to her only last week, all excited and eager to start her new job. Sarah Davidson, four months pregnant. The sight of her dead body had been too much for Tracy.

It took her a while to settle down. David brought her a tuna sandwich and a Pepsi, which she gratefully accepted.

Al offered her a contraband Cuban cigar, which she politely declined. John slipped to her side when he thought the other two were not looking and apologized for calling her 'woman.' Tracy accepted the apology as graciously as she could. She was still not sure whether to trust these three men, whom she had dubbed 'the Triumvirate.' But she did not see that she had too many choices. If they had meant to harm her, they never would have rescued her from the killers of Dr. Howard earlier. Moreover, the vehemence with which they expressed their desire to destroy Bukhari and the entire ISI network sounded very real.

However, her instinctive distrust of anything to do with the Federal Government made her hesitate in offering help, however conditional. If these were government men, what were they doing hiding out in an abandoned building in the middle of Washington, D.C.'s worst neighborhood? Which side of the fence were they on? If David was such a good friend of her father, how come Bill had never mentioned his name? David had told her stories about Vietnam, but they could easily have been made up. She had no way of authenticating their veracity. Unless she called home and spoke to her father...

Tracy signaled for David to come and talk to her. She studied his face. It had aged unevenly. From certain angles, he looked twenty; from others, sixty. She decided she had only one test she could try on him. If he answered correctly, she would co-operate with them. After all, she could not spend the rest of her life in a decaying house.

"Mr. David..."

"Just David."

"David what?"

"Just David." He replied with a smile.

"Is that your real name?" quizzed Tracy. She found the secrecy a bit amusing.

"It's real enough."

"David, you know my father."

"Very well. One of the best individuals and officers I've ever met."

"Why did he resign from the Navy?"

"He never told you?"

"I don't think a prematurely retired Admiral would want to discuss something of that nature with his ten-year-old daughter."

"His daughter hasn't been ten for a while."

"His daughter's a doctor in training, not a spook. She uses her brain for science and medicine, not espionage."

David sighed deeply.

"After Vietnam, your father became something of an intelligence legend. He took all the energy he had in him and instead of using it to chase Charlie up and down the Mekong, he used it to track Chinese moles who had penetrated the Federal government in Washington."

"Like the Manchurian candidate?"

"Exactly! Like the Manchurian candidate!" David was pleased with the analogy.

"Your father was a prison bloodhound," offered Al, who now stood to his senior officer's side.

"Counter-intelligence suited your father just as well as counter-insurgency did back in 'Nam. It was as though he could just walk out on the Mall, sniff the air and know what to do, whom to peg... "

"Your father made more enemies this side of Richard Nixon than anyone else we know," Al said. "Problem was, he was too good at uncovering Chinese spies. That conflicted with Kissinger's legacy of appeasement of China."

David continued. "Some higher-ups in the State Department thought they could get rid of him if they could only get him back into action. The chance came in 1982 when the US military took up position off the coast of Lebanon in response to the Druze attacks on Northern Israel.

Seeing those marines garrisoned in Beirut infuriated your father. He begged the brass not to garrison those leathernecks out in the open. He argued they were sitting ducks for terrorist attacks. The brass demanded proof of any intended terrorist plot. Proof - he screamed, at them, you want a newspaper headline in advance! Nobody listened to him. The explosion killed all those marines also killed a big part of him too. He felt personally responsible. He was in Beirut when it happened. A few minutes here or there and he would have been in the blast zone. In his letter, he said any military that had such a callous disregard for the safety of its own personnel was not worth serving."

"So, he heard the blast?" Tracy asked softly.

"Yes, he did," replied David.

"Is that why he can't stand electronic noises?"

"No, that's only part of it. He can't stand noises because he claims he heard the electronic buzzer going off when the bomb detonated inside the marine camp. Like a loud, cheap clock radio, he said. At first, I told him he was getting his ordinances mixed up. It was a car bomb, not a remote-controlled job. He insists, though, that he heard something. After a while, I quit telling Fighting Bill Hopkins otherwise."

Tracy bowed her head down, as though about to say grace with unclasped hands.

"Who exactly are you guys?"

"We're your tax dollars at work, the CIA," Al said under his breath.

"Why didn't you say so from the beginning?"

"Well, we don't like to declare ourselves. It's an old habit." Al was clearly uncomfortable.

John bailed Al out. "Miss Hopkins, before you stand two of the greatest agents the CIA has ever seen, excepting maybe Wild Bill Donovan and the original OSS gang during World War II." He began with the formal introductions. "Ol' Dave here started while Kennedy was still in office. Poor fellah never left. Kept finding some way or other to get assigned to all the wars, covert or overt, the agency has been involved in. Our man here speaks well over a dozen languages, including Farsi, Arabic, and the manner of English that is still spoken in our native South, ain't that right, captain?"

David smiled.

John continued, "Al came on board with the Agency right around the time of the first Reagan administration with his Ph.D. in Arabic something or other. The Agency noticed something. These two guys are smart, but they can't stand the thought of sitting behind a desk. They go out into the field, they get things done, but they don't get killed. Casey loved both of them. Let'em both do all the Wild Bill stuff they wanted. Tagging along with GI Joe in Beirut or parachuting into Afghanistan to meet with the *Mujahideen*."

"I figure if I stick around long enough, someone in charge will actually bother to listen," David interjected. "The three of us met in Afghanistan and have been together ever since. I saw a lot of stuff there I wish I hadn't seen."

"We all saw too much during that last operation, Ms. Hopkins. It produced some long memories," Al added.

David began to explain the origins of their nexus.

"Let's begin with Bukhari, whom you know so well. The brain behind Bukhari is a most sinister man, one who could outdo Professor Moriarty. His name is Ghazni. Mohammad Ghazni of the ISI, Pakistan's secret service. Six years ago, Ghazni, the second most-feared man within the ISI, risked his entire career in an attempt to develop and perfect a biowar weapon the likes of which the world had never seen."

Al piped in.

"Supporting Ghazni's efforts was Abid Sahabuddin, the head of ISI." Al drifted off. "The last time I saw him was when we told him we were leaving Pakistan, with the Afghanistan imbroglio still unsorted. He stood erect, his cold steady eyes never left my face, and though his mouth never said it, I knew we had made an enemy that day…anyway, Sahabuddin saw the advantages of Ghazni's ideas, and gave them priority status."

"Who is this Saha-whats-his-name?"

Al continued, giving a brief sketch of the man.

"Sahabuddin is a well-known danger to us. One of Pakistan army's rising stars, he was offered a prized post in the ISI when it was created out of the army. His initial task was to organize terrorists in East Pakistan - modern-day Bangladesh - against the elected leaders of the province, which was at the time trying to secede from Pakistan. To do so, he had to work with willing locals who were guided by their priests and leaders of the Islamic fundamentalist party, *Jamiat-e-Islami*. The experience gave him a unique exposure to his country's religion, and a fundamentalist viewpoint he hadn't known before. We heard from then on, he thought of nothing but the global domination of Islam, from Tunisia to the Philippines, and ultimately the whole world

"When the Soviets invaded Afghanistan, Sahabuddin was given the task of organizing the *Mujahideen*. By 1980, as deputy director of ISI, he controlled billions of dollars flowing into ISI's coffers. The position facilitated his making important contacts among members of U.S. Senate and Congress, contacts that came in handy more than once."

Al saw Tracy grimace, and he appreciated the gesture.

"Yes, our own Congress. He also made contacts in the banking circles and learned the art of laundering money. While in control of the

Mujahideen's purse, he made sure fundamentalist factions like those of Gulbuddin Hekmatyar got the lion's share, while the secular factions got peanuts."

"And the U.S. government allowed it to happen?"

"We made some mistakes. Really, really stupid mistakes. The CIA agents in charge, Milt Reardon and Frank Anderson, should have known better. They were so caught up trying to emulate Lawrence of Arabia they missed the whole point. If only they had half the sense of T. E. Lawrence! The goal of getting rid of the Soviets, at any cost, was the prevailing mentality, even if it meant Islamic fundamentalists came to power in Afghanistan. David and I had warned them, but they didn't listen."

"God, we sure do some idiotic things." John burst out. "Like selling arms to Iran, so they can use them against us. Just think what would happen if one of those Stinger missiles we gave to the *Mujahideen* brought down one of our planes!"

While Tracy looked on, shell-shocked, Al continued.

"After the Soviets were driven from Afghanistan, Sahabuddin was rewarded. He was made the head of ISI, probably the most powerful position in the country. However, the appointment came at an unfortunate time for him. Having won the war, the U.S. lost interest in Afghanistan. Pakistan, no longer a front-line state, was not an important ally anymore. Pakistan's nuclear ambitions, human rights violations, child labor, and heroin smuggling became important issues. That's when I think Sahabuddin turned into our enemy. He thought he and the ISI had been used and discarded. Adding insult to injury, he lost control of the *Mujahideen* factions as they fought with each other. We don't know what exactly happened subsequently, or when, but the next we knew, he had gone off the deep end. At least, that's the way it appeared to us.

"With the suspected connivance of Nazarullah Babar, Interior Minister in Benazir Bhutto's government, he siphoned money from the remnants of U.S. aid to Pakistan. He trained mercenaries from other Islamic countries for use in guerrilla wars. But, that was only the beginning of his plans.

Afghanistan's semi-arid land was ideal for opium cultivation. Realizing this, he encouraged opium farming, increasing acreage from 40 acres in 1978 to 140,000 acres in 1994. The ancient Silk Road was reopened, and heroin flowed through it, right into the heart of U.S. and Europe. From an annual 200 tons in 1978, 3500 tons of the white gold reached its destination in 1994. The profits filled ISI's coffers. With his ill-gotten gains, Sahabuddin recruited students studying in madrasas, the religious schools, at the border between Pakistan and Afghanistan. Somehow, he convinced them the gun was a natural ally of the holy Koran, and they were organized into an army."

David uttered his next words slowly and dramatically.

"The Taliban was born."

"Under the remote-controlled guidance of Sahabuddin, the Taliban struck quickly. While the erstwhile *Mujahideen* factions were fighting among themselves along ethnic and religious lines, the Taliban took them by surprise. Capitalizing on the splintered opposition, they quickly gained control of the Southern half of the country. In less than two years, they reached the capital, Kabul. Seeing an enemy at the gates, the bickering *Mujahideen* patched up. Secularist Burhanuddin Rabbani was installed as the President, Ahmed Shah Massoud as the Prime Minister. Together, they halted the Taliban. Matters had stood there, and the war continued. For a while. But the seeds of bitterness had been sown with the poppy, and the harvest was equally bountiful."

"So, it was a civil war, between the government and the Taliban?"

"Not really. It was more international than you would think. Iran and Russia backed the *Mujahideen* government. Why? Iran's Shia Muslim government didn't want a rival Sunni Muslim government destabilizing its Eastern borders. A secular government was preferable. Russia, on the other hand, didn't want to see an Islamic theocracy to its South. The secular *Mujahideen* led government was much more acceptable. Politics, as they say, makes strange bedfellows.

"The Taliban was backed by Pakistan and indirectly by Saudi Arabia and Kuwait, our dear allies from 1991 Gulf War. The Taliban, with Allah on their side as well, were convinced they could not loose. History proved them right. They finally did overrun Kabul, and Massoud's army crept away in the stealth of the night to the Northern mountains and established its base there.

"The Taliban had won its first war. The next was to come."

Tracy held her breath.

David continued where Al had left off.

"Sahabuddin had carefully considered his options. He had a country from which to launch his global ambitions. He had an army. He had a goal. How to achieve the goal was his problem.

"He did not have an appropriate weapon.

"The Islamic world was, and is, weak and divided, without a clear leader. Countries aspiring for leadership have similar resources and capabilities. This has led to petty wars, such as the one between Iran and

Iraq, draining their resources. Nothing stands out that propels any one country to leadership. Not money, not land, not population. Nothing.

"What they needed was a superweapon.

"If a country had a superweapon, it would make that country the leader. The bickering countries would unite behind that country, and an essential goal of Islamic unity would be achieved. In addition, with such a superweapon, the West could be defeated, achieving the second goal of pan-Islamic domination. The problem was, what would the superweapon be?"

That's it, Tracy thought. Biological weapons!

"Nuclear weapons? For a long time, countries in the Middle East had tried to obtain nuclear weapons. Iran, Iraq, Libya, and Syria have been foremost in this attempt. They have failed. The International Atomic Energy Agency has kept a close watch on nuclear technology and its ingredients, depriving the nuclear wannabes the joy of securing even a single bomb. There is, however, an exception. Pakistan."

"You remember John said we do some really stupid things? Well, here is another. We're supposed to spread democracy throughout the world, right? Well, we slept with Pakistan, a dictatorship, for three decades. It didn't matter, so long as it was our ally during the cold war. So, how do we treat our allies? We turn a blind eye when they develop nuclear weapons. We did it with Israel, and now we've done it with Pakistan. Anyway, to cut a long story short, Pakistan clandestinely acquired nuclear weapons technology. While the Reagan administration looked the other way, they built twenty-five nuclear bombs. In 1990, under pressure from pragmatic Senators like Larry Pressler and congressmen like Stephen Solarz, President Bush, after much dilly-dallying, finally acknowledged Pakistan may have the bomb. U.S. military aid to Pakistan was cut. It was too little, too late.

"We heard Sahabuddin wanted the bomb. It was to be his superweapon. However, successive civilian Pakistani governments balked at his plans. The reasons were simple. Financially, Pakistan was, and is, a basket case. Without the help of the West, it will be ruined. If Pakistan uses the bomb, even pro-Pakistan hawks like Congressmen Dana Rohrabacher of California and Dan Burton of Indiana won't be able to stem the tide of anti-Pakistan actions. In fact, Pakistan had come close to being named a terrorist nation. It had taken persuasive diplomacy by the Pakistan Caucus in the House of Representatives to stop it from happening. On its part, Pakistan bent over backwards to arrest and deport Ramzi Yousef, the mastermind behind the early 1990's World Trade

Center bombing, and Amir Kansi, who assassinated our colleagues in Virginia. The situation ameliorated somewhat. Using nuclear weapons to assert supremacy would change all that."

David added his bit. "That's when Sahabuddin went nuclear, if you'll pardon the pun. He reportedly told his Prime Minister he was fed up with cowardly politicians. He must have felt he had to branch out on his own and create his own superweapon. One that could be easily made and used.

"Biological weapons.

"Sahabuddin had been on the prowl, trying to find someone in Pakistani academic circles who could create such a weapon for him. In Lahore, he ran into Ghazni. Ghazni was, and is, a professor of microbiology at the medical school in Lahore. The medical school Bukhari graduated from. He was trained at London's King College and has an international reputation in science."

Tracy's widening eyes confirmed the last statement. She remembered seeing the short, plump man at Mayo Clinic when he had come to give a guest lecture. She especially remembered the uproar he had caused when his glasses fell and broke and he had to order new ones.

"What is less known about Ghazni is he is one of the most active members of Jamiat-e-Islami, whose visions of the future influenced Sahabuddin. Still less publicized is the fact Sahabuddin convinced him to become the chief of ISI's biowar program. In this capacity, Ghazni exhibited a Dr. Jekyll/Mr. Hyde persona his students would have found difficult to believe. He approached his goal with a single-mindedness and cruelty that sometimes scared even Sahabuddin, let alone us."

"How come we are so powerless to stop the likes of him if Pakistan is so financially dependent on us?" Tracy was nonplused.

"Unfortunately, that's another long story. It has something to do with spineless politicians and confused State Department policies."

"Anyway, you were saying about Ghazni?"

"Ghazni was and is a firm believer in biological weapons. He likes them because they're silent, cheap, deadly, and extremely difficult for international agencies to regulate. This is well borne out by the fact many countries have worked on and amassed biological weapons. The US and Russia are known to have worked on biological weapons. It is suspected Iran, Syria, Iraq and North Korea have produced biological weapons. These include anthrax, typhoid, pneumonic plague, etcetera.

"If they're so good, why hasn't anyone used them as yet?"

"Well, biological weapons have their drawbacks. First, the perpetrator is just as likely as the victim to be exposed to the agent, especially in the long term. This is particularly true for viruses such as smallpox and even bacteria like anthrax. One could, in theory, fight a war wearing protective gear, but it would be too cumbersome for an army on the move. Besides, biological weapons take time to act; especially those ingested orally through food or water. Perhaps the greatest drawback, however, is the fact that all weapons amassed so far use known pathogens. An army can be vaccinated against a variety of pathogens, thus circumventing the usefulness of biological weapons. If a bug does manage to break loose, it can be rapidly identified and countered with appropriate antibiotics.

"We found out the evil professor had a new idea. He decided to create an entirely new bacteria by combining parts of existing ones. Recombinant technology, something you know a lot about. The result is a bacteria that is not known to exist. No army can be vaccinated against a bacteria that isn't even identified. When an army is exposed to such a weapon, diagnosis can be difficult, if not impossible, because the bug won't respond conventionally to any known test. You probably know this better than I do. The new bacteria, the 'superbug', could be engineered to be fast-acting, to be delivered by the fastest route - inhalation - and to be resistant to some or all antibiotics. Finally, Ghazni proposed the superbug not be used in a conventional war, but as a terrorist tool. A means to terrorize Western civilization, wreck the economy, and decimate our population.

"Unfortunately for the mad scientist, tools to create such a superbug aren't available in Pakistan. Therefore, he recruited medical students who would be willing to undertake such a project in the U.S. Naive, full of patriotic fervor, and brainwashed, they became his fifth column, unwitting pawns of a deadly conspiracy. Ghazni helped many of them find positions abroad. Tuition was paid, visa problems mysteriously solved. Universities in the U.S. - their budgets tight due to congressional cutbacks - were very happy to obtain hard-working, free labor. The Westward infiltration began many years ago. With Bukhari, it may have reached a climax. The climax that you saw in the St Mary's MICU."

"I find this so hard to believe!" Tracy interjected. "Doesn't anyone in the government know, or care?"

"The problem is, everyone's too greedy. The Congressmen on the ISI's payroll don't care. Do you think Dockhorn gives a damn about anything? So long as there's a buck to be made, they don't care who ultimately pays for it."

"So, are you a part of the non-caring government?"

"We care enough to be doing this on our own, Tracy. That's why we're hiding in this godawful place because no one in his or her right mind would think of looking for us here. And why we need your help because we can't turn to the Centers for Disease Control or any other governmental agency. If we did, we'd be caught. If the Senate or Congress catches wind of what we're doing, we'll be strung up from the highest lamp post."

Tracy hung her head, depressed by all this information.

"How do you fit into this?" Tracy queried John.

"Well, Ms. Hopkins," John answered, "I had two brothers with me in the service during the Gulf War. One never came home. One wishes he never had because of the poisons eating away at his body, poisons that no one seems to know anything about, but we think are the germs he got exposed to over there. It's to stop those kinds of germs that we need your help."

"Why didn't you capture Bukhari and find out from him? Why didn't you find out from Howard the details of Bukhari's work?"

"If we went after Bukhari, we would tip our hands. We would win in the short term, but not in the long term. As far as Howard is concerned, we neither trusted his science nor his judgment. We would have asked someone else to help us, but when Howard told us he was bringing you, we thought you would be perfect."

Tracy was finally beginning to see the CIA renegade's point of view. Still, she wanted to speak to her father and seek his advice before agreeing to co-operate.

"Let me call my parents first," she insisted.

Chapter 25

This was the first time Andrew had heard his sister scream. The combination of panic and agitation in her voice made the young man scramble to smother the telephone receiver in the folds of his sweatshirt, attempting to deaden the sound.

"Shhhh, not so loud," he cautioned. Andrew worried the noise would wake his injured parents, who were trying to rest after a harrowing evening. They had enough to worry about in Ogden without Tracy falling apart.

After Bill had expelled Charlotte Kennedy yet again, an uncomfortable tension, as tactile as the heat and humidity of a Texas summer had blanketed the house. As the evening had worn on, Doris had grown more distraught. Rory's call earlier had only increased her agitation, and Bill had reached the point where he could not console his wife any further. Andrew had escaped to his room since there wasn't anything useful he could do upstairs.

At about 8:30 pm, feeling stiff in his joints and in the mood for a snack, Andrew left his room. He climbed up the narrow stairwell that led to the utility room, which in turn opened into the kitchen. As Andrew approached the utility room door, he noticed the light was on. His father's discipline would never allow an unessential light to be left burning. Andrew quickened his step, wondering if there had been bad news about Tracy.

They would've let me know; they would've told me.

The door between the utility room and the kitchen was securely closed. Andrew assumed somehow his parents must have overlooked turning off the utility room light. He grinned to himself.

They're getting old and forgetful!

He flicked off the light with one hand and, still grinning to himself in the dark, pulled the door open with the other. As he stepped through into the dark kitchen, his left foot caught on something in his path and he stumbled into the kitchen. Though light on his feet, he almost rammed into the freestanding gas range in the middle of the kitchen. After catching his balance against the grill, he gingerly moved towards the light switch. Everywhere he stepped, his feet touched debris. As his eyes accommodated to the dark, he sensed something was terribly wrong.

He flicked on the light and was greeted by absolute devastation. He had tripped on his mother's KitchenAid mixer which was lying on its side on the floor. The entire kitchen had been ransacked, as though a squadron of vandals had stormed through, seeking only to leave chaos and ruin behind them. Turning around, he saw the dining room had suffered an equal amount of damage. He ran from room to room, turning on every light, frantically calling for his parents. The only thing he heard was the sound of his feet crunching over the wreckage.

Andrew ran upstairs. Sweeping through the rooms, including his parents' master bedroom, he saw nothing was amiss. A thousand sinister possibilities raced through his mind. Had his parents been kidnapped? Was it a robbery? Why would robbers destroy so many valuable things so indiscriminately? What had they been after? Could they still be in the house?

Though neither a hunter nor a collector, Bill kept something of a household arsenal and made sure everyone in the family knew how to operate a handgun properly in the event of an emergency. In an attempt to be inconspicuous, Bill had constructed a hidden gun locker in the anteroom connecting his garage workshop to the house. Disregarding any caution, Andrew ran to the locker and found it open. He noticed one of the MAC-10 'Streetsweepers' had been taken.

A thudding sound caught his attention.

Andrew cocked his ear. The sound appeared to be originating in the garage. Impetuously, he grabbed the first weapon he could reach, a .38 police revolver. He concluded the only thing he could do was to enter the garage through its interior door. Otherwise, he would have to go back to the utility room, fetch the keys that unlocked the rolling garage door, and then open it. If an intruder were to take a shot at him, he or she would have considerably more opportunity to do it if Andrew stood in full view as he raised the garage door.

He was considering heading back to his room to call the police when the thudding noise stopped. Andrew crouched down and, instead of calling the police, approached the garage door. Turning off the overhead light, on all fours, he quietly opened the door.

To his relief, there were no gunshots aimed at him. His eyes, now adapted to the dark, scanned the garage at floor level. He spotted no feet, or anything to indicate someone equally low to the ground was waiting for him, ready to spring out. Andrew also did not spot any body part above the top of the car, so unless the intruder was less than four feet tall, and could float in the air, the only place he or she could be was in one of the cars.

The thudding resumed Andrew discerned the banging sound was coming from the car parked closest to the welding rack. He needed to crawl over to the closest light switch, unfortunately, located on the opposite side of the garage. On his belly, he shimmied over, moving as slowly as possible.

Reaching the switch, he cocked the hammer of his pistol and stood up on his knees. As he flipped the switch, the bright industrial-strength overhead lights blinded him with their incandescence. Holding one hand up to shield his eyes, Andrew stood up and waved the pistol, hoping to flush out his hidden adversary.

As his eyes slowly adjusted, he was able to make out two heads in the Shelby Mustang his father had been working on earlier in the day. Andrew stood upright and bolted for the car. He peered inside to see the bloodied figures of his parents in the front seat. His father cradled the missing shotgun. He had been trying to hold it up and keep it pointed at the door, but it kept slipping in his tired hands and hitting the metal frame of the car, each time banging loudly.

The sight made Andrew nauseous, but he controlled himself and opened the driver's door. His father, blood saturating the front of his body, grabbed hold of his son and drew his face down to his split lips.

"No police. Don't call the police..."

Chapter 26

"The police may show up any moment now. Hurry up!" Ziad commanded Bukhari. "You are delaying us."

Ziad's men had unpleasantly surprised Tariq Bukhari in the parking lot of Mayo Clinic. Since then, he had more or less been Ziad's captive, which made him very disagreeable. Bukhari's attitude, in turn, irritated Ziad to no end. Accustomed to being immediately obeyed on the battlefields of Afghanistan, Ziad was close to erupting at what he considered Bukhari's blatant insubordination. Bukhari followed Ziad's finger pointing at a clock hanging prominently on a kitchen wall.

"You have thirty seconds Dr. Bukhari, thirty seconds. One, two…"

The control officer commanded the doctor to shoot the bound and gagged woman straining against her bonds on the tile floor between them. The other two ISI agents looked on with a mixture of annoyance and amusement. They had no idea of what was transpiring between Ziad and Bukhari, but they saw this as a great opportunity to witness bloodshed, seemingly for sport.

Bukhari was having difficulty removing his gaze from the clock on the wall. The clock was shaped like an enormous, flat, black cat. The clock face occupied its belly. With each second, its tail moved in one direction, the tongue moved in the opposite direction, and each eye rolled independently.

"KGB style, Dr. Tariq. Right at the base of the skull."

Ziad had learned enough American slang to deliver the words 'Dr. Tariq' with just the right amount of condescension so the acculturated doctor felt the implied insult.

"Twenty-nine, thirty. Your time's up." Ziad snatched the gun from the doctor. Bukhari watched as his nominal protector placed the cobalt-blue nozzle of his huge, silenced .45-magnum handgun against the nape of the terrified woman's neck. Though Bukhari had no hesitation in killing with a biological weapon, using a gun in such a cold-blooded manner went against his grain. They were opposites, Bukhari realized. Ziad would never use biological weapons but had no qualms about killing with more conventional tools.

Ziad gave his charge an enormous grin. Bukhari knew Ziad would take great pleasure in reporting Bukhari's refusal to follow an order in the field to the top ISI brass.

The recent events were a blur in Bukhari's head. He could almost recall the first hours following the superbug operation with a kind of nostalgia. News of the St Mary's deaths had spread throughout the world. Ghazni had demanded incontrovertible proof of ctb's efficacy. Well, he had received much more proof than he bargained for.

Upon safely reaching Wildwood, Senator Dockhorn's palatial estate, Bukhari had allowed the glow of triumph - well, partial triumph - to wash over him. However, Ziad's recriminations about the deaths in the unit, and the lost vial had vexed the doctor to no end.

"Idiot! You call yourself an agent? You killed people you didn't intend to, lost your weapon, and alerted everyone about ctb. You've even blown our cover with Dockhorn. Is that the work of a good agent? Keep quiet till I tell you otherwise. Understand? Ghazni will deal with you later."

Ziad had told him they would remain in Wildwood until the situation settled down enough for them to leave for Chicago and then Pakistan. However, Bukhari was adamant they should kill Tracy as punishment for stealing the vial. At this point, the vial itself hardly concerned him. If she accidentally punctured it and all of North America perished, so be it. He would hand Ghazni an unexpected gift. All he cared about now was personal revenge, but Ziad was not interested in flying to Utah for that.

Then, quite suddenly, Ziad had changed his mind. After talking to Thor Martin, he came to the conclusion the vial had to be retrieved, whatever the cost.

Exhausted but determined, Ziad and Bukhari, along with Kufa and Iqbal, the two agents who had accosted Bukhari in Mayo Clinic's parking lot, caught a flight to Salt Lake City. After landing, Ziad searched the short-term parking lot for a lock to pick, figuring renting a car would leave a paper trail. He found and appropriated a large van and the quartet burnt the rubber off the wheels to get to Ogden. Ever the cab driver, the ISI control agent easily found the Hopkins family house.

The house had been built in the middle of a five-acre hillside lot. The driveway meandered through several hundred yards of light forest before arriving at the front door. The nearest neighbor's house was well out of sight. Ziad guessed the driveway functioned as the only entrance or exit. He explored the street further. The Hopkins' house had been constructed at the end of a very long cul-de-sac and occupied the space at the very top of the bulb. Ziad discovered a dirt road at the base of the hill at the edge of the property. He decided to park the van there rather than risk being trapped in the driveway, should the police somehow be alerted.

The ISI control agent had gambled Hopkins would rig alarms to cover the front and back approaches to his house but leave the flanks uncovered on the assumption no one would have that much time or energy to devote to assaulting the house.

In light dusk, Ziad led his team to the property immediately adjacent to the Hopkins home. Ziad was pleased by Iqbal and Kufa's composure as they reverted to their *Mujahideen* form. Meanwhile, in harsh whispers, Ziad threatened to shoot Bukhari if he kept making loud noises and banging into trees. The quartet passed Charlotte Kennedy's back yard around 7.30 in the evening.

Scouting around, Ziad discovered a well-worn footpath heading towards the Hopkins' property. Stepping lightly and quickly, he was delighted to discover a gate in the fence between the two lots. Years ago, Charlotte Kennedy had taken it upon herself to grade the path between the houses and install the gate, 'to be a better neighbor.' Bill had immediately installed security equipment covering this approach. After Charlotte's ceaseless, overwrought protestations, Doris convinced Bill to allow her access. With great reluctance, Bill had agreed, in the process leaving a hole in his security system.

Ziad signaled the three men to follow him through the gate as he led them toward the Hopkins household. He wanted to establish who was inside before surprising them. His instructions from Martin had been clear; the Hopkins must not be killed, despite what Bukhari wanted, and the vial must be retrieved. Beyond that, Ziad had a free hand. Martin had suggested they search Ogden first for Tracy and the missing vial before proceeding to Jackson. Almost all flights landed in Salt Lake City anyway, and Ogden would be en route to Jackson. Ziad and Martin had never needed to work together on such a plan before, but Ziad felt no inclination to disobey Martin's instructions.

The ISI control agent had ordered no shots to be fired until he gave a signal. Undetected, the agents reached the pool next to the back patio. They saw someone pacing the living room, silhouette outlined against the window. Bukhari's imagination took wings, and he immediately assumed the silhouette was Tracy's. Standing up, he awkwardly emptied an entire clip of ammunition into the windowpanes.

The silhouette vanished.

"Idiot! Who told you to fire?" Ziad cursed Bukhari.

Now that the element of surprise was completely lost, he waved his men on to a mad rush toward the house. Bukhari fell behind, struggling to reload his weapon. When the men rushed into the living room after shooting down the back door, they came upon a woman vainly attempting to hide in the pantry and a man who was running from the room. Ziad immediately cornered Doris and put his hand across her mouth, while Iqbal and Kufa chased Bill.

Bill had wanted to get to his gun collection. With a gun, he was sure he would be able to not only defend himself and Doris but destroy the attackers. He had lost precious time lying next to the window, making sure the firing had stopped. That had cut down his lead over the intruders, and then Doris' scream arrested his progress even more. He hesitated for a moment, trying to decide whether to go back to her or proceed to the gun closet. That moment was all his pursuers needed.

Iqbal and Kufa caught up with Bill, and Iqbal swung his gun at the ex-navy man. Bill's face erupted in a fountain of blood, and he lost balance. The second blow, this time administered by Kufa, hit him squarely in his solar plexus. Unbalanced, unable to breathe, he fell to the floor. The two men carried the fallen Admiral to the room where Doris was being held. Silently, the couple was made to stand side by side.

"Who are you?" Ziad demanded, wanting to make sure of his prisoners' identity.

"Who are you?" Bill countered.

Kufa slowly walked over to Doris and placed his gun on her temple. With great deliberation, he cocked the trigger.

"Let me ask again, who are you?" Ziad spoke slowly.

Bill decided this was not the time for heroics.

"I'm Bill Hopkins. What do you want?"

Bill could not even begin to guess who these men were, and why they had broken into his house. Ogden was too quiet and sedate for gang violence. Unfortunately, there was always a first time for everything. He hoped they would not become statistics of some senseless and brutal violent crime.

"Where's Tracy?" Ziad came straight to the point.

Tracy? Why are these people interested in Tracy? Why do they think Tracy's in Ogden? Where on the earth is Tracy, anyway?

"I don't know!"

In a mad rage, Bukhari began indiscriminately destroying everything he could get his hands on, smashing chairs, tables, and lamps, strewing the pieces everywhere. He attacked with vigor every knick-knack Doris had collected over the years and destroyed them before her horrified eyes. Within a few minutes, the room began to look as if a tornado had passed through it.

"That's enough!" Ziad restrained his charge. Turning to Bill, he restated his query.

"Where's Tracy?"

"He's telling the truth! We don't know where she is. What do you want from her? What do you want from us?" Doris shouted in anger and desperation Ziad recognized as the truth

"Where do you think she is?" he asked.

"In Rochester, where else?" Doris snapped. This was information these men could easily get, and there was no point raising their ire without reason.

For a moment, Ziad was taken aback. They had searched her apartment earlier, without luck. Could she still be in Rochester, hiding somewhere else? If so, why did she send the package to Jackson?

"Are you sure she isn't in Jackson?"

"Jackson!" Bill and Doris had looked at each other. These men knew a lot about Tracy. How? Why?

"Who are you?" Bill's intelligence-minded brain could not let it pass.

"Never mind who we are. Answer the question."

"She isn't in Jackson," Doris replied with certainty.

"How do you know?" Ziad had persisted.

"Because that's what Rory said." Immediately, Doris wished she had not said that. The demeanor of the four men began to change.

"Who's Rory?" Bukhari barked.

Neither Bill nor Doris replied. Seething with anger, Bukhari got up and hit Bill on the face, drawing blood from his lips.

The doorbell rang.

Everybody stared at the door as if a ghost had just walked in. Ziad looked away from his victims, the gun dangling in his hands. Bukhari jumped at the reverberating sound of the bell and began quietly approaching the door. Kufa and Iqbal loosened their grip on Bill and gaped at Bukhari, wondering what foolish antics he was up to now.

"Bukhari, what are you..." Ziad started but never finished.

Bill neither wondered who was at the door, nor what Bukhari was up to. He saw his chance and made full use of it. His hands partially free, he suddenly raised them and brought them down with ferocity on the noses of Iqbal and Kufa. With a yelp, they let go of him and dropped their weapons. Ziad saw Bill hit his subordinates and was in the process of pointing his gun at the navy man when Bill's shoe caught him under the chin. As Ziad swung his gun up to fire at the navy man, Bill's loafer caught him under the chin. His lower jaw met his upper jaw with a force nature had never intended when it designed the mouth for purposes of mastication. The stocky ex-*Mujahideen* fighter lost his bearings and crashed onto the floor.

Grabbing hold of Doris, Bill ran from the room. As soon as he passed the door, he locked it from the inside. Without pausing for breath, he picked up the streetsweeper from the gun cabinet. Dragging Doris behind him, he quickly made his way to the garage. If necessary, this was where he would make his last stand.

"Damn!" Ziad was furious at this turn of events.

The Hopkins had escaped him and were now hiding in a house he did not know. His days in Afghanistan had taught him an important lesson; he who knew the terrain had the advantage. Clearly, he was at a disadvantage. He had learned something about a Rory in Jackson but could hardly search all of Jackson for this Rory.

The doorbell rang again.

Bukhari opened the door with a jerk, and a woman fell into the house.

It took Ziad and his company little time to learn Charlotte Kennedy's name, where she lived, and what she was doing there at this time of the night. Most importantly, they found out who Rory was and where he could be found. The ISI men went through the house and tore up all the telephone lines, making sure the Hopkins could not call for help. They missed one telephone, in Andrew's room.

The quartet relocated to Kennedy's house. Ziad wondered what to do with her. Martin had forbidden him to kill the Hopkins but had not said anything about anyone else. And Ziad knew he could not let the whining and whimpering woman live because she would call the police as soon as they closed the front door, if not sooner.

While wondering what to do, Ziad began to explore the house. It was much larger than the Hopkins household, and, during his perambulation, he found the door to the garage. Ziad stole inside the garage and encountered one of the most beautiful vehicles he had ever seen. Captivated, he gazed at it for what seemed like an eternity. Finally, with great reluctance, he left the garage. Cars were Ziad's Achilles heel, and Charlotte Kennedy paid the price for it.

Ziad learned from her it was some French thing her late husband had accepted as a payment on a natural gas lease down in Texas. Leaping up, Ziad announced the time had come for them to proceed. While Iqbal and Kufa rummaged through Kennedy's purse for the car keys, he ordered Bukhari to shoot her. After watching Bukhari dawdle, he finally snatched the gun from his hands and put a bullet into the crying woman's head.

Chapter 27

John was afraid the sound of Tracy's crying would bring in the police. Granted, it was highly likely no unit would respond to the call. However, there was always the possibility they would take the call simply because it would be preferable to more urgent calls that required a response.

Almost ten minutes earlier, John had wrestled the telephone receiver out of Tracy's hands. The news of the assault on her parents had been too devastating for her, and David had spent some time trying to comfort her.

After a while, she had regained enough of her composure to tell them about the attack. She could not remember all the details Andrew had struggled to provide, but from what little they had to go on, both David and Al knew the attack had been deliberate. Someone had traveled to the Hopkins home in the hope of finding Tracy there. It was a surprise - a wonderful surprise but a surprise nonetheless - that Bill and Doris were still alive. After Tracy had finished narrating her tale, she became a bit more self-possessed. Her voice had gotten stronger as she confronted the men around her.

"All right, you want to know what Bukhari was making? The truth is, I don't have the faintest clue. I have no information for you."

"Well, we didn't expect you to know off-hand what he was making. We were hoping if we gave you access to what he was working on, knowing his abilities and habits, you would be able to figure it out faster than someone in, say, Los Alamos."

Why Los Alamos? Who's in Los Alamos? What's going on there?

"You'll have to get the other vial first," she told them.

"That's no problem. We know where it is and have access to it."

David's answer surprised Tracy. How could he have known about her package to Jackson?

"You mean, you know about Rory?"

It was David's turn to be surprised.

"Who's Rory?"

"My fiancé in Jackson. The one I sent the other vial to!"

Tracy had no idea her words would have such a profound impact on the three men. The news surprised and terrified them.

"The other vial? We thought Howard had the vial!"

"No, he didn't. I switched vials. Howard had a dummy vial, with saline in it. The real vial, the one containing whatever Bukhari made, is on its way to Jackson. I sent it to my fiancé, Rory!"

"My God, Tracy, does he know what it is? Does he know how to handle it?"

"If I know Rory, he'll have a pretty good idea of how to take care of it."

"What do you mean by that?"

"Oh, never mind. But if you still want the vial, we'd better move fast. Let me call him first."

Tracy had no luck reaching Rory, but without missing a beat, she told the men what her next course of action would be.

"All right, here's the deal. I'll do whatever needs to be done to assess and analyze Bukhari's bug. I'll even help you get the vial back. In return I want something. I want you to find and punish the men who attacked my parents!"

Chapter 28

Tracy's parents were in a tizzy. It was obvious the attack represented a very serious threat to all of them. What Bill did not know was who exactly was behind the attack, and until he found that out, he was loath to approach the local authorities. That was how he operated. He would get all the facts, and then present it as a *fait accompli* to the police.

Doris was furious over the threat to her family and the destruction and loss of so many cherished possessions that had taken her years to collect. She wanted to get even and get even fast.

Andrew was the least hurt of the three, but the most shocked. Kids - even adolescents - assume their parents will always be there. His parents' sudden brush with mortality had shaken him deeply.

The first to formulate a plan of action was Doris. She knew of Andrew's computer hacking, but her maternal feeling had come in the way of better judgment, and she had turned a Nelson's eye on the whole matter. Bill, on the other hand, was so averse to computers he had no inkling of what his son was capable of. Doris decided to keep him in the dark on the matter for the time being. She told her husband she was going downstairs with Andrew to console him, and with Bill's grunting acceptance, dragged the boy to his room.

Once the door was locked, Doris put Andrew on the spot.

"You're pretty good on the Internet, aren't you?"

"What do you mean?"

"You do a lot of hacking, don't you?"

Andrew did not want to lie, but he did not want to admit to the truth either. He kept quiet, wondering if this was his mother's idea of consolation and if this was really the best time for her to give him grief about hacking.

"I want you to do something for me." She told him.

"What do you want me to do, mom?"

"I want you to do some hacking for me!"

"What?" Andrew was beginning to wonder if the events of the evening had unbalanced his mother.

"You heard what I said."

Andrew eyed his mother carefully. Her black eyes were blazing, and her chin stuck out resolutely at an angle that would have made a cubist proud. Her high cheekbones seemed even higher, flushed with anger and determination. Andrew had never seen his mother like this.

"Wha, what do you want me to find out?"

"Let's find out more about Tracy's laboratory. Let's find out more about Howard. Let's find out more about Bukhari!"

Andrew sat down meekly in front of the computer. His mother had given him a tall order, and he was not sure what, if anything, he would find.

The screen came to life, and with it, Andrew became transformed. From an unsure boy who had witnessed a tragic evening, he became an intense artist, his eyes blinking in harmony with the cursor on the screen. Like a master pianist, his fingers glided effortlessly over the keyboard, with results equally profound. Using his UNIX compatible machine, an Apple Performa, he accessed the main computer at the University of Minnesota in Minneapolis, and using it to hide his tracks, he accessed the database of Mayo Clinic.

"What are you doing?" his mother queried.

"Let's go to accounts." Andrew ignored the interruption. His experience had taught him of all the branches in a company, often the easiest to break into was the accounting department, the branch most businesses tried, ironically, the hardest to protect. However, since so many people within the organization needed access to it, accounting was rarely secure.

Accounts it was. All the monetary transactions of Mayo were at his fingertips, and millions of entries swam across the screen.

"Try research," Doris suggested.

That narrowed it down a bit. To a few thousand.

Andrew started scrolling through the names, looking for the head of Tracy's laboratory, Dr. Dan Howard.

"Where's he hiding... where's he hiding... there he is!" He shouted triumphantly.

Dan Howard, Ph.D. Andrew clicked on the name.

"Grants: ten million dollars," they read in unison.

"That's a lot." Doris gasped as she realized the enormity of the sum.

The screen continued to spill its secrets.

"Duration: five years."

"Amount spent: three and a half million."

"What now?" Andrew wondered out aloud.

"Um, where did the money come from?"

Andrew's hands flew over the keyboard again.

"Routed through The Union Bank of Switzerland."

"Why on the earth is he getting money from Switzerland? He should be getting money from the National Institutes of Health." Doris was stupefied.

"Let's see whom the account belongs to."

The screen had the answer.

Abid Sahabuddin.

Andrew delved deeper. The money had been transferred to the United Bank of Switzerland from BCCI, the Bank of Credit and Commerce, International, Karachi, Pakistan.

BCCI got Andrew's attention.

"Isn't that the Pakistani bank that went under? It was also called the Bank of Crooks and Criminals, International!"

Pakistan got Doris' attention.

"That's where Bukhari is from!"

Andrew logged off and an alternate screensaver came on, showing America's National Parks in all their beauty.

Mother and son sat for a while, wondering what to do with all this incredible information. Finally, Doris broke the silence.

"Let's go talk to your father. He may have an idea of who this Sahabuddin is!"

Chapter 29

Ziad recited Sahabuddin's name like a mantra to keep himself in check. He was terribly frustrated and was having a hard time containing his warrior instincts in the small town of Potatoflower, Idaho, off US 89 between Ogden and Jackson.

The stolen car that had so enchanted and captivated him had become his ruin. Unlike anyone else in Ogden, and probably Utah, Charlotte Kennedy drove a constitutionally temperamental Citroen; a model no longer made. Like its owner, the needle-nosed car was difficult to maintain under even the least challenging circumstances.

However, it was a classic, and Ziad had fallen in love with it on first sight. The four ISI agents could not believe its smooth ride as Ziad had slowly, carefully driven the Citroen out of the slain woman's garage. None of them had ever ridden in such conspicuous comfort.

"What a ride, what a ride. What a fantastic car!" Ziad even smiled at Bukhari. Miles passed by pleasantly for the four men, their mission almost forgotten, as if they were off to see Yellowstone National Park.

Their collective love affair with the Citroen lasted almost two hours, until about midway through Idaho. Had Mr. Kennedy been alive, he would have remonstrated his wife for spending too much time pestering the neighbors and too little time looking after the car. On its last mechanical legs, the car carrying the four agents limped to the only open service station on the highway at 1:00 am.

"What on the earth happened to it? Stay inside, I'll check the motor." Ziad instructed the others. It was no use. The motor looked more foreign than the language in which the instructions were written, and he was at a complete loss.

"What now?"

"Let's ask the station manager if he can fix it."

Approaching the manager with their request, he shook his head, "Sorry, but it's against regulations for me to leave the station, and it's also against regulations for me to work on cars."

"We're visiting scientists on our way to a conference at the University of Wyoming in Cheyenne. We need to be there for our session in a few hours. Can't you please help us?" Bukhari pleaded.

"Sorry, but I can't. You'll have to wait for the mechanic." The station manager apologized.

Ziad knew the man was telling the truth. Nonetheless, his instincts were to pull out his gun and shoot everyone and everything that stood between him and the vial. With great difficulty, he controlled himself. He recited the name of his commander the way a priest recites holy verses. Remember the mission, he reminded himself. Nothing must impair the success of the mission. If he shot someone or stole a car, he was sure he would never make it to Jackson without an army of state troopers buzzing around him like a swarm of angry bees. With everything else going on, that was the last thing he needed.

They needed to sleep, anyway. Rory would have to wait. Tomorrow would be another day.

Chapter 30

Day did not come soon enough for the Hopkins household. The night before, Bill had recognized the name Sahabuddin, and what he was up against. Andrew observed some kind of inner fire had come to possess his father, the likes of which he had never seen before. Bill Hopkins was as full of energy as if he was in the jungles of South East Asia again. It took all of Doris' persuasive abilities to keep him in the house through the night. She was not sure what he would do, but it was bound to be dramatic. In all the hubbub, Andrew was relieved no mention was made of his hacking habits, though he was sure it would come to haunt him later.

As if the excitement in the house was not enough, a visitor had shown up at their door early Tuesday morning. Andrew had never heard of this person before, who went by only one name, David. The one good thing to emerge from David's visit was knowledge of Tracy's whereabouts.

"Don't worry about Tracy. She's okay. Very tired, somewhat angry and confused. She has a cold she's fighting. But other than that, she's fine."

"Doesn't sound as if she's okay. At least she should have come home for a while. I should've spoken to her before she took off again." Doris retorted.

Apparently, they had all flown in from D.C. on a redeye, reaching Utah early in the morning.

"Where's she anyway?" Andrew burst in.

"Well, she's gone with a couple of my colleagues to Jackson to retrieve something."

"What thing? What was she doing in DC, why was she with you?" There were too many mysteries here for Andrew to let slip by.

"Pull up a chair. Get ready for a rather long story." After clearing his throat, shifting uncomfortably in the chair, and humming and hawing, David finally told them the events of the past 36 hours.

Afterwards, Doris set about trying to restore some order to the house - it was her way of releasing stress. At least she knew where her daughter was, and with whom. What Tracy was trying to do still concerned her. Doris wondered where last night's attackers were. For that matter, she wondered where her neighbor was. Charlotte Kennedy had not poked her head in all morning, which was very uncharacteristic of her. Well, she said to herself, maybe Bill's insults had finally taken their toll. She would make it a point to go over and see her later in the day.

Although he regretted intruding on the Hopkins household, David felt elated to be back in Bill's good graces. It had taken the two men a good half-hour to make peace. Finally, after much venting, Bill forgave David for not supporting him on Beirut; and David forgave Bill for not forgiving him for almost twenty years.

With not much to do but wait for Tracy and her companions to return, they sat around the kitchen table, nursing cups of coffee.

As he heard the story, questions began to form in Andrew's mind faster than he could come up with answers. It just did not make sense. Who was fighting whom? And for what?

Emboldened by his curiosity, he posed a question to the two men seated across from him. "Dad, David - why are you doing this? Who are you fighting?"

David shot a look at Bill, wondering if he was going to answer. With a nod of his head a quirk of his eyebrows, Bill shifted the responsibility back to him. David sat there, slowly twirling his coffee, as though hauling up the perfect answer from an invisible magic well within the coffee cup. Finally, the twiddling stopped.

"What we're doing may appear surreptitious and sneaky, Andrew, but sometimes, to uphold the law, you have to break the law."

Bill erupted into a long stream of obscenity-laced laughter. Doris came out from the kitchen to see what had caused her husband to act in such a fashion.

"Nam's long over, old boy," he was saying.

Doris quickly leaned over the table to refill their coffee. She recognized the pitch and tone of her husband's voice from the last time he had conversed with David, just hours before tendering the resignation of his naval commission. She gave him a look that said, 'not here, not now.' Bill caught himself and quieted down. Andrew saw the exchange and smiled to himself. It amused him his mother's look could do what the US navy and various other government agencies could not.

David resumed. "This game, like the one before it, is about world domination. About cultural domination, masquerading as religious domination. About blocs of humanity far larger than any one nation. We're about to enter a new phase of wars, this time over religion. Communism is dead, long live religious fundamentalism!"

Andrew leaned in to hear David's words more closely.

"Simply put, Andrew, the West, and the nations of Europe, especially

Western Europe, have dominated the world for the past five centuries. This domination has been possible because of the great technological and scientific superiority the West has enjoyed. With the diffusion of Western science and technology around the globe, other nations, other cultures, believe it is time for a change, where they are in charge and people of European origin follow. The West has served its purpose; its tools and knowledge have been distributed. Now it's time for us to relinquish the world's center stage and go away."

"And how do these other countries hope to convince the West to relinquish the trappings of power and prestige?"

"In most of the world, organized religion provides the means of achieving their goal. Whatever religion it may be, it's the easiest way of rallying people, of mobilizing them."

"Religion, the opiate of the masses!" Andrew had heard the famous quotation from Karl Marx.

"What you say is slightly simplistic since religions cross the North-South divide. Christianity, for example, is prevalent in European as well as African countries, rich as well as poor countries." Bill countered.

"Of the world's major religions, Christianity is the only one that spans the North-South divide. The remaining don't, and they resent the domination of Christianity. Since Christianity is dominated and controlled by the West, they, by extension, have another reason to hate the West."

"Well, I don't know about that, Dave," Bill interjected. "You can't categorize all religions as the same. I don't see any Buddhists running around, trying to overthrow Christianity and rule the world."

"That's true, I guess," David conceded. "My point, however, remains valid when you consider the religions that are based on aggressive conversions. That means Christianity and Islam, religions that emphasize conversions as a way of propagation. In short, it's 'believe in our way or else you'll go to hell.' It's the proselytizing that makes all the difference."

"Why the emphasis on proselytizing?" Andrew found that rather silly. Why care so much about conversion?

"Proselytizing sets up opposite camps, because it emphasizes converting others to one's point of view. We don't like it when someone tells us we'll go to hell if we don't convert, and the same applies to other religions. It becomes 'our way' versus 'their way', and when both sides claim sole proprietorship to the path to God, the opposing camps end up going to war."

"Since you point to Christianity and Islam, what's the difference between us and Muslims?" Andrew was beginning to regret having slept through his comparative religion classes.

"Muslims are derived from the same tree as Jews and Christians. They accept the Old Testament, just like Christians and Jews. The difference lies in the acceptance of messiahs. Christians accept Jesus as the Messiah and Son of God. Jews don't accept Jesus as The Messiah, but as a prophet in a long line of prophets. Muslims, similarly, don't believe he was the Son of God, but just another prophet. They believe Christians deviated from the word of God, and Mohammed was then given the task of saving humankind. He was the last and greatest prophet, and his word supersedes all. Thus, in their view, the Koran is more sacred than the Bible. So you see, it is a contest between prophets, not between Gods."

Bill saw where David was going.

"Since prophets, like all religious and mythological figures, are by-products of their culture, a religion propounded by a prophet is based on his cultural heritage. Is that what you mean?"

"Exactly! In effect, the difference between Christianity and Islam is not about God, but about prophets, and their respective cultures. That's why this is a cultural war, masquerading as a religious war."

Andrew looked around him as his father and David got increasingly immersed in theological discussions. His mind started to drift, just as it had during religion classes. His roving gaze rested on the clock on the mantelpiece for a brief moment and then moved on.

It was only 8:30 in the morning.

Chapter 31

Potatoflower's only mechanic arrived at 8:30 am. He glanced at the Citroen quickly and perfunctorily.

"Well, well, I've never seen one of these before. I've no idea what to do with it. You'd best take it to some other station." To Ziad's angst, the mechanic displayed as much enthusiasm about the car as a dental hygienist would have in performing a rectal exam.

"Maybe you could try." Ziad forced out through gritted teeth as he pulled a wad of bills from his pocket. The bills seem to provide the mechanic with enough enthusiasm to saunter over to the car.

Taking a walk to control his temper, Ziad began to scout out the town's terrain. What he discovered did not suit him at all. US 89 was the only identifiable road leading either into or out of town. The town boasted a booming population of almost two thousand, and it appeared every one of them was up and circulating between the diner next to the service station and the local supermarket across the street. Ziad contemplated stealing a car but realized he would not be able to drive twenty meters before all two thousand citizens, a significant number of them dressed in hunter orange and heavily armed, gave chase. The wily ISI control agent had enough cash to buy each agent a used car from the lot next to the supermarket. However, the used car dealership was closed and, if the sign on the door was to be believed, would remain closed till the owner returned from a fishing trip.

Ziad resigned himself to the fact the only course of action left open to him was to wait. As he returned to the service station, he was greeted by the sight of the mechanic holding an infuriated Bukhari at bay with a lit acetylene torch. Bukhari had gotten himself trapped in a corner of the service station, out of reach of any object to use as a weapon. The other two agents were roaring with laughter at their compatriot's self-inflicted plight. The mechanic had expected the other two to rush him from behind, but after detecting they had no intention of getting involved, he devoted more energy to taunting his entrapped victim.

Ziad approached Potatoflower's mechanic.

"Is there a problem?"

"Yea, this jerk here keeps insulting my skills as a mechanic. I done told you I don't know anything about this car, but I'm doin' the best I can.

I don't need this jerk makin' comments.

"Don't worry about him, he's an idiot. Ignore him and keep working on the car," stuffing a week's pay into the man's palm. As though he had been on the take for his entire life, the mechanic shut off his torch and pocketed the cash. The wad of hundred-dollar bills made him a convert with a speed that would have made Jimmy Swaggert envious.

"Well, here's the problem. See the water pump? It's got a huge hole in it. That's making the engine overheat." The mechanic pointed.

"Can you fix it?"

"No, the hole is too big. You need a new pump."

"So do that."

"Can't. We don't have any pumps that'll fit this car. Ford, yes. Chrysler, yes. Chevy, you bet. Citroen, no." The mechanic wryly noted.

"Can you order one?" Ziad continued to explore all options.

"We can order one from Salt Lake. Will need to have it sent by special courier. You'd have a new pump in a few hours. It'll cost you quite a bit, though."

"Don't worry about the expense. Just order it and get it in fast.".

The ensuing six-hour wait was interminable. Ziad thought it best they park themselves at Magenta's, the town's only non-chain diner, and wait for the hours to pass. The diner and its considerable charms could entertain them for only two hours. Bukhari's whining about the vial and Tracy's treachery tempted the senior ISI agent to shoot the doctor right then and there.

After leaving the diner, the quartet invested half an hour in circumnavigating the town, finally returning to the service station where they had started.

"Why don't you try the video arcade? It just opened up, a couple of blocks behind the station." The mechanic suggested, eyeing the wad of money in Ziad's pocket. He was hoping for a good tip.

He had reckoned in country blocks, not city blocks. The four agents walked almost three miles to a small arcade, packed with the county's collection of truants and young delinquents.

By the time they returned to the service station, around 1:00 pm, the mechanic had just started installing the new water pump. The four men collapsed into four small hard, interconnected plastic chairs lined up against the glass paneling of the wall opposite the station's cash register. A steady parade of local customers passed by and stepped on each agent's toes en route to the station's soda machine.

The most battle-hardened of the three ex-*Mujahideen*, Ziad recovered his strength first. He noticed the time as he raised himself to stretch. 1:30 pm. Ziad calculated he and his party had approximately four hours to find Rory before dark. The senior agent stepped outside the service station's small office to smoke a cigarette. As he struck his match against a rain gutter, something caught Ziad's eye.

Maintaining his nonchalant stance, he used his peripheral vision to concentrate and soon recognized something. Rather, someone. Allowing the smoke to obscure his face, Ziad peered hard at the two gas pump islands. A man was topping off the tank of his car at the self-service pump.

Ziad looked more closely and saw Al had not changed at all. He had not put on any weight or lost much hair since the last time they had met.

Ziad quickly slipped the safety catch off his pistol.

He knew if Al walked into the office to pay for his gas, the agency man would recognize the three ISI men. He would certainly raise an alarm of some kind, and even if Ziad's party could somehow shoot its way out of Potatoflower, they would not get too far.

The senior ISI agent resolved to meet his end fearlessly, like a true warrior. As he looked around the mountains and expansive blue horizon, he rationalized there were worse places for a man to die. However, death once again ignored him.

An attendant met Al halfway between the pump island and the office. Ziad watched as the CIA agent withdrew a money clip, peeled off a few bills and handed it over. Al looked carefully around him before opening the door and sliding in.

Ziad counted two other heads in the low-slung Lincoln Continental as it slowly came to life and pulled out onto the highway. With utmost calm, Ziad strolled over to the mechanic and inquired of the legs and torso sticking out from under the car how much longer the repairs would take.

"An hour," replied the half-hidden local.

"Make it fifteen minutes and you'll get another," the wily Ziad proposed as he dropped two weeks' pay on the mechanic's exposed chest. Summoning superhuman speed and professional knowledge of which he had been previously unaware, the mechanic installed the new water pump in ten minutes. With the car running better than it had in years, the foursome said goodbye to the lively and cosmopolitan Potatoflower.

Ziad noticed Al's car had accelerated rather slowly out of the service station, white smoke billowing out of the exhaust pipe. The engine was obviously not in the best state of repair. Ziad realized it would be better to catch up with the CIA-mobile slowly, guessing Al and his passengers could only be heading for Jackson as well. On the highway, Ziad toyed with the idea of allowing Al to lead him wherever it was they had to go. Tossing out the idea, he resolved that the occupants of the Lincoln would not reach Jackson alive.

Al and his companions were unaware plans were being made for their funeral. Tracy was lost in her thoughts of Rory. It had been almost five months since they last met, and she looked forward to seeing him again, although the circumstances could have been better. She tried to suppress a smile as she remembered the first time they had met. It had been at a fraternity party, where more alcohol was served than was legally permitted in the State of Utah. Students of all sizes were being dumped into a swimming pool, and the last dry person left standing would be the winner of a very large keg of beer.

Tracy had arrived a bit late, only to find herself the only woman high and dry. One of two contenders for the prize picked her up and ran to throw her into the pool. Tracy shrieked as she felt the sinewy muscles swiveling under her dress and looked directly into the eyes of her cave-man. Something about Tracy's gaze re-ignited the process of evolution that nature had taken centuries to perfect, and the cave dweller became a civilized human. He put her down gently, smiled, introduced himself as Rory, and asked her out. That had been almost six years ago.

She yearned to see her ex cave-man and lean into his strong physical frame. She also desperately needed his abiding political level-headedness, which was not based on apathy or ignorance, but on knowledge and logic.

John, too, was lost in his own world. Mile after mile, as was his habit, he attempted to articulate his impressions of the beauty through which the Lincoln passed. Al used to his colleague's poetic attempts ignored him. Tracy, reluctantly tearing her mind away from Rory, tried to follow along from the backseat and offered encouragement.

"You cannot help but notice the majesty and beauty of Mother Nature. For fleeting moments, our self-importance is dwarfed by the imposing mountains. Firs and pines dot the landscape and mountain streams gush in their youth. Small wooden bridges cover bubbling streams and beg visitors to stand and stare."

John swept his gaze from Al in the driver's seat to Tracy in the back. "Well?"

Al remained stone silent.

"I liked it better when you said, 'burbling streams' instead of 'bubbling.' More onomatopoeic that way," offered Tracy, exhibiting her erudition as well.

John began to consider her editorial comment.

In the rearview mirror, Al caught sight of something very peculiar. It was a car, painted an unmistakable metallic lime green. Almost needle-nosed, it was moving infinitesimally closer across the tinted glass of the Lincoln's mounted reflector. It had been bearing down hard and then had suddenly slowed down, as though it recognized the Lincoln. For the next few miles, dozens of cars had closed the gap between the Lincoln and its escort and passed them both. Al recognized a professional was tailing them.

He speeded up, and so did the following car. Al slowed, and so did the needle-nosed car.

John and Tracy saw something was amiss.

"What's wrong?" John was sure it was not just high-altitude sickness that was making his colleague drive in such an erratic fashion.

"We've got a tail."

The hunter and its quarry crossed the state line into Wyoming.

"A Citroen, no less. Well, a lime-green Citroen doth not a successful tail make. Show 'em, Al." John suggested.

"In a minute, John. Who would be tailing us in a such a car?" Al tried to guess who would follow them in something as exotic and anachronistic as a Citroen.

"Maybe someone who's seen far too many Austin Powers films." Tracy turned to look at the car behind them at a stretch of straight road. She could see the driver in the Citroen as clearly as he could now see her. She screamed.

Conditioned by years of training, Al resisted his urge to pull the Lincoln off the road. Distracted from his aesthetic frame of mind, John disconnected his seat belt and un-holstered his pistol. Al placed a free hand to steady John and keep him in the front seat.

"Tracy, what's wrong?" John asked as he began to move to the back seat.

Through quick breaths of panic, Tracy struggled to explain.

"It, its Mrs. Kennedy's car! But she isn't driving it!"

"Who's Mrs. Kennedy?"

"Our neighbor in Ogden!"

"You sure it's her car?"

"Yes, look at the license plate. It's her vanity license plate!" she replied.

Al quickly flicked his eyes to the rearview mirror. The Citroen had begun accelerating and was bearing down on them again. Its front license plate read like a movie marquee: 'CHOCL8'.

Al trusted the Lincoln's V-8 engine to lift them away from any immediate contact, giving him and John time to prepare themselves for action. John had already removed the police shotgun from its rack and yelled at Tracy to get down on the backseat's floor.

Al pressed his foot down on the accelerator. The engine coughed.

Al began pumping the gas. The engine coughed.

John was halfway between the front and back seats.

The Citroen flared out into the oncoming traffic lane. Al saw guns protruding from its windows.

"Watch out!" he shouted.

Ziad had concluded the Citroen could never knock the huge Lincoln Continental off the road. The best he could hope for would be to pass it and let Kufa and Iqbal open fire. Noticing the Lincoln billowing white smoke, he surmised it was because Al was trying to accelerate. As he sped, he ordered the others to stay down and not to fire until he gave the word. As the Lincoln coughed and failed to speed up for the second time, he gave the signal.

From the side windows, the I.S.I agents pumped the Lincoln Continental with solid bursts of fully automatic weapon fire. Ziad kept the Citroen steady, giving the shooters an excellent firing platform.

John had fired at the back window, blasting it to pieces. He even managed to get a shot out of it, but it hit the back of the Citroen as it was speeding up. He turned around desperately to fire at the car that was now dead even with them. John saw the hateful looks on the faces of two men as they hung out of windows, holding their automatic weapons. The looks changed to excited anticipation like hyenas licking their lips before killing a wounded antelope in the Serengeti. Then John saw the guns blaze and heard them strike the Lincoln.

The senior ISI agent heard the satisfying sound of screeching tires. He swung back into his lane, in front of the Lincoln, and looked in the rearview mirror. He saw the big car lose its bearing, swinging from side to side. Then, in slow motion, it careened off the edge of the mountain road into the deep chasm below.

Chapter 32

Rory gazed up at the steep mountain walls that formed the chasm. His body ached from the rigors of the day. He lifted the rubber paddle from the icy waters of the Snake River, swollen from the snows of the Grand Tetons that had been melting over the past few weeks. Laying the paddle down on the gunwale, he enjoyed the smooth drift of his raft towards the landing spot on the shore. In the dusk's fading light, he fingered his large hemp medicine bag and thanked the nameless god or goddess of the river for giving him a successful journey.

He had started later than usual and had navigated all the runs of the river. He had seen lonesome eagles soar, nervous deer skittish at being spotted, and bears rummaging for food. He had seen remnants of winter avalanches, with hillsides stripped of trees, except for a few scarce survivors clinging to the steep incline, their roots meeting the sky. The river ran briskly, and he anticipated a good season. A full river that did not overflow its banks promised a healthy tourist crowd.

However, the wondrous panorama failed to comfort him. He was worried about Tracy. He had been disturbed when he had received the package with its terse instructions. He had tried to call her, with no luck. He knew he should worry when Bill called him, looking for his daughter.

Only something of Himalayan proportion would make the old geezer call me!

Rory had been looking forward to Tracy's return to Utah. For the first time in four years would they be living in the same time zone, in the same state. They would be able to see each other in intervals not dictated by the considerations of long-distance travel and school holidays.

The raft reached its bank at the unloading zone. Rory hopped out, pulling a towrope over his shoulder to beach the craft for the night. The thought of Tracy consumed him. He scarcely felt the chill attacking his wet legs as he emerged from the water.

A sudden sound brought him out of his reverie. Rory tried but was unable to identify its character or its source. Water began splashing around him. Innocently, he wondered if somebody was playing a prank on him by throwing pebbles into the water from the shoreline.

These pebbles, however, made a rather dull, thudding noise.

Gunfire!

The kind Rory heard the solitary time Bill had taken him to the firing range in one of the military man's attempts to frighten the gun-hater away. Rory threw himself into the shallow water. Miraculously, none of the bullets that were angrily slapping into the water hit him. Though his body touched the beach's sand, he dog-paddled backwards, keeping low in the water.

Who's trying to waste me?

A different gun sounded. Lower. Deeper, like a cannon. Rory tried to remain unobtrusive behind the paddle of the raft.

A firefight had erupted between the shoreline and the beach.

"Rory! Rory!"

Rory peered over the edge of the paddle. For a moment his brain refused to believe what his eyes were telling him.

Tracy? Tracy!

Finally, his brain caught up. He leaped from behind the raft.

"Get down," he screamed, tackling Tracy in the Snake River's shallows and pulling her behind the raft. The guns began to explode again. The deep-sounding gun went off repeatedly, silencing the automatic weapons with its loud, interdictory fire.

During a brief lull in the gun battle, Rory decided they would be better off fleeing the firefight unfolding before them. Holding his fiancé behind his back, Rory slowly pushed the raft back into the current. He flipped Tracy over the gunwale, launching himself after her with one move.

It was better, he thought, to chance the river than to risk being cut down by the battle on the beach. Lying on top of Tracy, Rory attempted to guide the raft into the Snake River's powerful current. The raft hesitated, seeming to prefer the safety of the shores than the risks of the river.

The heavier weapon fell silent.

Two figures leap-frogged from their safe positions in the tree line and headed down to the beach. One figure took up a position behind a small dock, vigilantly scanning the tree-line. With a whistle, the sentinel summoned the other figure to approach, who in turn signaled a third. The third person hobbled, struggling with a bound figure. Crouching low, the second figure returned to relieve the third. The bound prisoner found himself by the river's edge.

"You'll be our guide," Bukhari stated imperiously to the terrified, shivering prisoner, Billy Hayes.

Billy Hayes and Rory had a lot in common. A few years older than Rory, Billy had helped train Rory to respect and master the wild river. In appreciation, Rory had always steered his excess business towards his friend. Every Tuesday evening, during the spring and summer, Billy and Rory made time to paint the town of Jackson red, like sailors who had just returned from a long cruise.

Billy had shown up at Rory's office a few hours early, hoping Rory was available.

"Hi, Daisy, Rory in?" He asked as he pushed the door open.

"No, he's still scouting the river. He said he wanted to scout the river further upstream, above your usual embarcadero. He might be late. I'm heading out soon, but you're welcome to stay here and wait for him." The secretary left him the keys after she left. Billy did not mind waiting. Rory's office subscribed to all the fun gossipy and sports magazines to which his pecuniary conservative office manager refused to subscribe.

At first, Billy did not think twice about the four men who showed up at the office looking for Rory. Some early tourists, he thought. Two of the four men before him wore city clothes and city shoes. The other two wore a kind of dress he had never seen before. None of them looked ready for a day out on the rapids.

"Where's Rory? We must see Rory." One of them, the slim, excitable man dressed in Western clothes kept insisting.

"He's not in right now. He'll be back very late today, so you can leave a message with me."

The four men spoke amongst themselves in a language Billy failed to recognize. Three of them left. One of them, sporting a large mustache that he twirled, sat silently across from him in the office's small outer room. Billy pegged him as the kind of person who, even if he knew everything going to happen for the next hundred years, would not disclose a thing, but sit there, twirling his mustache.

Billy knew he was in trouble when the three men came back carrying guns. Not believing in arguing with guns, the rafter got up slowly, holding his hands up, his face in utter confusion.

>>A hold-up? In modern-day Jackson?

Without any explanation, the man who looked like a tree stump with a mustache bound Billy's hands behind his back.

"Where's Rory?" The mustache twirler asked.

"He's rafting in the river."

"Take us to him." It was a command Billy felt would be unwise to discuss or disobey. He was sure they would have no compunctions about shooting him then and there if he refused. They drove in silence to the unloading zone by the river, a few miles from Jackson.

Ziad had decided they did not have the time to wait for Rory. They would go to him instead. He had parked his car and was on his way to the riverbank with his comrades when the shooting began. Ziad had no idea who was shooting at them, or why. All he knew was the raft with Rory on it was on the banks of the river, and he could not get to it.

A figure cut loose from the trees and hurtled down to the raft.

"That's Tracy!" Bukhari shouted. Immediately, he began to fire at the raft, but his shots were wild, and Tracy was able to get into the raft without any injuries. With a roar, Bukhari took off after her.

Tracy turned and looked at Rory. Her eyes were wide, her lips trembling.

"That's him! That's Bukhari!" She cried out.

With Tracy's package and brief note still fresh in his mind, Rory realized Bukhari's presence here could mean only one thing. Trouble! Now the strangers were running towards the raft. That could also mean only one thing. Trouble!

About thirty feet separated the two groups and Kufa and Iqbal, now in the lead and were reducing the distance at a fast pace. Bukhari and Ziad brought up the rear, dragging Billy.

Rory was galvanized into action. Using all his strength, he pushed the raft into the river.

Twenty feet separated the two groups.

The raft continued to inch backwards.

Kufa, running faster than Iqbal, was now only ten feet away.

The raft stopped.

Kufa was in the river, wading towards the raft.

The raft changed direction and started inching forwards, as the river's current started to catch hold.

Kufa saw the raft was moving away from him. He was only three feet away. If he waited any longer, he would miss it. He gambled. Planting both feet on the riverbed, he sprang towards the raft with all his might.

Frozen with horror, Tracy had been watching Kufa approach the raft. She saw him leap, hands outstretched, and grab the side of the raft. She saw him pull himself up with his right hand and place his left hand inside the craft. The sight of his hand in the raft broke Tracy's paralysis. She picked up a paddle lying on the floor and swung at Kufa with all the force she could muster. But Kufa saw the blow coming. Just before it struck his head, he let his right hand off the raft and ducked, while holding on with his left hand. The blow bounced harmlessly off the side of the raft. Seeing an opportunity, he quickly grabbed the paddle with his right hand and jerked it, yanking Tracy's arms in the process.

Unprepared, Tracy completely lost her balance. She fell into the center of the raft, leaving it wide open for Kufa to board. With a sick feeling in the pit of his stomach, Rory watched Tracy's vain attempt at stopping Kufa, and the ease with which Kufa thwarted her. Though he was focused on guiding the raft, he knew he had to do something, and do it quick.

Just as Kufa was starting to hoist himself into the raft, Rory saw a particularly vicious eddy and guided the raft into it. It was a large, swirling pool of water, hungry for sacrificial victims. With huge gulps, it attempted to swallow the raft and its passengers. It sucked with all its might, and the raft quivered and shivered, trying desperately to stay afloat. The power of the river was pitted against the buoyancy of the raft. The battle raged for a few tense seconds that seemed to stretch into eternity.

Rory and Tracy, familiar with the basics of rafting, hugged the floor, while Kufa, less informed, tried to get up. Unable to maintain his balance in the wild raft, he stumbled backwards, flipped over the side, and fell into the river. The hungry river accepted him as a sacrifice, and let the raft go. Kufa was sucked into the maelstrom. Water poured into his eyes, nose, and lungs. Gasping, coughing, choking, he fought the omnipresent water as he went down. He was still struggling when his head struck the jagged rocks at the bottom of the riverbed. The force of the impact split his skull open. Blood poured out, mixing with the turbulent, muddy water. Only then did the river relent, releasing the mutilated body.

It floated, lifeless, for all to see.

Ziad, Bukhari, and Iqbal had watched the scene from the dock. They watched Kufa die. They saw Tracy and Rory escaping down the river, and they did not like what they saw.

Motioning Bukhari, Ziad dragged Billy to a raft anchored on the shore.

The pursuit began anew.

Chapter 33

Al gave pursuit in the car. The events of the afternoon were already a distant memory.

The battered Lincoln had flown off the road into the ravine below. It flipped and tumbled as it went careening slowly over the edge of the road. The car eventually came to a halt by landing on the branches of a tree just a few feet from the edge of the road. The tree gave the bent and disfigured car refuge, nestling it in its mighty branches. There it lay like a hunted animal, gasping its last breath.

John, without the restraints of his seat belt, was less lucky. He lost his moorings and went flying out of the car as the passenger-side door opened, his scream echoing in the ravines. He missed the tree and hit the rocks at the bottom of the ravine with all the force gravity could muster, breaking many bones in his body.

Al, still behind the wheels, assessed the situation very quickly. It was only a matter of time before the fortitude of the tree gave way, and the car would crash down the ravine. Carefully, trying not to upset the delicate balance between car and tree, he opened his door.

"C'mon Tracy, slow and easy." Coaxing Tracy out with him, he exited, helping Tracy climb carefully down the branches till they reached the ground. Then, to Tracy's shock and consternation, he went back to retrieve a large case.

He had then hailed and commandeered a Buick, using the gun from his large case and his badge. National security, to Tracy's sardonic amusement, was once again the operative word. The Buick had taken little time to reach the unloading zone. Unlike the ISI men, Tracy knew exactly where to find Rory and they got to him just in time. While Al gave cover, Tracy had joined Rory to warn him and to help him escape.

Much to Al's chagrin, he saw the ISI men slip away while he was reloading his gun. Without a good vantage point from which to shoot, he decided to give chase in the car. As he swung out onto the road, he realized he had overlooked a small but important problem. He would be driving on the right side of the road, hugging the mountain wall, leaving him without a view of the canyon or the river. The oncoming traffic had the best view but driving on it would be suicidal.

Al was desperate enough to choose a dangerous solution. He decided to drive on the left-hand curb of the road, in between the protective railing and the oncoming traffic. The curb was narrow and graveled, and it did not make for the best driving conditions. Despite the railing, the slightest miscalculation on his part would send the car into the Snake River. A slight oversight on the part of oncoming traffic would lead to a fatal crash.

The canyon was steep, with jagged rocks dotting the slopes. The wind howled at him, and cars coming from the opposite direction swerved and honked at him, reminding him of his folly. Al knew of his folly quite well. The advantage, though, was he could travel faster than the rafts on the river, and he hoped to be able to overtake them.

Ziad's raft was making rapid progress, and he was ecstatic. He kept a close eye on Billy, while Bukhari and Iqbal paddled furiously. Since they had manpower advantage over Tracy, who was paddling alone, they were catching up quickly.

Rory had been aware for a while the situation was grim. He was trying his best to use the river's speed to his advantage. Uncontrolled speed at this point was particularly tricky since the river had become very treacherous. Grade-four rapids were common, and some grade-five rapids were appearing. As the decline of the river became steeper, the river ran faster - much faster. Rockslides had created shallow streams, with small dams and islands. The chances of running aground, or of shredding the bottom of the craft, were dangerously high. He was well aware if either of those happened, he was sunk. He had negotiated this stretch only once before for the thrill of it and had vowed not to return in a hurry.

Rory was now in a hurry.

He heard shouting in the rear. Turning around, he saw the other raft. It looked like a Viking ship on a quest of conquest and it was catching up fast.

"They're gaining! Paddle faster!" He begged Tracy.

Tracy was near total exhaustion. She was not used to this much exertion, and, on top of it, her illness had left her weak. While her shortness of breath and cough had improved a bit, the weakness remained. Desperation, the mother of innovation, made her consider other options. She looked around to see if there was anything she could do to help Rory, besides paddling till she dropped dead. There were paddles, jackets, and buckets in the raft, but nothing worthy of a weapon. Then she remembered.

"Rory!" she shouted, "don't you keep a fishing line in here?"

Rory was nonplused. This was hardly the time or place to think about fishing.

"Why?" he queried.

"I don't have the time to explain! Just tell me where it is."

"It's in the box back here."

She crawled toward him on her hands and knees. The pitching and rolling of the craft made progress very difficult. Waves of water inundated her, throwing her off balance, but with extraordinary effort and resolve, she managed to reach the box between his feet. Tracy struggled to pry it open, but the lock had partly rusted. She picked up a paddle and hammered at the box until it finally opened.

The raft behind them was getting closer and Tracy could see Bukhari's teeth as he smiled broadly in anticipation. With renewed energy, she dug into the box and pulled out the fishing tackle. Making sure the point was sharp, and the attached line long, she tossed the hook into the river. Tracy had picked out a boulder jutting out of the river as a landmark, and when the raft following them reached that point, she planned to yank on the line. She hoped the hook would pierce the bottom of Bukhari's raft and sink it.

Bukhari had a clear view of Tracy. He saw her crawl toward Rory, pick something out of the boat, and throw it into the river. He began to get suspicious when she held onto what appeared to be a thread that extended away from her. It looked as if she was flying a kite underwater. Although Bukhari did not know what she was up to, he instinctively did not like it. He lifted his paddle and swatted at the line.

Tracy saw Bukhari hit the line with a paddle. Fearing he might break it and put her plan to naught, she yanked at the hook. Just as she pulled, Bukhari got his paddle under the line. The combined force of the two made the hook react like an incensed wasp, and it sank its teeth into the bottom of the raft. As the pull on it continued, it ripped a long gash in the raft's fiber before making a clean getaway.

A tremor ripped through the raft, and it began to drag. Billy was the first to feel the effects, just as the driver of a car is the first to notice a blowout. He had seen the battle between Bukhari and Tracy and had guessed what had happened. While his captors were distracted by the battle, he jumped out of the raft. The river was preferable to these lunatics, he thought. At least he could swim in the river.

Ziad looked over to Iqbal and barked some orders, then scampered to fill Billy's place.

Iqbal stood up as best he could and picked up an oar, handling it like a spear, with the blade as the shaft. He took careful aim and hurled it, like a javelin, at Rory.

Rory was concentrating on maneuvering the raft and never saw the missile coming.

Tracy saw it, and shrieked, "Rory! Watch out!"

Instinctively, Rory turned to look. The handle hit him squarely between the eyes, knocking him off balance. As Tracy watched, horrified, Rory fell into the front end of the raft, his arms flailing. His head hit a bucket with a dull thud, and he lost consciousness instantly. The raft, having lost its navigator, began to float sideways, slowing down considerably.

This was the opportunity Ziad had been waiting for. His craft, though ripped, was now moving faster than Rory's, since it was floating straight down the river. As soon as the two rafts came close enough to each other, Bukhari leaned forward and grabbed Tracy's raft. Using all his strength, he held the two crafts together, allowing Ziad and Iqbal to board the other raft. Bukhari then jumped on as well, leaving the disabled raft to sink alone.

He and Tracy were now a few feet from each other. They stared, Bukhari with a sneer on his face, Tracy with a look of sheer horror. Neither moved for a few seconds.

Tracy retreated to the end of the raft.

Bukhari stood in front of her.

Iqbal was to her left.

Ziad was to her right.

Chapter 34

Tracy's alone with Ziad and his men, and Ziad's advancing towards her!

Al had pulled off at a scenic overlook, surveying the panorama from his vantage point. The river, twisting and turning like a contortionist, was clearly visible. Its angry roar and white froth chilled his bones. Straining his eyes, he could see a tiny, brightly colored object floating in the river.

I'll bet that's one of the rafts.

Due to the distance, Al could not be sure. He took out his rifle and used its telescopic lens to identify the raft and its cargo better. As he focused the telescopic sight, a young girl came into view. She was holding a paddle like a baseball bat, ready to swing it. Three men confronted her. He recognized Ziad and could only guess the identity of the other two. It did not matter.

He focused his attention on what he could see, and what he could do. At this distance, it was hard enough to hit a stationary object, let alone one that was constantly moving and bobbing. He selected the easiest target and pulled the trigger twice in rapid succession.

Iqbal, his broad back facing Al, was standing still, laughing at Tracy's attempts to stop Ziad, when the first bullet hit him. A soft-nosed bullet, it made a small hole as it entered the body. Once inside, all hell broke loose. It shattered into thousands of small projectiles, each with a will of its own. They pierced, ruptured, and shredded every organ they came into contact with. Then they collectively exited. A large hole formed where Iqbal's chest had once been, and his innards decorated the floor of the boat.

The force of the bullet threw Iqbal off balance, and he was about to fall when the second bullet hit him. It flung him into the center of the raft, on top of the unconscious Rory, while his entrails splattered Ziad in the face.

"Got one son of a bitch!" Al shouted with satisfaction.

Ziad and Bukhari stared at the fallen Iqbal with bewilderment. Ziad realized this had to be the work of Al. He had not died, after all! Damn! Ziad had no idea how many men were involved, or where they were. He vainly wished for a gun. All he could do at this point was to try to survive.

His choices were limited. He could jump into the river and try to escape, or he could try to take Tracy hostage, using her for cover and negotiate a surrender. One look at the river convinced him the latter was the better plan.

Bukhari did not care much about the shooting or its implications. Like Captain Ahab, his attention was focused entirely on revenge. He dove at Tracy's legs, knocking her off balance and she fell to her right, arms flailing, just as Ziad moved toward her.

As the senior ISI man lifted his foot to step toward Tracy, her arms hit him in the middle of the chest. The blow came at an inopportune time. He was unsteady, with one leg planted on the raft, the other in the air. At that moment, the raft pitched suddenly, and he lost his balance, clutching at the air in from of him, hoping to right himself. He failed and let out a blood curdling scream as he went overboard.

Ziad suffered from hydrophobia. It had afflicted him ever since his childhood when he had gone swimming in an irrigation canal. An operator upstream, unaware of the child's presence, had opened the sluices just as Ziad started swimming. The sudden torrent of water had overwhelmed the little boy and he had almost drowned. Nearby farmers had rescued him, but the experience left an indelible scar. Ziad lost all enthusiasm for swimming, hating any collection of water larger than a bucket. In the excitement of the moment, he had forgotten all about his phobia. Falling into the river the memories of his near drowning four decades ago came flooding back.

Ziad froze. Cold, turbulent water smashed against his face again and again. It entered his eyes, his nose, and his mouth.

Air, air, I need air.

All he got was more water.

Must get out, go up, which way is up?

He could not breathe. Panic drove out all lucid thought. Amid wild, uncoordinated, ineffectual thrashing, Ziad sank. Water filled his lungs and he lost his buoyancy. He slid to the riverbed as he lost consciousness, becoming one with silt, rotting plants, and dead animals the river had claimed in its journey.

After shunning him throughout his life, death finally embraced Ziad in its cold, clammy arms.

"Damn!" Al shouted, half in anger, half in satisfaction. He saw Ziad go overboard, but he also saw Tracy being tackled.

Bukhari had slid behind Tracy and pinned her down, his left arm around her neck, his right arm ensnaring her hands. His legs covered hers, leaving her no room to move.

The valiant raft turned the corner.

Al could not see the raft anymore. He considered running down the road, but the river was too fast for him. He ran to the car instead and headed to the next pullout point. He did not like the odds. First, Tracy was no match for a large man. Second, neither of the two survivors - Tracy or Bukhari - were adept at negotiating a fast-moving river or grade five rapids. And right now, neither of them was guiding the raft.

The raft continued on its perilous pilgrimage. Without a guide, it ran into troubled waters. Buffeted by rolling waves and smashed by eddies, it rose and fell as if on a hellish roller coaster. Water poured in as it struggled to stay afloat, turning the blood in its center into a crimson tide.

The sloshing water slapped Rory in the face, rousing him. Groggy, he looked up, but his vision was blurred, and he had difficulty focusing. He was also having trouble getting up, there seemed to be an enormous weight on him. With effort, he propped himself on his elbow. Just then, his eyes began to focus. A man lay across him, and pieces of flesh were scatted inside the boat. The strange sight sickened him, and he almost passed out again when he heard his name being called.

"Rory!" Tracy was overjoyed to see Rory move. She had feared the blow and subsequent fall had killed him.

As Rory focused his attention on Tracy, another strange sight came to view. She was lying in the raft, not too far from him, pinned down by another man. He had his arm around her neck and appeared to be quite willing to wring it. Rory stared at the man, still struggling to comprehend what was going on.

"Rory," growled Bukhari. He did not like this at all. In a short span of time, he had lost all his comrades, and with them, the upper hand. No, he did not like it at all. He sat glowering, his gaze fixed on Rory.

"Rory, help!"

Rory began to remember. Scenes of the chase came back to him. The man holding Tracy was the one who had been chasing them. Rage kicked in.

"Let her go!" he commanded, as he pushed the lifeless body off himself and got up on his hand and knees.

"Stay there! Take a step closer and I'll kill her."

"If you do that, I'll kill you." Rory returned evenly, his pacifism dead and buried.

The two men stayed in their respective positions, waiting for the other to make the first move.

Tracy made the first move. While Bukhari was distracted, his grip on her neck had loosened just a bit. It was just enough for her to bring her mouth onto his arm and bite it with all her might. With a resounding yell, he let go of her and Tracy quickly scrambled away from him.

At that moment, the raft ran into a grade-five rapid. It swirled around like a discus in the hands of a thrower and was flung into the air. It flew, turned on its head, and inverted, throwing everything and everyone into the river.

Bukhari was thrown the farthest downstream, well past the rocks. He was mostly interested in self-preservation now and took his opportunity to getaway. Closest to the right bank of the river, he started swimming towards it.

Tracy and Rory were also thrown downstream, barely missing the rocks. As the powerful currents threw Tracy about, she completely lost her bearings. She made a valiant effort to sort out her position, but her strength began to ebb. She was about to give up when she felt an arm around her waist.

Rory had seen Tracy go under and had jumped after her. The swirling, muddy waters made it difficult for him to find her. He groped around desperately until he came across her soft body, putting his left arm around her and pulling her up so her head was above water. With great difficulty, he changed positions so his arm was across her chest. Then, with powerful strokes, he started swimming towards the left bank.

It was a difficult task under the best of circumstances. The speed of the current was incredible, and the river seemed determined to keep them in its clutches. With tremendous effort, Rory managed to reach the shore, pulling Tracy to safety. He put her on the bank and collapsed next to her. They stayed that way for a while, gasping and panting. After what seemed like an eternity, he turned to her.

"Are you okay?"

"Yes!" She smiled. "Thanks." She swung her arms around his neck and kissed him.

"This has been the most exciting rafting trip I've ever taken," Rory commented. Tracy gave a short laugh. Suddenly she remembered Bukhari.

"What happened to Bukhari?"

"Who, the guy who was holding you? He was Bukhari?"

"Yes, the one and only!"

"I have no idea what happened to him. Maybe he drowned?"

They sat up and looked around. There was no evidence of him. No lifeless body floating in the river or dashed on the rocks, no footprints on the sand. They peered at the opposite bank. Nothing.

"Who were the other guys?" Rory had only a vague idea whom he had been battling.

"Bukhari's co-conspirators. God, Rory, what a nightmare."

"You can say that again."

"I'm sure they were trying to get you because of the vial. They somehow figured out it was with you. I hope there aren't any more of them."

"Who knows, there may be," Rory remarked prophetically.

"By the way, what did you do with the vial?"

"Exactly what you suggested I do."

"Thanks."

They sat on the rocks for a few minutes, hugging, whispering and ruminating. Finally, Rory got up.

"The sun's beginning to set, and it's time to get out of here. The question is, how? No rafters come to this part of the canyon."

"So what do you plan to do?"

"I should probably go and get help. There's only one way I can think of."

"And what's that?"

Rory looked up at the canyon wall.

"I'm gonna climb those slopes!"

Tracy looked up at the dangerous mountain walls.

"You're kidding!" She saw the determined look on his face and realized he was not. She tried to dissuade him.

"Sooner or later, someone will send a search party. If we wait here, they'll find us."

"Who'll send a search party? Billy's the only one who knows about us, and I have no idea what happened to him."

"Al knows about us, too!"

"Who's Al?"

Tracy realized a lot had happened to her that Rory did not have the foggiest notion of. She spent a few minutes filling him in on her exploits of the past two days.

"So, do you think he would go to the police?" Rory queried. "It sounds to me like he would want to avoid them at any cost."

Tracy was not sure what Al's next step would be. Would he be secretive enough to risk their death rather than seek the help of the local authorities? She just did not know.

"Why not spend the night here? We could trek upstream in the morning. It'll be daylight and we'll be well rested."

"We don't have a bank to walk on all the way. The mountain slopes meet the river directly for quite a while, and we won't have any place to walk. More importantly, if we stay here, we'll be dead by morning. As soon as the sun sets, the temperature will plummet. I won't be surprised if it touches freezing point by midnight. In our wet clothes, we don't stand a chance."

"I still don't like the idea of your climbing that steep slope all by yourself. I should come with you."

"I don't think that's a good idea. The road 's far away, with steep mountain walls in between. Climbing the mountain will be difficult, even with appropriate gear, which we don't have. In any case, you don't have the experience and you're in no shape to climb. Don't worry about me. I'll be fine."

Hugging Tracy, Rory started on his trek. He had gone only a few feet when Tracy ran up to him.

"I'm coming with you."

"Now what?"

"What if Bukhari's lurking around somewhere? I don't want to be here alone if he comes back!"

Rory had to concede she had a good point. He held his hand out for her, and they started their climb together.

Meanwhile, the raft continued its journey down the river alone. As it went through the next set of rapids, the jagged rocks attacked it with ferocity, and its bottom was shredded. The unforgiving currents slammed the injured raft into tree limbs jutting out of the river. The inflated sides were punctured, and air leaked out of it. Maimed, lifeless, its shell floated on down the river.

Chapter 35

"Where's the damned raft!" Al was exasperated.

He had driven like a maniac to the next scenic overlook, waiting for the raft to show up. It was a while before it did.

He did not see anyone in the raft, or what was left of it. Nobody at all. *Had everyone in it died?*

He stood there for a while, brooding, till the blaring sirens of a police car drew him out of his reverie.

Hank Cooper had been about to end his shift with the highway patrol when the first call had come in. It had been a routine day till then. He had given out a few speeding tickets, helped out a couple of stalled cars. Not much in the way of violent crime took place in Jackson. The police had become accustomed to well-behaved citizens and tourists, and in turn, were laid-back and helpful. The system worked - under routine circumstances.

The first call came in around half past four. Some upset tourists were telling wild tales about gunshots and drowning deaths. He was heading to the unloading dock to check it out when the second call came in. Many drivers had called, complaining about some idiot driving on the curb. On the curb, he thought! If they wanted to kill themselves, there were simpler ways to do it. He was directed to attend to the second call first since it was a crime in action.

He was speeding in the direction of the last call when the third one came in. Someone had pulled off into a scenic viewing area and was shooting into the canyon. From the description of the car, it appeared calls two and three were related. He stepped on the gas, turned on his sirens, and made haste to where the car had last been seen.

He saw the Buick Regal parked at a scenic viewpoint. A solitary man was standing in front of the hood, staring into the canyon. He had a rifle with telescopic sights in his hands.

This could be dangerous, Hank thought. He parked some distance away, pulled his gun out of the holster, and shouted into the megaphone.

"Drop your weapon and put your hands on the car!"

Oh great, Al thought. Here we go with the Hollywood routine. He complied silently.

Hank waited before making the next move. Nothing seemed to be amiss; nobody seemed to be hiding in the back seat of the car. He got out slowly, hand on his gun, and approached Al.

"All right. What's going on here?"

Reluctantly, Al responded.

"I'm with the CIA. There are a bunch of terrorists down in the canyon."

"Right! And Tarzan's swingin' in the trees. Do you have any identification on you?"

Slowly, with great deliberation, Al removed his driver's license and CIA identification card and gave it to the police officer. Hank looked at the cards carefully, then studied the man in detail. The man in the picture certainly looked like the man in front of him. Hank had to consider the strong possibility that the man in front of him was telling the truth, but he wasn't finished with his inquiry.

"So, what's going on around here?"

It took Al five minutes to give him a brief sketch of what had transpired. The sincerity of his delivery helped convince Hank.

Hank was a mountain man at heart, not given to musing much about religion or philosophy. The only time he had anything to do with them was when his wife forced him to attend church, which happened about once a year. Hank was a practical man who knew the terrain and weather in the area very well. He was very aware of the possibility everyone on the raft was dead, and if alive, in grave danger. It was the time of year when hibernating bears woke up and went foraging for food. They were irritable and likely to attack at the slightest provocation.

That was not the only danger.

The weather was very fickle at this time of year and the temperature fluctuated wildly over a twenty-four-hour period. It could be warm during the day, and below freezing at night. The temperature swings could be fatal. It was five in the evening now, and darkness was falling swiftly in the mountains. There was not much time left.

"We have to move quickly. Let me speak to my captain."

He went to the car to call his headquarters and was back in less than a minute.

"They're going to call a chopper in. Follow me to the unloading dock. They'll pick us up there."

The Jackson police force, though small, had helicopters at its disposal. They were needed for rescuing lost hikers, evacuating injured skiers and sometimes for routine business in the winter when roads became inaccessible. The force had a well-trained team of pilots, and one of their best was available.

Hank escorted Al to the deserted unloading dock fairly quickly with sirens wailing and lights flashing. He instructed Al to park his car in a corner of the lot so the chopper would have a place to land.

It did not take the helicopter much time to get there. The pilot, Alex, motioned them in. He had been briefed about the mission and knew its urgency. The passengers had barely closed the door when he took off again.

The route was dangerous since Alex would have to follow the river closely to get a clear view. Which meant flying in between the walls of the ravine and as daylight faded, it became riskier by the minute.

The helicopter flew fast over the river. They knew where Rory and Tracy had last been seen, and they approached their last known location in a hurry. That was the easy part. Then, their eyes peering into the canyon, straining to spot any bodies on the rocks or floating in the river, they began to move forward. Slowly.

They saw nothing for a while.

Suddenly, Al shouted. "Look, down there!"

A solitary man stood there, waving his shirt.

Billy had managed to reach the shore after jumping out of the raft and, like Rory, realized he could not walk on the edge of the river. However, unlike Rory, he was not adept at rock-climbing. He decided to stay put, shivering, waiting for help to arrive.

Hank trained his binoculars on the guide.

"Is that one of them?"

Al borrowed the binoculars.

"No, it isn't."

"Well, we have to rescue him anyway," Hank said firmly. He could not play favorites.

Alex realized the conflicting emotions his passengers were experiencing. They could not leave the poor man down there but taking him to a police station or hospital would take too much time. Finding a way out of the dilemma, he let a rope down with a life jacket attached to it. If the stranded man had any common sense, he would secure himself to the jacket so they could ferry him up the canyon, let him go, and return to their original mission.

Alex's plan worked to perfection. Billy was let off at the nearest scenic viewpoint, where he unfastened himself. Hank shouted to him through the din of the rotors.

"Are you okay?"

Billy gave the thumbs up sign.

Hank shouted to him again.

"I've radioed the headquarters and let them know you're here. Someone will come and get you. Stay here till they come."

Billy gave the thumbs up sign again.

The chopper returned to the slopes.

Chapter 36

Rory and Tracy were halfway up the slope and in deep trouble. They were cold, wet, tired, and hungry.

It was dark, and Rory could not see good crevices to use as holds. Groping at the mountain wall, he clawed on to any crevices he could find and then hung on. Wearing only shorts and old tennis shoes provided hopelessly little traction. More often than not, the shoes would slip, and he would be left dangling in the air, holding on to the mountain wall with his bare fingers. After repeated attempts, he finally managed to get a good toehold and gain some inches. The process was repeated again and again.

Tracy was in worse shape. Though Rory had attempted to help her by tying himself to Tracy with his shirt, she did not have the strength or the stamina to haul herself up the mountain wall. She tried her best not to become too much of a load on Rory by attempting to climb by herself. However, her success in finding holds was far worse than Rory's, and she spent a lot of time dangling, slipping and sliding. Rory would move only when she had a firm hold, and she would do the same for Rory. Their progress had been slow and painful.

Initially, the slope had an inclination of sixty degrees and they had climbed that part fairly easily. About halfway up, the angle increased to seventy-five degrees, an incline even professional mountaineers would not have attempted without pitons, ropes, and hammers.

Rory and Tracy had nothing.

Tracy looked up, and her heart sank. The edge of the mountain could not be seen, only the sheer walls. She looked down and felt like throwing up. Jagged rocks pointed accusing fingers at her. All she wanted to do was to lie down and sleep, for a long, long time. Maybe Rory was right. She should have stayed back. At least he would have lived.

"Rory!" She yelled.

"What?"

"I don't think I can go on."

Rory paused before answering.

"Yes, you can. Just concentrate on one step at a time."

"No, I can't. I don't have the strength to do this. I want you to go on without me."

Rory was stupefied.

"Don't be silly. I won't go on without you."

"Listen to me. I don't want us both to die. Go on up, I'll stay on here as long as I can. If you get help in time, I'll be fine. If not, remember, I love you."

Before Rory had the time to reply, she started to untie her end of the shirt that bound them together.

"Tracy, don't!"

It was too late. She was free of the shirt. The only thing stopping Tracy from falling was her tenuous hold on the mountain wall.

Rory's head began to buzz. He thought it was from the shock of what Tracy had just done. He clung to the wall, a foot above Tracy, wondering what to do next. He could go down and re-hook himself to her, but she was holding on to the only crevices he knew on the slope.

The buzzing grew louder. It wasn't his head. Must be those damn mosquitoes! They were everywhere.

"Rory, do you hear that?" Tracy had heard something too.

"Hear what?"

"That sound. Isn't it a chopper?"

That was it. A helicopter.

"Yes, I hear it! Loud and clear!" They hung on to the slope with renewed hope.

Alex and his new crew were looking intently at the river but had not seen anything. A raft had been observed a while ago, lying on the shore, stuck to the roots of a tree, but it was not the one Rory and Tracy had been seen on earlier. They hadn't been able to see anyone near the raft, so they had carried on.

Dismay began to set it. They had been at this for a while and were failing. Now night had fallen, making their search even riskier. They began to wonder if it was futile.

Tracy saw the helicopter first. It was moving very slowly, hugging the river, its blades barely missing the slopes. A searchlight emanated from its belly, stabbing the darkness, sweeping the river and embankments. She could see the outlines of ghostly faces pressing against the windowpanes, peering into the darkness. It was strange, but one of the faces almost looked like Al. Tracy did a double take. It was Al.

"Al!" She shouted at the top of her voice.

Rory looked at the helicopter with intense interest but could not see anything initially. After a brief while, he was able to see tops of heads but not the faces - perhaps, he thought, because he was higher than Tracy.

The helicopter continued its search. It was now abreast of them, at a slightly lower altitude. The crew was concentrating on the river and the bank, where they expected to see the missing duo, and was completely ignoring the walls.

"Al!" Tracy half-shouted, half-screamed.

The helicopter continued moving forwards.

"Rory!" She shouted.

"What?"

"They're going to miss us! They're looking down, not up here where we are."

The chopper was now a few feet in front of them. A few more feet and it would be too late.

"I wish I could get their attention."

"Is there a rock near you?"

Rory immediately understood what Tracy was suggesting. He groped the wall around him for a loose rock. He found one, but as his finger touched it, it began to roll down. He desperately leaned over and grabbed it, almost losing his balance. With great difficulty, he straightened himself.

The helicopter was ten feet away from them.

Rory took aim at the rear section of the craft, which was the closest to him. It was also at a safe distance from the rotor, and therefore the least likely to bring the helicopter down. He hurled the rock over his head with all his might.

Alex was concentrating on flying the helicopter, using his crew as his eyes.

"See anything?" He asked.

"No, nothing," Al replied dejectedly.

Silence permeated the helicopter as it slowly made its way forward. The stillness was interrupted by a loud clang that seemed to reverberate in the cabin, making the chopper trembled as if in agony. Alex instinctively raised the nose of the helicopter and started taking the craft up.

"What the hell was that?" Hank thought the rotors had hit the mountain wall or a tree.

Alex concentrated on stabilizing the craft before answering.

"I'm not sure. I don't see any trees around, and we're not as close to the slopes as you might think."

"It sounded as if a rock hit us."

"Maybe one fell off the slopes."

"This is dangerous. We should be flying higher." Hank had been involved in many rescue operations and had come to the conclusion it was pointless to risk his life unless absolutely necessary.

Alex seemed to agree, and the helicopter began to head vertically up. It was still about ten feet in front of Tracy and Rory, and level with them.

"They still haven't seen us!" Tracy wailed.

"I don't have any rocks left. Can you look around?"

Tracy was scared to let go of the mountain but realized it was their only hope for rescue. Gingerly, she began to feel around her. Her feet hit a loose pile of rocks, and they cascaded down the mountain.

Al was looking at the sheer face of the wall beside the craft when his attention was drawn to falling rocks.

So that was it. One of the falling rocks had hit the helicopter.

Out of curiosity, he followed the path the rocks had taken. The path ended in a pair of legs. Al stared at the legs. He was definitely seeing things. As the chopper continued to rise, the pair of legs acquired a torso, and then a face. The face was staring at him, full of fear and hope.

It was Tracy.

Tracy!

"Look! Look! It's her! She's right there!" Al walloped Hank across the shoulder in his excitement.

Hank turned to see what he was looking at. The silhouette of a girl could be seen in the moonlight, hugging the wall, face turned towards them, mouth open in an unknown cry.

"Al!" Tracy yelled, sure this time, she would be heard.

The helicopter continued its slow ascent.

A man was now visible a few feet above the girl, in an identical posture.

"That must be Rory!" Al shouted.

The helicopter stopped moving.

"They've seen us! They've seen us!" Tracy was ecstatic.

The helicopter hovered at the spot.

"What are they doing? Why are they waiting?" Tracy was worried at the slightest delay.

Hank and Alex conferred. Poor visibility and the mountain wall made this a difficult situation. The only saving grace was Rory's background, and it soon became apparent they would have to capitalize on it. The searchlight was trained onto the slope, blinding Rory and Tracy.

Hank opened the right door of the chopper. The rotors were making quite a din, and he could hardly hear himself talk. Pulling out the megaphone, he shouted into it.

"If you can hear me, turn your head to the right and the left. Don't let go of the mountain! Understand?"

The heads turned to the right and left.

"Rory, we're going to go up and drop you a life jacket. Grab it and secure yourself first. Understand?"

The head turned to the right and left.

"After you secure yourself, you'll have to grab Tracy and pull her up with you. Can you manage it?"

Rory's head turned to the right and left.

Rory took a big gulp. He had never done anything like this. The closest had been when, as part of his rock-climbing training, he had rappelled down a mountain wall with someone strapped to his back. This was clearly different.

The helicopter resumed its ascent. It went up about twenty feet and then stopped. A life jacket came down toward Rory, swinging wildly from side to side as the wind from the rotors pushed it around. It stopped when it was about a foot from his head.

Rory did not move.

"Why isn't he moving?" Alex was puzzled.

"Don't know. Let me ask him." Hank used the megaphone again. "Is there a problem?"

The head turned to the right and left.

"He indicated there's a problem. What could it be?" Alex hoped Rory hadn't developed cold feet.

"Maybe we're too high. Go down a bit," Hank suggested.

The chopper came down a couple of feet.

The life jacket swung from side to side, a foot below Rory's head. He took a deep breath. This was it. He had to turn and jump at the jacket with perfect timing. The slightest miscalculation and he would be impaled on the sharp rocks below.

The jacket swung away from him. It reached its high point, and then slowly retraced its arc, heading in his direction.

Rory turned and leaped into the air.

A gust of wind blew at the jacket and slowed it down.

Rory was expecting to hit the jacket head-on but missed it. He desperately threw out his right hand in the direction of the jacket.

His hand got caught in one of the straps, and he clung to it with all his might. Like a spider dangling from its web, Rory hung on to the jacket, while everybody watched with bated breath. Slowly, using all his strength, he tried to pull himself up. It was like attempting one-hand pull-ups, and Rory was unable to pull it off. When he failed, he threw his left hand onto his right and tried again. This time he was successful. After he got a good grasp of the jacket with both hands, he began to climb into it.

Swinging like a pendulum, he managed to secure himself in the jacket.

Then it was Tracy's turn. She was clinging to the wall like an ant, her head turned to see how Rory was faring.

He cupped his hands around his mouth and shouted at her, "I'm coming to get you! Catch me tightly as soon as I touch you!"

"Hurry! I can't hang on much longer!" She yelled.

Rory swung toward her but missed her by a wide margin. The rope swayed in the opposite direction then headed back toward her.

Straight toward her.

They were on a collision course. They stared at each other with horror as they came closer and closer. A few feet separated them. Instinctively, Rory stuck his legs out, and they landed on the mountain wall, on either side of Tracy.

A few inches separated them.

Rory grabbed hold of Tracy just as the rope was beginning to retrace its path.

Tracy still hung on to the wall.

"Let go, Tracy! Let go!"

The rope began to pull on Rory. Soon, he would either have to leave her or risk having his shoulder pulled off by the rope.

"Now!" He pleaded.

Tracy let go.

The rope started its return journey, its swing dampened by the increased load. Rory and Tracy hung on for dear life.

"Can you see what's going on down there?" Alex suspected success since the weight had changed but wanted to make sure.

"They're fine! Rory has Tracy. They're okay."

"Let's head to higher ground." Alex was beginning to worry about how long the helicopter would be able to handle the weight, and how long Rory would be able to carry Tracy.

"Good idea," Hank agreed.

The helicopter slowly lifted and headed toward a landing site. Less than an hour later, they were at the police headquarters in Jackson.

Chapter 37

"Let's call the police." Hilda Brakeman suggested.

"No, you're over-reacting." Dan Brakeman, her husband of the past two days, differed.

They had spent the late hours of the evening arguing over whether they had heard gunshots from the direction of the Snake River. Their discourse had started as a pleasant enough honeymoon tiff. Exchanging New York City for a week's worth of camping in the Grand Tetons, the Brakeman's were at first delighted to hear something approximating the sounds of home emanating from the great American wilderness.

Their bickering started over the question of the caliber of the gun that had been fired. The ballistics topic quickly turned into a full-scale spat over the Upper West Side location of their apartment. He insisted if they lived closer to the river, they would hear less gunfire. She insisted whatever gunfire they heard was the product of his over-stimulated imagination and nothing would ever coerce her into moving more than two blocks from Central Park.

Meanwhile, Dr. Tariq Bukhari was convinced he had died and gone to hell. He was covered in a film of cold, wet mud, his clothes were in tatters, and his shoes long gone. He felt nothing, and his eyes saw only crudest shapes and visual sensations. After some time, Bukhari discerned a bright light, twinkling far away. Lacking any reason to disabuse the notion, he decided to head for it. The river had been especially harsh on the doctor's body. As he approached the light, he could hear shrill, raised voices.

"Shhh, be quiet." Hilda Brakeman remarked.

"Shut up yourself. And quit yelling." Dan Brakeman replied angrily.

"No, I mean it. Just shut up and listen." She put a finger in front of his lips.

Bukhari's leaden footsteps resounded like the tramping of a large animal in the forest.

"Don't worry. Animals don't like fire. They won't come into the camp" Dan Brakeman whispered.

Husband and wife screamed simultaneously at the sight of a disheveled Tariq Bukhari. Fatigue had robbed the ISI agent of any normal speech. He beseeched the terrified couple in a constantly-shifting monosyllabic mix of Pushto and English. The Brakeman's could have handled a mugger with a ski mask over his head and a gun in his hand. However, the sight Bukhari presented was too much for them. After a few seconds, the couple ran away, preferring the unknown dangers of the forest.

Bukhari did not understand why the couple had fled. However, it did not matter. Like a hungry animal, he marauded through the Brakeman's' campsite. While in a frenzy of attempting to satisfy his hunger, he discovered Dan's cellular telephone. Realizing what it was, he held it gently in his hands, cherishing it like a miner handling an enormous nugget.

Ziad, with his guerrilla fighter's prescience, had drilled Bukhari for just such an occasion. From the deepest recess of his memory, the doctor recalled Thor Martin's secure, private number.

After a couple of rings, the telephone was picked up.

"Thor?"

"Yes."

"Thor," Bukhari gasped. "I need your help!"

Silence greeted his cry.

"Thor!" He half shouted, half cried.

"Who's this?" Came a hesitant, cold reply.

"Bukhari. Tariq Bukhari. I'm in a lot of trouble. Please, I need your help. Now!"

"Where are you?"

"In Jackson. We..."

"Where's Ziad?"

"Dead. They're all dead. The CIA is killing us."

Silence. Then, 'click'. The telephone had been hung up. All Bukhari heard was the dial tone.

He stared at the telephone in disbelief.

Did Thor mishear me? Why did he hang up?

Slowly, in his numbed state, Bukhari began to comprehend he was now truly alone.

Chapter 38

"Once again, taking on the establishment alone?" Doris sighed, resigned.

For the first time since he had resigned his commission in the United States Navy, Bill Hopkins was wearing the sparkling white uniform of an Admiral. He had not put on a solitary pound in the years since he had last worn it. Originally, in his rage, he had intended to burn it. Doris had persuaded him otherwise; she reminded him of all the men he had commanded. If he went ahead with such an action, it would be as though he were denying the memory of all the men who had served with him.

Bill did not say a word to his wife as he readied himself. He hated anything theatrical and melodramatic. He hated having to resort to something as melodramatic as holding a press conference.

Doris moved over to her husband and began minutely fixing his tie and adjusting his collar.

"Bill, are you sure..."

"Yes. And no, you're going to stay here. God knows who's going to be watching. For all we know, we may be fugitives in twenty-four hours. I don't want your pretty face turning up on the cover of some supermarket tabloid." The two embraced warmly.

"7:30, sharp."

"Aye, aye, sir."

Bill had deliberately selected the most innocuous place he could find to rent for a press conference. The Sportsman's Room at the Real Motor Lodge next to Salt Lake City's airport met his requirements. The local media had shown up, complete with a few stringers. A local UHF channel agreed to broadcast the proceedings live on Wednesday morning.

At the appointed time, Bill took the podium. Clearing his throat, he began as though addressing a roomful of his men just before the start of a dangerous mission.

"Ladies and gentlemen of the media, thank you. I'm William Holman Hopkins, once an Admiral in the United States Navy. In 1983, I resigned my commission and concluded my career a good ten years early to protest a series of events long since forgotten. I have elected to address you today in my uniform as an indication of the gravity of the news I have to share.

"You are all aware of the tragic event occurring at St Mary's Hospital in Rochester, Minnesota two days ago. Several theories and explanations have been put forward to explain the terrible deaths of the two dozen patients, nurses, and doctor.

"As of last Friday, my daughter, Tracy Helen Hopkins, was an MD/Ph.D. student in good standing at Mayo Clinic. For reasons that will be explained later, she came to acquire direct knowledge about how those innocent men and women met their demise.

"We believe they were murdered. Next Monday, my daughter plans to return to Rochester and offer the Olmsted County District Attorney a full, sworn testimony identifying the persons behind St Mary's murders. I cannot and will not at this time divulge any names. However, for your future reference, my daughter was the last person to see Dr. Dan Howard, the professor from Mayo Clinic who is missing, alive. Let me inform you that based on what will be revealed in full to the District Attorney's office, Dr. Howard is dead.

"I was and still consider myself to be a sailor. I make no pretenses about knowing anything about medical science. However, I would like to question the assertions made by Senator David Dockhorn of Minnesota. For reasons best known to himself, Senator Dockhorn mentioned in a press conference this past Monday the deaths at St. Mary's were the result of a freakish outbreak of a drug resistant strain of >>pneumococcus. Ladies and gentlemen, on my honor, on the honor of everything good and true this uniform represents, allow me to inform you no such outbreak occurred. The deaths were caused by something far more sinister. I will also assert the Senator, despite his innumerable efforts at public welfare, is no more a scientist than me. For reasons that will become clear on Monday, Senator Dockhorn was incorrect, willfully and knowingly incorrect, in attributing this rare disease as the cause of St Mary's tragedy. That's all."

A shower of camera flashes immortalized Bill Hopkins. Questions started pouring in and Bill Hopkins answered them as best as he could without revealing too much. The assorted stringers immediately contacted their networks. Within the hour, Bill Hopkins had become the most featured man in America, and David Dockhorn the most scrutinized.

Chapter 39

Thor Martin carefully scrutinized David Dockhorn's face for any clues to his thoughts or hints of his plans. The Senator had returned to Minneapolis on Tuesday night to attend a series of fund-raisers. The last event, a symphony ball, had lasted late into the night. At the last moment, he had decided to spend the evening in the city and head to Wildwood estate in the morning.

The suddenly un-retired Bill Hopkins press conference had caught Martin by surprise. The aide had perused the highlights of the Admiral's service file while investigating Tracy earlier in the week. Nothing had indicated the ex-navy man would have anything to do with the media. Martin struggled beneath the weight of Bill Hopkins' statements. Calls were flooding the Senator's local and national offices.

Even after all the years they had spent together, Martin could not predict how Dockhorn would react to any given situation. Mostly, he behaved as though he was a baseball coach glancing at the batting averages of the opponent's lineup. Sometimes the Senator deliberately laughed off the direst emergency while exploding over a minor issue.

Martin had taken the liberty of waking up his late-sleeping boss at 10:00 am on Wednesday. A half-hour later, Dockhorn had already watched the videotape of Bill Hopkin's press conference three times. After the third viewing, he stood up from the table of his private office and loudly cracked his knuckles.

"Take care of the situation, Thor. I've got other things on my mind."

"I've already drafted some possible courses of action which require your approval."

Beckoned by the downward tilt of Martin's chin, the Senator resumed his place at the conference table.

With a sure, practiced cadence, Martin began to outline his proposed counter-attack.

"First, a press release will be issued thanking Bill Hopkins for his interest in the public health of Minnesota. However, we will encourage him to remember by his own admission he is not a trained scientist and/or medical professional, and he should refrain from contesting the results of an investigation fully supported by both you and the citizens of Minnesota."

Drowsily, Dockhorn nodded his assent.

"That's fine, what else?"

"Nothing else, that's it."

"That's it? That's it? That's hardly enough."

"It should be. There's no point blowing this up too much."

"Thor, this situation is unique, and it requires an appropriately unique response."

"We'd better be careful of the response. It could be as bad as the problem."

"How's that?"

"We both know the loss of lives earlier this week at the St Mary's MICU was hardly caused by the spontaneous appearance of some mystery disease. I.S.I.P was responsible for those deaths. Why did you choose the words I.S.I.P. anyway?"

"It was Sahabuddin's idea, another way of saying ISI's project. Anyway, that's beside the point. Let's get back to this situation. I don't like your suggestion. This problem requires a permanent resolution."

"Permanent resolution? What kind of permanent resolution?"

"I would like you to think of and then implement the most appropriate permanent solution."

"I'm sorry Senator, but I don't follow. I guess we could call in some favors from the regional IRS—keep Bill Hopkins in tax court for the next thirty years. Is that what you mean?"

"That won't solve the problem. Tracy will still be around to testify next week. We need a permanent solution before then. For Bill Hopkins and his meddlesome daughter."

"I'm sorry, Senator, then I don't understand what you're driving at."

"Thor, I'm not interested in drama. What the hell's gotten into you this morning? Why can't you understand what I am talking about? Damn it, boy, are you going soft?"

"Do you mean murder?"

"What?"

"Do you mean we should have the old man and Tracy murdered?"

"I … yes, you're getting the idea."

"Maybe do in the entire family?"

"Yes, like in a car accident."

"You know sir, I haven't heard anything from Ziad since Monday."

"Thor get off your goddamned soapbox and get to work. You know about my old and dear friends from Pakistan. You know my most fervent hope is we all grow older and dearer together. If you haven't heard from

Ziad, find him! Call Sahabuddin or whoever else who might know his whereabouts. Find the vial. Get to work, boy! Are you hungover?"

"No, sir."

"Well then, stop acting as though this is your first day on the job. Now, if you'll excuse me, I need to be on the links within an hour."

Martin had never heard the Senator invest so much carte blanche in his decisions before. The tall, blonde aide smiled as he walked out the door. As he left the building, he nodded to Dick Abbott and his FBI men who were waiting outside.

He had also never worn a wire before.

Chapter 40

Bill Hopkins removed the wires attached to his navy uniform at the press conference. It had gone as planned, and his house was soon surrounded by news crews from around the globe.

Bill looked around him with some pride. His daughter was home unharmed. She still had a hacking cough but was feeling better. Doris was in a much better frame of mind, and that always made the navy man feel he had done his marital duty. In his eyes, Andrew had suddenly grown into a man, and he promised himself he would take the young man on a motorcycle tour, regardless of what his mother said. There was only one fly in the proverbial ointment.

Rory sat across from him in the living room. Bill had to concede if it were not for Rory, his daughter would be dead. A hard fact for him to swallow, if he were to be honest with himself. What was making matters worse was the vial. Rory would not disclose what he had done with it.

"You know, Rory, you're being childish. You cannot possibly expect to keep a biological weapon in your possession. Just think what would happen if something went wrong. Millions of people, Tracy, us, we'll all be dead!"

"Relax, pop. It's in a very safe place."

Bill cringed at being called pop, especially in such a familiar fashion. However, since he had no control over it, he ignored it.

"Can you hear yourself talk? Safe place? Do you know anything about keeping biological weapons in a safe place?"

He looked beseechingly at Tracy.

"Can you ask him to tell us where it is, or to give it to the FBI, or to David or Al?"

David and Al looked on hopefully. This was their insurance policy against political repercussions from their actions.

"Can't!" Rory replied briefly.

"Can't? Can't! Listen, you snot-nosed hippie, you've no idea how dangerous this is. See what happened to the people in Rochester? You're asking for it to happen again, only on a much, much bigger scale." David was beginning to lose patience.

Rory stared at David, who stared back at him. It was a stalemate.

"Tell 'em what you did with it, Rory," Tracy finally interjected. She could tell the situation was getting ugly.

"All right. I destroyed it!"

"Destroyed it? What do you mean destroyed it?"

"Just that. Destroyed it. A friend of mine works in a laboratory in Jackson. I took it to his autoclaving machine yesterday morning, soon after I got the package and Tracy's note. I autoclaved the damned vial at 500-degree centigrade. No bug could survive that temperature. Even the organisms in the hot springs at Yellowstone would not be able to survive it. Nothing was left of the vial. Nothing."

David and Al saw their dreams vaporize.

"Why the blazes did you do that?" Al asked in shock.

"Because I'm fully aware of how dangerous biological weapons are. No one should have them. No one. Not even you. I'd rather destroy it than give it to you because you're just as likely to use it on someone else later on."

"Are you crazy? Has the CIA ever done anything that stupid?" Al was amazed by the kid's total lack of patriotism.

Rory was just as amazed someone working for the agency could be so naive.

"Maybe they didn't tell you this during your indoctrination at the agency, so let me tell you. Your CIA isn't as pure as the driven snow. It has a long history of subverting freely elected governments and killing people if it suits their purpose. Look at Allende in Chile and Mosaddeq in Iran. Look at all those Latin American dictators trained at the School of the Americas. Look at the drug running your nifty unit did in Cambodia and maybe even in the inner cities of this country. If you expect me to trust an organization with a track record like that, you need to have your collective heads examined!"

The CIA men glared at Rory, wishing they could strangle him. Tracy smiled at him. Doris nodded understandingly. Andrew looked at all of them with stupefaction. He wished he was at his computer, lost in a make-believe world.

Chapter 41

Imran looked at his men as they gathered to attack. All five of them were nervous and excited. This is what they had been sent to the US for. Finally, the time had come. Imran remembered the six fallen men and wondered how these, the last of his troops, would hold up in comparison. He fingered the pink vial in his vest, next to the long, curvaceous dagger he always carried.

It was early Thursday morning.

"Wait for my signal. Be still until then." Imran spoke in a hushed voice. They still had time to kill.

Imran reflected on Afghanistan. A land he was proud to admit he was from. Though a generation younger and a few billion dollars poorer than Omar, Imran had suffered the same sort of dissatisfaction as Omar, but at a much younger age. The young Afghan had run away from his dwindling family and desolate village to join the *Mujahideen*. He had been fascinated by politics and enticed by *Jihad*. The most important reason for his joining, however, was in that devastated country, he had nothing better to do. In this, he was not alone. There were many others like him in the hills of Afghanistan - men who came from all over the Muslim world to become modern versions of *El Conquistador*.

During the struggle against the Soviets, Imran had become well acquainted with Sahabuddin, Ghazni, and others in the ISI. He had spent a few years studying them, learning from them, and emulating them. They had tried relentlessly to enlist him into the ISI, but for reasons the ISI never understood, Imran always refused. The reason was simple - Omar had made him a better offer.

The relocation to Afghanistan had succeeded very well for Omar. He quickly began building the nucleus of what could generously be called an armed force and a political movement. It wasn't long before Omar came to believe far too much in his own authority, thinking the high hills surrounding his camps echoed his voice as a sign of nature's fealty.

Shortly after joining Omar, Imran had quietly begun to question his loyalty to the Saudi leader. It occurred to him one fine day while hiding behind rocks and listening to bullets whizz by his ear, that Omar was an imperialist, just like the Soviets. Different race, language, and religion, but the same goal - the domination of others. It was true for Pakistan and

ISI as well. No one was interested in Afghanistan, or the people there. Everyone used the locals as cannon fodder for their selfish goals.

Imran began to make different plans for himself and contacted the CIA. Not that he was under any illusions about the agency. He did not expect them to liberate Afghanistan and pump it full of money. He just wanted the agency to help him liberate his country of Omar. Later, he hoped the policy would apply to all foreigners in Afghanistan. However, for now, he just wanted to get rid of Omar.

Soon after Imran's change of heart, Omar called upon him.

"The stars tell us we have to act. You have long waited for a special assignment. Now I'm giving you the chance. Take a few men with you to America. Wait there for a few months and further orders will follow."

Their first mission was to take place on American soil. It would be a win-win situation in the spirit of the Tet offensive: a good chance existed the operation would be successfully conducted. If, on the other hand, the operation failed, and everybody in the group died, it would still shake up both the Saudi and the American governments, and it would lend prestige to the Ash-Sham movement.

Initially, Omar did not give Imran any specific targets. He was told to get acclimatized and acculturated in Washington, DC.

While setting up shop, Imran was contacted by his new friends, Al and Dave. Imran respected them as the finest case officers he'd had the privilege of coming across. They seemed to understand and genuinely care about Afghanistan without any pretensions, unlike other CIA operatives like Milt Reardon and Frank Anderson. They understood men like Imran, Omar, Sahabuddin, and Ghazni. They understood men whose lives, thoughts and ideas were shaped by forces other than prime-time television and a daily commute. They understood the world, especially his corner of the world, was moved by ideas that could build or destroy societies, not just the promise of a bi-weekly paycheck, a movie, and a bag of popcorn.

Imran felt sorry for these men. They represented a government that had atrophied to the point where it was now incapable of dealing with anything that did not resemble it. The CIA refused to recognize the grave threat posed by the ISI because the CIA did not know how to think like the ISI. The agency worried how it could stretch its budget to keep an eye on all parts of the world, whereas the ISI dedicated its budget to controlling the world.

David had asked Imran for his help in eliminating Howard. Since he, Al, and John were still in the agency, they had qualms about doing the job themselves. Killing an American citizen, no matter how justified, was severely discouraged. The CIA would rather someone else handle that kind of work for them in return for, of course, a generous reward. Imran did not have a monetary reward in mind, though. He felt he was too small a fry to destroy Omar, the billionaire, on his own. All he wanted was help in destroying Omar's operations.

Like strangers on a train, they agreed to swap murders. Unlike strangers on a train, both parties would carry out their parts perfectly.

With a jerk, Imran came back to the present. Omar had given him and his men their first job. The Saudi Defense Minister, the same Prince who had Omar arrested, would be paying a visit to the Upper East Side mosque on Thursday morning before going on to the United Nations. Omar ordered the US unit of Ash-Sham to attack the mosque directly. He wanted the Prince dead, whatever the cost.

The men had traveled to New York, taken the #6 Lexington subway, and emerged at the 105th street stop. They had walked to the mosque, prayed, and waited near the entrance for the Saudi Prince to show up.

There was no mistaking the minister when he finally arrived an hour late, with all the pomp and ceremony the royal family demanded. A big, black, bullet-proof limousine drove up to the entrance of the mosque, surrounded by a fleet of smaller, less expensive makes. Police motorcycles and cars blared sirens as ordinary citizens looked on in irritation at the regal parade. Dressed in a traditional white, silk dress, the Defense Minister regally exited the car. With his security men running circles around him, he slowly began ascending the stairs to the mosque.

Imran was trying to figure out the best angle of attack when all hell broke loose. The Ash-Sham men, tiring of waiting and knowing heavenly rewards awaited them, ran out in the front of the onlookers. The sight of five men running toward the minister with drawn guns drew an immediate response from the security team. They had already been warned by an anonymous caller of a possible attack and were fully prepared. The guards already had their weapons out, and they used them before the Ash-Sham men did. In a chatter of gunfire, the attackers perished.

Imran had seen the Defense Minister hit the ground at the beginning of the action and knew he was unhurt. He looked around and noticed that of the Ash-Sham men, he alone was left standing. Imran then looked down and noticed that the front of his shirt was soaked.

A bullet had torn through his shirt and vest, hitting the vial and shattering it into tiny pieces. It had then gone on to enter his body, treating it with an equal amount of disrespect. However, in its hurry, it missed the heart and exited before its work was done. As Imran fell from the impact, his thoughts were on biological weapons, not his own injuries.

May Allah be praised; the vial didn't contain the superbug.

Chapter 42

"So, the vial's lost to posterity. Now we won't have any idea of what it was really all about, will we?" The Senator asked.

Al and David sat uncomfortably in the resulting silence. They occupied the center table, and their inquisitors sat in a semicircle around them.

Senate Intelligence Committee hearings are never pleasant, especially when conducted behind closed doors. Initiated in 1976 after Senator Frank Church had begun investigating the freewheeling ways of the CIA, the committee was one arm of the Senate that took its oversight responsibilities very seriously. The Director of CIA and the Chief of Directorate of Operations sat behind Al and David, while Thor Martin sat next to them.

Al glanced at Thor. The former stooge of the deceased Senator Dockhorn had undergone a radical transformation. Joining the Concord Coalition, a non-partisan group devoted to ensuring a corruption-free government, he had acquired a sense of humility and responsibility that impressed the CIA men. Speaking to the committee before David and Al's testimony, he had placed the blame for the superbug incident entirely on the former Senator. In the process, he had implied it was to humanity's advantage that the Senator, confronted by the FBI and facing the prospect of spending the rest of his life behind bars, had turned his gun on himself. Thor had gone out of his way to shower lavish encomiums on the renegade CIA men, and to describe how they had saved the world from a biological meltdown.

David had been pleased by Thor's testimony. The Senate would be less likely to go after him when the onus of the disaster fell on one of their former colleagues. David knew he could not use the Plausible Deniability escape clause, a loophole allowing the agency to wink at the escapades of its men so long as they did not get caught because they had just gotten caught. The escape clause had been created because of the inherent dichotomies in the agency's mission. David called it the HAL complex. Like the computer in '2001: A Space Odyssey', the agency had to subvert the very rules it was created to protect when it could not protect them by legal means.

"Yes, unfortunately." He replied briefly in answer to the senator.

David and Al then recounted the events of the past few days, and how the episode had led to the deaths of John and the ISI men. After he had finished, and questions of details were answered, the Senators became more personal.

"We still don't quite understand why you went out on your own. We don't as yet know what motivated you to start a cell within the CIA without the knowledge, consent, or approval of your chiefs."

David and Al looked at each other. Al let David answer.

"We had been working in Pakistan for a while, sending in reports about the rise of Islamic fundamentalism. We had been sending in reports about the drug trade fueling the Taliban's rise, and about terrorists throughout the world. All our reports were ignored by the likes of former Undersecretary of State Lawrence Eagleburger, Robert McFarlane, and Madeline Albright. The reasons were, and are, simple. Senator Dockhorn, along with some of you who now sit in judgment and who are beholden to the ISI, blocked all our efforts. Administration officials, some of whom I have mentioned, still locked in the cold war mentality, made sure our warnings were ignored."

"There isn't any evidence Pakistan has supported terrorism." The Congressman from Indiana was furious.

"You prove my point, congressman, too many politicians have blinders on. Have you ever wondered how Amir Kansi was able to live in Pakistan for years after killing two CIA employees, despite an international manhunt? Has it occurred to you what Ramzi Youcef, the mastermind of the World Trade Center bombing in the early 1990s, was doing in Pakistan? Have you wondered how American civilians were killed in broad daylight in Karachi, while our administration looked on helplessly? Even you must know the administration has labeled >>Harkat-ul-Ansar a terrorist organization, one that kidnapped and brutally beheaded Hans Ostro, the Norwegian, and an American, Donald Hutchins. Who is behind this terrorist organization? The whole world now knows Pakistan is the one who created the Taliban."

"Pakistan is a democratic country. These things happen in an open society where people have the freedom to do what they want. Remember, it was an American who blew up the Federal Building in Oklahoma."

"If it's a free and open society, why is there no freedom of the press, no freedom to practice any religion other than Sunni Islam? Why was a Christian, Ayub Masih, condemned to death under the blasphemy law for preaching Christianity? Why did Bishop John Joseph have to commit suicide to bring the world's attention to a law targeting Christians and other religious minorities? The hardworking and forbearing people of Pakistan want a good and honest life, just like people elsewhere. However, since they gained independence in 1947, a nexus of crooked dictators and fundamentalist politicians have hijacked their aspirations. They have been asked to sacrifice their freedoms for a glorious future, which never comes for them, but only for the corrupt few. The ISI epitomizes the corrupt nexus that has destroyed Pakistan and has made the land destitute."

An uncomfortable silence greeted David's last remark. Seeing no one was going to challenge him, he continued.

"We were becoming increasingly fed up with the inaction, but the Brown Amendment in 1996 did it for us. As you all know, the legislation, sponsored by Senator Hank Brown of Colorado, ignored our concerns and reports, and reinstated aid to Pakistan. We felt that to make a difference, we had to go out on our own, especially since we believe the threat of Islamic fundamentalism is more dangerous than Communism."

"More dangerous than communism? You must be out of your mind."

"Not really, Senator. Capitalism, the foundation of our society, and communism are based on materialism. Our differences are in the distribution of wealth, freedom, liberty, and the fact we believe in God in addition to material goods, whereas the communists don't. Nevertheless, both are materialistic ideologies. It's the main reason Khrushchev blinked during the Cuban missile crisis. He realized a nuclear war would wipe out the only entity his system believed in, namely material goods, whereas we had something to fall back on, however intangible it may be."

"Are you suggesting we wasted our time fighting communism?"

"Not at all. Though we are both materialistic, capitalism is progressive, and we encourage the fittest to prosper. In contrast, communism is regressive, where the fittest are penalized for their abilities. Such a system inevitably collapses under the weight of its own incompetence. As it did, with some help from us. However, that was the easy war. The difficult one lies ahead."

"What do you mean?"

"We are now fighting enemies who play by entirely different rules. Maybe I shouldn't use the word 'now', since the fight has been going on for a thousand years, since the Crusades."

"We know all about these enemies you talk about, enemies such as Hezbollah and Hamas. They are of nuisance value, and we don't think they can do any substantive geopolitical damage."

"I think the ISI is more dangerous than either of the two organizations you mentioned. It has global ambitions, whereas the other two are local. In any case, collectively, these groups are very dangerous. Despite all the damage they have done, no concerted effort has been made to infiltrate or destroy them. In the case of the ISI, we have actually helped them!"

"Don't you think you're overstating this religion business?"

"No. These organizations are based on beliefs that are diametrically opposed to ours. They don't care about material goods or materialism. They don't even care about their personal existence. All they care about is the ultimate victory of their goals, their faith, and their theology. Just take a look at the Iran-Iraq war, where children wearing amulets were sent to the front. Take a look at the numerous suicide bombers attacks in Europe and our bases in the Middle East, such as the bombing in Jobar, Saudi Arabia. Other than during World War II, during the siege of Leningrad, how many communists can you count who resorted to tactics like that? That's the kind of fanaticism I'm talking about. That's why we consider them so dangerous, and that's why we risked our lives and careers to stop them."

The Senators saw the determined look on the faces of David and Al. They had no idea how to proceed. As heroes who had averted a biological accident of unimaginable proportions, they could not be punished. On the other hand, they were simply too independent for the politicians to tolerate easily.

David felt a hand on his shoulder. He turned around to note the CIA Director had stood up and was motioning him and Al to do the same.

Thor Martin saw the two agency men get up and follow their superior officer out of the room. He could have sworn the CIA head was suppressing a smile and had given the two men a quick wink. As the Director led his men out, his arms around their shoulders, the Senators realized one thing.

The Director was going to stand by his men. Anything more than a slap on the hands would cost the politicians dearly.

Chapter 43

Dr. Tariq Bukhari had no inkling of his fate. He had long lost the ability to track the passage of time in hours, days, or even weeks. Those responsible for arresting, imprisoning, and torturing him had been so proficient in their duties he could scarcely remember the almost four decades of life he had lived before this month-long incarceration. His body was so wrecked he could feel the decay rotting his skin away. However, the lifelong rage that had fueled him since childhood gave him the energy to rail against the blackness of his surroundings. Alas! To be born in poverty and destitution, spend a lifetime escaping it, only to be consumed by it in the end.

Bukhari's profound self-pity came to an abrupt halt as two guards roused him.

"Get up, dog!" they yelled.

Contemptuously, they hoisted the manacled doctor by his armpits and hauled him outside. The four weeks of imprisonment had all but destroyed Bukhari's ability to walk. The guards had to drag him by the manacles shackling his arms and hands over the rough stones lining the Kharg Palace's floors, like a truck pulling a trailer with a flat tire over an unpaved road. Though numb for so long, Bukhari was still able to feel barbs of pain shooting through his body from his newly bloodied feet.

"Hurry up!"

He tried in vain to keep in step with the heavily armed duo leading him through a gray maze of cold stones. His rage demanded a show of strength, however pitiful. He must not flinch in the face of what could only be his execution.

His prison, the Kharg Palace, had once graced Kabul in the manner of a beautiful lotus blooming in a sewage pond. Besides being the residence of any man foolish enough to assume the throne of Afghanistan, it also represented the most secure corner of the kingdom. At first sight, the Kharg Palace suggested whoever occupied its throne ruled an empire so vast its capital had to float above the clouds. However, as countless contestants and invaders had discovered, Kabul could be as hostile and impenetrable as its remote, highland outposts.

However, that Sunday, even in ruins, the royal grounds still exuded an undeniable air of command and presence. Built centuries ago, perhaps with some mystical foresight of the future, the lower levels of the palace were strong enough to withstand the destructive power of modern weapons. The dungeon where Bukhari was confined had suffered little perceivable damage despite the barrages and counter-barrages of countless wars, and darkness, as always, dominated its passable corridors. Weak hand-held torches provided the only illumination for the guards and their prisoner. As the trio made its way upstairs, light began to filter in through the wrecked, wretched walls.

Bukhari could discern entering a great chamber. Though a denuded shadow of its former self, the chamber, where the royal palace guard once gathered for muster, had survived well enough to retain its own particular brand of authority. He felt warmth - no, heat, actual heat. Through his exhaustion, Bukhari slowly realized he stood beside an improvised fire pit. Besides driving the dank chill from the air, the flames provided light. For the first time in weeks, Bukhari's eyes took in objects larger than fists, boot heels, and sticks. He carefully turned to examine his guards. Each of them wore the filth of battle as though they had just come in from storming the walls of Kabul with scaling ladders. Bukhari perceived dim, distant shapes of other unmistakably armed figures patrolling the perimeters of the chamber as though it was an encampment.

Hands on his shoulders propelled Bukhari forward towards the fire pit. He wondered if he was to be executed by being thrown into the fire. Suddenly, the weakened doctor's forward motion was stopped, and he collapsed to his knees. Looking up, he saw four figures coalescing around him and he struggled to see their faces in the fire's amber glow. He anticipated more beatings and cringed reflexively from their undelivered blows. One of the guards brutally yanked at the chains around Bukhari's feet, smashing his face into the stone floor.

Bukhari's four judges maintained their slow approach toward his prostrate form. Two decades of savage guerrilla war and espionage had made these men masters of drama. Taken together, all of Red Army helicopter gunships, anti-personnel mines, and booby-trapped toys parachuted into villages could not match the theatrical effect of a patrolling sentry's throat being cut by a single, unsalaried Afghani guerrilla driven only by his belief it was what Allah had wanted him to do.

The guards yanked Bukhari up from the shallow film of his own blood and forced him to squat on the hard stones. Two of the four figures halted. An AK-47's muzzle jammed itself into the nape of Bukhari's neck. The doctor managed to look up, and his gaze bisected the room, herding incandescence to one side and darkness to the other. With his crushed mouth, he attempted to smile. In his crazed mind, the fire had grown to command the entire chamber for the sole purpose of allowing him to die grandly illuminated.

Two shapes crossed the boundary from dark to light. Bukhari watched them carefully. He wondered if they were talking in his native Pushto language. Curious, he rocked forward to catch their words. He watched as the two figures threw objects repeatedly into the fire. He could not quite tell what they threw, though the pair stood only a few feet away from him.

One of them marched towards him and with a flourish held something up close to his face. A photograph. An old photograph. Slowly Bukhari recognized his official identification photograph, the one taken on the first day of training at ISI. Chains snapped, and Bukhari's head was whipped upwards. The other figure came close. Dr. Tariq Bukhari groaned as though he had aged sixty years and was sinking away on his deathbed.

The man who had created a perfect biological warfare weapon, a weapon that could destroy Western civilization, trembled as he recognized the pitiless countenance of Mohammed Ghazni, the head of ISI's biowar weapons project. Abid Sahabuddin, the chief of the ISI, came to stand next Mohammed Ghazni. In silence, they stared at the prostrate, pitiable prisoner.

The heat Dr. Tariq Bukhari had at first so thankfully welcomed began to torment him. The iron shackles girding his wrists, ankles, and waist greedily absorbed the fire pit's close heat. Yet the shock of actually seeing Ghazni standing not more than two yards away nullified the doctor's pain.

Bukhari's loyalty to Ghazni had remained unshaken. After all, it was Ghazni who had arranged for Bukhari to be smuggled into Pakistan from the mountains of Wyoming. Using the cell telephone, Bukhari had called the Pakistan Embassy in Washington after Thor had hung up on him. The name Ghazni had worked miracles that night, and Bukhari thought of it often throughout the ordeal of his incarceration and torture. He had always felt if he could just speak to his mentor and explain what had really happened, he would understand.

Ghazni obviously must not know what happened, how I had been betrayed.

Upon finally seeing his commander once again, Bukhari's first inclination had been to greet him with warmth and reverence. However, the guards held the doctor's chains tightly and he reared up like a feeble horse in a stable.

The man in charge of ISI's biowar weapons program did, however, refrain from throwing his once-favorite pupil's photograph in the fire. In America, Bukhari had read of how the Taliban had decreed all photographs within Afghanistan had to be destroyed - burned in public under the harsh, suspicious gaze of the religious police. In other regions of the Central Asian underworld, it had become quite fashionable to announce the demise of an adversary by burning his photograph.

Ghazni had inadvertently kicked up some dust, which landed on Bukhari's photograph. A sinking feeling took hold of the bound ISI agent. This was it. The scene playing out before him was to be his trial.

"My lords," Ghazni began dramatically, using the ancient Arabian form of address, "happy dies the man who knows his son will never bear arms against the house of his father."

Two of the three figures standing around the fire murmured their assent. The figure closest to Ghazni remained perfectly still and quiet.

"My lords," the ISI plenipotentiary continued, "happy lives the man who never fears his son will one day betray him for false profit."

The chorus approved Ghazni's statement once again.

"My lords, happy is the son who buries his father after a long, prosperous, peaceful life. Unhappy is the father who must attend the funeral of a treacherous son, bent on the destruction of his father's lands and house."

Bukhari struggled vainly against the warming iron around his neck to say something. His guards pulled at the chains, indicating they would choke him should he utter the shortest word.

"Tariq, gaze upon the men whom you have not succeeded in depriving of their flesh."

The doctor's head flew up with a jerk.

"Nadir Shah, tactical commander of Taliban, the man most responsible for shaping and holding the lands of Afghanistan free from the hands of godless, mercenary vultures who seek to deprive the God-fearing of their justly earned victory over the forces of Satan."

Bukhari began to choke from the heat of the collar. He knew about Nadir Shah and recognized the beady eyes, broken nose, and unshaven beard. He trembled at the sight, for Nadir Shah was known for his lack of compassion. A rapacious man, he enjoyed making his opponents miserable and then putting them out of their misery in the most miserable way.

"Mahmoud Ghori, political chief of Taliban, the man charged with ensuring the soldiers always know exactly what it is they are fighting for and whom they are fighting against." Piercing eyes, accentuated by hollow cheeks and a sharp aquiline nose, gazed fiercely at Bukhari.

"I believe you are aware of the name of our most honored commander, Abid Sahabuddin."

Bukhari failed to contain his astonished gasp at the mention of the ISI's commander-in-chief, and by extension, the most powerful figure in all of Pakistan, and the de-facto ruler of Afghanistan.

The chief of the ISI's biowar program placed himself between the roaring fire and Bukhari's dissolving face.

"And I, Tariq? I am your father."

The doctor wondered where this would lead to. Would it be nothing more than a very uncomfortable, public scorning where Ghazni would register displeasure after displeasure, but in the end would welcome him back into the fold? Right before the man whom they all served with such unquestioning loyalty, the legendary Sahabuddin? Or was this just another theatrical episode in his long torment?

"And, according to our law, I have asked my three lords, these three heroes in the struggle against the evil which has consumed the entire world, to bear witness to my calling you my son no longer, to banish you from the heart you have so cruelly broken. You were the one, Tariq. You were the one chosen by Allah to give us what we needed to ensure His divine victory. You have the intelligence. You had the very best training. You had the loyal service of the noble Abolhassan Ziad. You had the weapon, Tariq. We needed your weapon. But you failed us."

The two-man chorus continued muttering its approval. Bukhari began to fear the collar band around his neck would soon neatly lop off his head with its heat.

"From the very beginning, I questioned my decision to select you. Schooled by the infidel, I could not help but wonder how long it would take for you to place the ways of the infidel above your ordained duties. America, how you do love it, don't you Tariq? Or should I say, Mr. Bukhari?"

Bukhari felt his collar chain finally loosen. His head fell forward, and he saw Ghazni throw more dirt onto his ancient ISI identity photograph with great deliberation.

"Yes, while you were out driving around in your sports car, Mohammad Ghori and Nadir Shah never gave up their armed struggles for our beloved cause that transcends countries. While you whiled away the hours in your laboratory, plotting our ruin, Abid Sahabuddin bowed his head under the yoke of the responsibility of keeping our faith from total ruin by the hands of those who abuse the people in the name of freedom, while looting their money.

"Perhaps, my lords, it is I who am to blame for the cowardly transgressions of my son before you. Perhaps I failed to instruct him properly, so he would understand why we had taken our offensive into the United States of America. Recall, my lords, America made us what we are today. Fight! Fight and die against the Godless Russians and come prosper at our table, they encouraged us year after year. Then, without so much as a proper good-bye, we were left hungry and alone to face a perpetual winter. Ah, as politely as children we knock upon the door and ask to be returned to our promised place. However, he refuses to answer the door, though we all know he feasts inside.

"But then Allah sends to us our lord Sahabuddin, a man who observes the situation and sees it for what it is, not for what we want it to be. Our lord Sahabuddin says if no one will answer our legitimate call, we must follow the alternate path. How easy was it, Tariq? Almost too easy. How many American Senators and Congressmen did we get pleading our case?

"And Tariq, you know very well the effort was hardly adequate on its own. This despite the fact the United States has fragmented. One section of the government hardly knows what the other is doing. That we outbid everyone else for controlling influence in the Congress, is but child's play compared to what we face on the battlefield. You, Tariq, could have given us every battlefield. What the American Congress would not give us, you could have. But you didn't!"

At Ghazni's command, Bukhari's guards pushed him back down into his own blood, spread like a carpet over the pocked and buckled floor of Kharg Palace.

Bukhari was sure this was his end. He would be executed before the fearsome four, his head joining that of Najibullah, the former ruler of Afghanistan who was castrated and then hung by Taliban. He closed his eyes, waiting for the sword to sever the connections between his spine and his brain.

He waited. And he waited. Nothing happened.

A hand caught him by the collar and lifted him up. Through half-closed, bloody eyes, he saw the cold unsmiling eyes of Sahabuddin gazing evenly at him.

"Tariq?"

"Y, yes." He managed to stammer.

"Do you still remember how to make the weapon?"

"Yes."

"Think carefully before you answer. Can you make it again?"

Bukhari did not have to think.

"Of course." Some of his bravadoes returned.

"Do you think that might be a good reason for you to want to live?"

Bukhari was being offered a chance. He took it with relief and thanks.

"It will be my only reason to live."

That was the answer the men had been looking for. As the guards hoisted Bukhari up and began to remove his shackles, Sahabuddin spoke again.

"If that be so before our enemies can regroup, make it. Then, in the name of Allah, we will let lose the germs of war!"

Epilogue

Tracy walked out of the building that housed her new laboratory. She wished she had the same joy on seeing her first creation as Madame Curie had when she initially saw radium shining in the dark.

Maybe I will when I make the antidote.

At least Tracy didn't have to hunt for funds like Marie Curie. She had funds and a support staff that would have made her former Mayo faculty members extremely envious. The flip side was she could not be published or be publicly recognized since her work was secretive.

"Isn't it ironic?" She had mentioned to Rory. "Dad tried so hard to make me a spook. He never thought it would come to this."

"The part I love is when you tell him, 'Sorry Dad, can't tell you that. It's classified'." Rory laughed. "The look on his face is priceless."

The moonlight lit the pathway quite clearly. It was a ten-minute walk through secluded trees to her house and she enjoyed the walk. The mountain air was crisp and clean. Little gusts of wind played with her hair, then moved on to tickle and tease the leaves on nearby trees. There was little ambient city lighting to obscure the stars, which were only too happy to give company to the moon.

Tracy was aware she had company too. That was a part of her life now. She suppressed a friendly wave at the shadows who followed her at a distance, knowing it would be frowned upon.

Hope they enjoy a walk in the moonlight as much as I do.

Even in the winter, she preferred to walk. It never got as cold as Minnesota, or even Utah. And the mountains were almost as pretty as those in Jackson.

Rory met her halfway. Without a word, they slipped their hands into each other's and continued to walk home.

"Will you be glad when it's over?"

"You know it's never going to be over, Rory. This is a part of all our lives now."

"Feel overwhelmed?"

"No, not really. Tired sometimes, since I've so many antidotes to create. But, in the end, we will prevail. We *will* have antidotes for all those germs of war."

ABOUT THE AUTHOR

Ketan Desai is a physician, scientist, entrepreneur and a writer. He is the founder/CEO of several biotechnology, nutraceutical and cosmetic companies. He has been a writer since the age of 16, started by publishing Op Ed articles then graduating to short stories and then a thriller, Germs of War. In Germs of War, he combined his medical and scientific knowledge, and childhood army background, to create a scenario of biological warfare. The events of 9/11 and subsequent rise of ISIS are testimony to the insights in the book.

www.ingramcontent.com/pod-product-compliance
Lightning Source LLC
Chambersburg PA
CBHW060327260626
47160CB00007B/2709